THE KILL SEASON

A KATE REID NOVEL
BOOK 10

ROBIN MAHLE

HARP HOUSE PUBLISHING, LLC.

Published by HARP House Publishing
May 2019 (1st edition)

For my mother

*She has always believed in me and continues to be my greatest
supporter in this crazy endeavor I have chosen as my career. I
would not have made it through the publication of the first Kate
Reid book, let alone this 10th book in the series without her input.
Trust me when I say nothing I write would ever see the light of day
without her getting a first look.*

I am blessed to have you in my life!
I love you, Mom.

1

Amid the backdrop of exquisite white sandy beaches, cloudless skies, and leafy hillsides lay the anemic dwellings of the favelas cast in shadow by Christ the Redeemer. The city of Rio de Janeiro sat perched atop the ocean's shores where the wealthy exploited its beauty, and the poor were kept at arm's length.

Rocinha was Rio's largest favela. More than half a million people resided in the urbanized slum which was hardly more than a series of shanties carved into the mountains. Controlled by the Amigos dos Amigos crime syndicate, those inside walked among drug lords, human traffickers, and thieves who operated freely and without repercussion.

Civil Police Investigator Pedro Sosa worked in the station-house on the favela's edge. A husband and father, Investigator Sosa straddled the line between right and wrong in order to stay alive. Everyone did.

He sat behind his desk with an oversized paunch and jaded

features and set his sights on a middle-aged woman donning a worn housecoat and sandals who had just entered. She shuffled toward him while he typed in his reports from the day before on an ancient computer.

"Minha filha está faltando." *"My daughter is missing,"* the woman said.

Sosa appeared indifferent before replying in their native Portuguese. "What is her name?"

"Adriana Santos. She is 24 years old and did not come home last night."

"Ma'am, she is 24. A young woman of that age rarely comes home when expected. Please come back tomorrow if you have not heard from her." Sosa dismissed her.

"No. You don't understand. It is not like Adriana. You must find her. I am afraid she was taken, like the others."

Sosa reclaimed marginal interest. "Like the others?" He looked at the wall behind him. Several pictures of missing young women were papered across it as though it was the latest in wallpaper decor. "Like them?"

"Yes," the woman replied. "I fear she is missing just like them."

Sosa understood the implication. The Amigos dos Amigos were known for kidnapping and human trafficking, though no one would dare cross them. Some of his closest colleagues were paid a handsome sum to look the other way, and he was no less complicit. "Fill out this form and I will file the report." Sosa handed her a piece of paper and when she stared at it with some confusion, it became clear she couldn't read. "Sit down. I'll do it for you."

He took down the woman's information and the last known location of her daughter. "I will do what I can for you, ma'am. But I would not hold out hope. This is Rocinha."

The woman stood with notable defiance. "All of you have blood on your hands. We suffer while you reap the rewards. God will be the one to judge you at the gates."

Sosa observed the woman as she left and a pang of guilt swelled inside him. A corrupt government, a tainted police force. What chance did the impoverished inside the favela have when those who were expected to protect them turned their backs?

He studied the report and noticed similarities to the other cases—the photos of the missing women who cast judgment upon him daily. Something changed in him, an intangible shift. Perhaps the time had come to remember who he was and why he was here.

Investigator Sosa stood from behind his desk, report in hand, and emboldened. He approached Inspector Gustavo Varela's office and knocked before opening the door. "Excuse me, sir, but I just received another missing persons' report."

Varela pulled away his glasses and rubbed his aged brown eyes before peering at his subordinate officer. "File it with the others."

"Sir, I think the time has come to take more seriously the claims of those who have loved ones on our wall."

The lines across Varela's broad forehead deepened. "Are you saying we do not take these allegations seriously? Are we not searching for clues regarding the missing every day? Would you care to explain then what our purpose is here, Investigator Sosa?"

He'd drawn the ire of his commander. This was not how Sosa wished to start off the day. For a man who pulled in an annual salary of only $15,000 US dollars or about 56,000 Brazilian reais, and a few extra when necessary, he was risking a lot for the woman who insisted God would be the judge of his actions. "Our purpose is to find the truth. Is it possible to ask for a gesture of good faith from the AdA? Perhaps they can offer insight?"

Varela gestured for Sosa to take a seat. "I understand you must believe what we do is futile and sometimes it is, however, approaching the Amigos dos Amigos could mean your face will be on that wall too. And that is not something I want to see happen."

"Then what can we do, sir?"

"What we always do."

Sosa nodded. "I see. Thank you for your time, Inspector." He returned to his desk and entered the report where it would linger in perpetuity.

Rio's civilian police force had been left behind. Cut backs, a depressed economy, recovering from the massive expenditures of the Olympics in 2016. All of it added up to a force rife with malfeasance. And Investigator Pedro Sosa was caught in the middle.

At the end of the day, Sosa prepared to leave and passed by his colleagues. "Boa noite." "*Good night.*" He pushed through the doors and into the evening air that was perfect this time of year. In another month, it would be winter and because Rio was close to the equator, temperatures didn't fluctuate much, but May was idyllic.

It was undoubtedly the most beautiful place in the world so long as one had the means to enjoy it. Rocinha was just 2 miles from the coast and was lined with extravagant homes, high-end restaurants, and retail shops. It was a paradise for the privileged few.

Investigator Sosa stepped into his compact blue Fiat Siena which had long passed its better days. His wife would never ask for a new vehicle because she knew it was out of their budget, for now and the foreseeable future. She was a good woman whom he did not deserve. They shared a child; a boy named Elias who had just turned six. Sosa was better off than most. He still had his family, unlike those who trailed in to see him almost daily speaking of missing or dead loved ones. No one cared. Sometimes he didn't care either except for this woman today. He couldn't shake her tenor as she spoke about her beloved daughter, Adriana, who would have been an ideal candidate for the AdA. She was exactly the type for which they searched, young, exotic, and far too naïve.

Sosa drove through the favela where he and his family also resided. The hillside shantytown had powerlines that cascaded down the streets in a web of tangled and dangerous intersections. Because he was on the police force, their family was left alone. That would change should he ever turn his back on the alliance he had formed with the controlling criminal organization. If word were ever to reach them about his inquiry with Inspector Varela, that alone could bring significant changes to his circumstances.

So he drove home, praying that no one would catch wind of his disloyalty. He drove through the crumbling streets between dilapidated concrete structures that were once painted beautiful hues, though the colors had faded into the landscape. Much like the favela itself.

THE INVESTIGATION INTO BOSTON FIELD AGENT CONNOR Murphy's death and subsequent shootings of two serial killers was scheduled to conclude today. It had been six weeks and it was coming to an end, though that hadn't made it any easier for Special Agent Kate Reid or her partner and supervisor Senior Unit Agent Nick Scarborough to find rest as the clock showed 5 am and the sun had yet to rise.

What would be contained in the final report was what both of them feared. While Unit Chief Cole assured the BAU team none of them would be held accountable, the fact of the matter was, he hadn't controlled the review, the FBI's internal investigators had. These were people Scarborough had encountered before. He'd been let off with little more than a warning then and neither knew if he would be so lucky this time around.

Nick sat up on the edge of the bed, his back exposed to Kate. She caressed his skin to offer comfort which would be a welcome gesture but would do little to assuage his concerns. "It's early. Are you getting up already?"

"Is it early? I can't tell." He stood and pulled on a pair of gym shorts. "I'm sorry if I kept you up too."

"Don't be. I'll go put on the coffee." Kate pulled her robe across her slender waist and tucked her long brunette hair behind her ears. She padded in bare feet along the cool tile floor until she reached the kitchen.

Gray light seeped in around the window blinds as signs of summer arrived via an early rising sun. Six weeks since the night they all listened as Agent Murphy was gunned down by a killer. Only Boston Police Detective King had survived and had spent this time exploring his own thoughts to try and understand how things escalated so quickly. It was impossible to know for sure. All they could do now was wait to be briefed on the report. The fate of the team would then be decided.

Kate poured the freshly brewed coffee into two cups when Nick entered. "Here you go."

"Thanks." He sipped on the coffee and closed his eyes for only a moment, ostensibly pondering the outcome. "On the bright side, it does seem like you and Quinn have reconciled."

"Only because we don't discuss what happened in Boston. I'm sure he's waiting until the verdict is in," Kate replied.

"But he has come around?"

"To a certain degree." She sipped on her own fresh brew. "I can't figure out if he's biding his time or searching for as much dirt as he can find before bringing anything to light."

"You make him sound like a villain," Nick replied.

"How else would you describe what he did? He was strategic in his approach, I'll give him that. Laying the groundwork by implying your decisions were faulty because you had been drinking." She laughed. "Good way to plant the seed of doubt about your leadership."

"I'm so sorry, Kate. I never meant for any of this to happen. Coming here—to Quantico. It was supposed to be a good thing for both of us."

She moved closer to him and placed her hand on his solid chest. "It has been a good thing. I love this team, almost as much as I loved our old one. And things with Noah Quinn weren't like this in the beginning. Maybe I can find a way. Maybe we both can, I don't know." She reached for her mug again. "Look, this whole thing will blow over and even if it doesn't, I don't think Cole will remove you from your position. You're getting help for a problem and it shouldn't be cause for termination."

"Even if he doesn't fire me, I can't afford to derail a reputation I've yet to finish building. I don't want them to know, Kate."

"So far nothing's come of it. So maybe I keep doing what I'm doing to stay on Quinn's good side."

He ran his fingers through the side of hair and held her gaze. "I don't know what I'd do without you in my life. You know that, right?"

"I do. And you know I feel the same. Today will be just like any other day. We have each other and we'll deal with whatever comes down the pike. It won't change anything between us."

"I couldn't bear it if it did." He stood from the barstool. "I better jump in the shower." He offered his hand. "Care to join me?"

"You don't have to ask me twice."

ROCINHA LAY BETWEEN THE NEIGHBORHOODS OF GÁVEA AND São Conrado where the well-to-do frolicked along the shores. Trendy nightclubs, cafes, and fashion malls lined the neighborhoods that were also home to some of the most expensive real estate in all of South America.

Gávea's luxurious mansions were in stark contrast to the undesirable elements of the favela only minutes away. This was where Adriana Santos came when she wanted to escape the realities of life in Rocinha. Her beauty was enough to get her in the door. Tonight, Adriana convinced her friend to accompany her to one of the most popular nightclubs in Gávea. Wearing borrowed dresses with stolen shoes, they were both allowed inside.

The nightclub was small and cramped with people pushed against one another, but that was the point. Music blared from the speakers above, shaking the floor beneath with its heavy bass. Lights flashed and people danced and no one cared that the aroma of sweat and smoke filled the room.

"Está quente aqui. Nós precisamos de uma bebida." *It's hot in here. We need a drink.*" Adriana walked to the bar and waited, though not for long.

An attractive 20-something man sporting expensive clothes and a stubbly beard approached the bar and leaned in next to her. "Posso te dar uma bebida?" *"Can I buy you a drink?"*

She gauged him from top to bottom and knew immediately of his wealth. "Sure. My friend is waiting so I'll need two."

"Of course." He turned to the bartender and ordered two cocktails.

Their small talk lasted only until the drinks arrived and when he handed them to her, she began to leave.

"Where are you going?" Perplexity masked his face.

She nodded to her friend and shrugged. "Obrigado." *"Thank you."*

He tipped his head and raised his glass to her. "Adeus."

She returned with the drinks and a smile on her face. "Here. There will be others. Just wait."

"How do you know this?" Gabrielle was her partner in crime and dearest friend.

"This is how it works. Don't worry, they're harmless. It's a different world here. You'll see." Adriana sipped on her cocktail and surveyed the packed dance floor. "Should we go dance?" Without awaiting a reply, Adriana finished her drink and made her way to the dance floor.

Her hips shifted beneath her sparkly dress and her feet moved in perfect harmony to the beat. Adriana was nothing short of perfection and she knew it. Unfortunately for her, she was born on the wrong side of town and this was but a glimpse of the life she could have led under the right pedigree.

The man who had delivered the drinks watched her as she swayed with others on the floor. He sipped on his cocktail and couldn't keep his eyes from her. She was flawless. He set down his glass on the bar and approached her again, offering his hand.

Adriana smiled and took it willingly and the two moved in unison.

He whispered in her ear. "Can I take you home?"

"Where do you live?"

"Gávea."

He didn't need to say anything more than that and she followed him through the club but stopped. "I have to tell my friend."

"She can come too," he replied.

Andrea spotted Gabrielle and rushed to her. "Come on. He's taking us to his house in Gávea." She reached for her friend's hand and both followed him outside.

The gentleman handed over his valet ticket and waited for the car to be brought around. "Thank you," he said to the parking attendant.

"Your Portuguese is very good. Are you American?" Adriana spoke in her native tongue.

"I am. Do you want to change your mind now?"

She laughed. "No." When they brought around his Tesla, her eyes widened and she gleefully turned to Gabrielle, nudging her in the process. For two girls who had nothing, this was beyond what they could've imagined. Adriana had been to this club plenty of times and had been seduced by plenty of wealthy men, but not this kind of wealth. This was American money and the idea excited her.

"After you." He held open the door as the women stepped inside.

Adriana was in the passenger seat and her friend squeezed

into the back seat of the small coupe. She waited for him to enter. "I don't think I asked your name."

"Scott." He pulled away from the club and onto the road. "And you're Adriana. What's your name, sweetheart?" He peered through the rearview.

"Gabrielle."

"Nice to meet you both."

"Where did you learn our language?" Gabrielle asked.

"I live here several months out of the year."

"This isn't your home?" Adriana replied.

"Only part-time. And I live with a friend. He should be there when we arrive." Scott continued along the winding roads and approached the coastal edge where the driveway of the mansion appeared. "This is it, ladies."

Adriana appeared astounded. "It's beautiful. Do you own it?"

"My friend does." He stopped at the top of the driveway. "Come on. I'll introduce you."

UNDER COVER OF NIGHTFALL, A LIGHT RAIN FELL UPON THE dirt that had been shoveled into the hole. Scott examined the work of his hired hand. "A little more just to be safe, though no one will bother to come look for them. We should also leave before the rain turns the road to mud."

The freshly turned earth was pushed back in, one shovel at a time until Adriana Santos and her friend, Gabrielle, were buried at the base of the lush hillside far away from homes or people or anyone who would take notice.

The man with him was a local and spoke little English. But he knew it was time to leave when Scott returned to the car. Only this wasn't the flashy Tesla in which he had driven the girls. This was a shitty Ford Fiesta that could have belonged to anyone. Seeing it emerge from the hills near Rocinha would be of no concern. And for this American in Rio de Janeiro, it was just another night on the town.

2

The cloud of uncertainty proved stifling for the FBI's elite BAU team. They sat in silence in the conference room while awaiting the outcome of the investigation. The head of the department, Unit Chief Cole, had already assured the team that they would not be held liable for what happened in Boston, but Senior Unit Agent Nick Scarborough felt differently. As the team leader, it was his call to allow Boston field agent Connor Murphy and Police Detective Terry King to go into that apartment alone with two killers. It had ended badly for them; one died, the other was injured.

The group of specialist agents, with two recent additions who had shaken up the status quo, had only just begun to gel and not all were happy with the regime change. That was where the real problem lay.

Kate Reid was among the best of the best the FBI had to offer and she had grown fond of each of these agents, with one exception. Noah Quinn remained an enigma. His boyish good-looks, well-dressed and polished veneer had lured her in to believing she was safe around him. That he wouldn't betray her trust, but he had. He also had yet to divulge to the powers that be what he thought he knew about Nick Scarborough, meaning he was likely awaiting this very moment to determine how he would play his hand.

"Good morning." Unit Chief Cole arrived several minutes late. "I'll keep this brief so you all can get back to work. First of all, I'd like to thank each of you for your assistance and cooperation in this investigation. I heard nothing but positive remarks from the Boston Field Office and you are all to be commended for your efforts. That said." He handed out the report. "Let's take a look at the resolution to this unfortunate episode."

Each team member reviewed the report, devouring it for any hint of blowback. Cameron Fisher was the second in command. The former New York cop chewed on his toothpick as he began to read. Eva Duncan, who sat next to him, was a hard-edged Chicagoan who had worked closely with Agent Murphy on the case. She might have been the one hit hardest by his death. And Levi Walsh, a former military man from Alabama who was responsible for coordinating with the local police. He felt the loss too. And last, but not least, Noah Quinn—Kate's supervisor and expert profiler. These were the people who had been there and witnessed, via audio, the events of that fateful evening that cost Agent Murphy his life. And now as they read the findings of the internal investigation, Kate pondered their reactions.

It was Nick Scarborough, the man in charge of this team, who broke the silence. "This appears to conclude that it was an error in judgement on the part of Connor Murphy that led to the shootout."

"That's right," Cole said. "As I recall in my initial response to the incident, I believed it had everything to do with Murphy's relative inexperience. And the committee agrees. I know you feel responsible for what happened, Scarborough, but this doesn't fall on your shoulders. It's time we all got behind you." He eyed Quinn. "I am aware some of you didn't agree with the decision, but it's easy to second-guess something when it all goes to hell."

This was the outcome Kate had hoped for, but what this meant for Quinn's intentions remained tenuous. Nick wouldn't be censured. He wouldn't be reprimanded in any way. So how would Quinn use this now? That was something both she and Nick would have to prepare for. There was no mistaking one thing, as much as she hoped Quinn would be an ally, he'd made it clear that night, as they listened to the horrific shootout, that he had no intentions of letting what he knew about Nick slide. It would be up to Kate to figure out how he planned to use it to his advantage.

"This was the right call," Fisher said. "I'll be the first to admit that I wasn't onboard with the decision to run the op that way, but had a more experienced agent been onsite, maybe things would've turned out differently." He turned to Scarborough. "I should've stood behind you on this one and I'm sorry for that. You'll have my full support and this won't happen again."

"That means a lot," Scarborough replied. "Thank you." He turned to the rest of the team. "Now that we can put this behind us, I'd like to move forward on the work we're supposed to be doing. I will be making some changes as it relates to how and when we get involved in investigations. Our priority is not in field work. We have field agents for that. While I understand there will be circumstances that require us to play that part, I won't put our focus on it. Our focus will and should always be to back up the field teams."

"Agreed," Quinn replied. "I'm glad we see eye to eye on that."

"I think we can all agree we should get back on the horse and do what the FBI pays us to do. So I suggest we all get back to work. Thank you for your time." Cole began to leave.

As the rest of the team left, Kate caught up to Quinn. "Hey, can I talk to you for a second?"

He eyed Scarborough as he left the room. "Sure."

She closed the door where the two remained alone and walked back to the table, dropping into a chair. "Look, I know you think what happened in Boston was Scarborough's fault." She waited for a retort, but he apparently had none. "And I'm sure you wanted someone to be held accountable. An agent died and that means something. I know that. We all do."

"What is it you want to say to me, Reid? That I was wrong. Your boyfriend was right. Things between you and me haven't changed. I still believe you could rise to be one of the greatest profilers out there. But that doesn't mean I have to cozy up to Scarborough. It's going to take some time to get past this one."

"I get it. But there's something I think you're keeping close to your chest. Something I'm afraid you might use to prove some point or to use as a steppingstone."

"And that is?"

She noticed he immediately took a defensive posture. "There's a side to Nick Scarborough I think you want to exploit."

"I don't think I know what you're talking about." He remained standing and folded his arms as if exerting authority over her.

"Come on, Noah. Please don't take me for a fool," Kate replied. "While you might think you know the situation, trust me, you don't. And to play that card would only tear this team apart. Is that what you really want?"

"What I want, is you."

"Excuse me?" she replied.

"I've made it no secret that I need you to work with me. Nothing's changed, except your reluctance has become intolerable."

"I'm sorry. You're going to need to step back a minute and tell me what the hell you're talking about. I have been very forthcoming with you."

"No, you haven't, and that's going to change. If you want to play ball, this is how we do it. I want to write a paper and I want you to help me. Kate, I'm telling you, with both our names on it, it will change the trajectory of our careers. That I can promise you."

"You over estimate what I can provide. You always have. I can see now that if this is how we get through our current predicament, then fine, I'll do what you ask. But this stays between us until you're ready to publish the findings."

"I can agree to that."

Kate retrieved her notebook and started to leave. "You'll be the one getting the short end of the bargain, I'm sorry to say."

He waited until she was out of earshot. "That's where you and I disagree."

POLICE INVESTIGATOR PEDRO SOSA STOOD BEFORE THE WALL of photographs, hands on his round hips, peering at them as if he knew them personally. All young and beautiful women. All from Rocinha. And all suspected to already be dead or victims of human trafficking, in which case, they might as well be dead. Rio was a dangerous city, more so now than in years past. And Sosa was torn between justice and safety for himself and his family. There couldn't be both. Not here.

For the time being, there had been no ramifications to his suggestion that he pursue the disappearance of Adriana Santos. Was it possible his supervisor, Inspector Varela, wasn't on the take? Possible, but unlikely. More likely was that he didn't want to see harm come to Sosa for the minor infraction. That didn't mean he would let him slide if he continued to dig into the situation. But what could he do to stop this? The people, his people, were suffering at the hands of criminals every day and to look the other way while it happened had begun to take its toll.

As he examined each and every photograph on the wall. With a furrowed brow, he retrieved a map of Rocinha and marked the locations of where the young ladies resided. They all lived in the area, but if there was a radius he could pinpoint, perhaps that would lead somewhere.

He began marking the addresses of the missing women and pulled back to view his findings. There was no definitive area, however, he did notice something unusual. The most recent of the women who disappeared were outside of the strongholds of the AdA, the Amigos dos Amigos. Could this mean the perpetrator understood that he was not to cross the organization? Or could it suggest a member of the AdA hadn't wanted his counterparts to discover what was happening? Either way, this was an interesting find and maybe it meant something. The only way to know for sure was to take it to Varela. It would require Varela's approval, and maybe he stood a chance of getting it. Sosa walked toward the Inspector's office and knocked.

"Come in," Varela replied.

"Inspector Varela, can I have a moment of your time?" Sosa asked.

"Of course. Sit."

"I would like to visit the AdA second-in-command, Luiz de la Costa, and discuss a situation I believe I may have uncovered."

Varela leaned over his desk with interest. "And what situation might that be?"

"The missing girls. I think it could be a rival gang seeking a turf war. We have seen this many times before, sir."

"Yes. But in regard to drug trafficking not human trafficking. I'm not sure this is the road you should take, Pedro. This could place you and your family in jeopardy."

"Yes, that is possible. But if I am to warn them of a possible impending turf war, might they want to hear from me then? And then I will understand if this is the work of the AdA or another gang."

Varela captured Sosa's gaze. "Why do you wish to pursue this, and why now?"

"Because I have a daughter and I would not want her mother to suffer what Adriana Santos' mother is suffering through. Nor myself. I can make this appear as a favor to the AdA. Warning them of problems that may arise. That is how I will show them my —our loyalty."

"Then you will not go alone. I will accompany you." Varela stood from his desk. "Is there no better time than now, Pedro?"

"No, sir. No better time." He was pleased by the support and held out hope that Varela could offer some rebuttal against the criminal organizations that were destroying not only the favelas but Rio in its entirety. Small and measured steps would be required, but this could be the beginning of something meaningful and Sosa prayed it would not cost either of them their lives.

They arrived at a known location of the upper echelons of the AdA. With armed guards outside the entrance, Varela approached first and displayed his badge.

"Inspector Varela here to see Senhor de la Costa. He is expecting us."

The armed member of the crime syndicate eyed the officers before nodding and allowing them entry. Once inside, more armed men appeared and both were subjected to pat-downs ending in the surrendering of their side-arms.

The building was far nicer than anything else inside Rocinha. While the AdA attempted to buy the loyalty of citizens inside the favela by offering basic public services and throwing lavish parties, they kept the true wealth for themselves. The money derived from drug smuggling and human trafficking, it was all used to funnel more wealth to their operatives, including the civilian police force.

Another of de la Costa's heavy lifters showed them to a room where the man himself was found. Varela and Sosa entered.

"Please, sit down, gentlemen." De la Costa gestured to the chairs opposite his desk. "Inspector Varela, I understand you have concerns regarding a forthcoming turf war. I am glad you came to see me right away. Please, explain your concerns."

Sosa followed his supervisor's lead and let him open discussions.

"Yes, of course, our inquiry into a missing persons' claim revealed something of interest that Investigator Sosa discovered."

De la Costa eyed Sosa before returning his attention to Varela. "Continue."

"What he discovered was that several young women in the

community have disappeared, but what makes that remarkable is that they lived in an area where it is believed the Terceiro Comando Puro are attempting to gain control."

De la Costa nodded his agreement. "Yes. This is interesting. However, at what point is this of concern for my operation?"

Sosa spoke up. "Well, sir, if the citizens become frightened enough, and that is beginning to happen, they might succumb to the demands of the TCP, disregarding your own."

"And are you hoping to make arrests in this scenario?"

Varela peered at Sosa before turning back. "At your command. We can make that happen."

De la Costa appeared to consider the officers' plan of action. "I will make the inquiry myself. This is something the generals and I should discuss with the TCP prior to allowing you to question any member of their organization." He stood. "I will relay the details. However, you must keep in mind, our arrangement still stands."

"Of course, sir. Nothing changes until you say so." Varela got to his feet. "Your time is sincerely appreciated."

The officers were shown out as they walked back to their patrol car. Varela stepped into the driver's seat and started the engine. "Progress was made today."

Sosa eyed him. "Yes, sir." But that wasn't how he saw things. It was status quo as far as he was concerned. De la Costa would do nothing except warn the TCP we were asking questions. It was in his best interest to do so. He would be seen as offering an olive branch, both factions looking out for one another. This couldn't stand. Not this time.

Upon their return to the station, Sosa and Varela walked inside.

"Thank you for your assistance, sir," Sosa said.

"These are dangerous waters you tread, Pedro. Do so carefully, yes?"

He nodded before returning to his desk and found something quite unexpected. A message lay on top of his keyboard. He retrieved the note that had a number written on it. No name, just a number. Sosa looked at his cell phone and considered making the call but thought otherwise.

"Sir?" He approached Varela again. "I need to run out for only a few minutes. It seems my wife has run out of petrol. I will need to bring her some."

"Certainly." Varela continued toward his office. "Give her my regards."

Sosa grabbed his car keys and started toward the parking lot. He needed distance and a payphone, which were in short supply here. In fact, there were only a few remaining and the nearest one was still a mile away. He drove until he made it to the last vestige of a pre-mobile phone world.

Upon stepping out, he approached the run-down booth and prayed the phone was still in working order. When he picked up the receiver, a dial tone sounded. "Thank you, God." With the slip of paper in his hand, he dialed the number and waited until the caller answered.

"Olá?" he asked.

"Pedro Sosa?" the voice said in return.

"Sim." "Yes." He waited while there was a short silence on the other end. Then the mysterious voice began.

"You are being led in the wrong direction. Neither TCP nor AdA have anything to do with the disappearances of the young women you seek."

"Then who?" Sosa asked.

"You are looking inside the favela for answers. That is not where you will find them. To find them, you must look outside. Gávea, São Conrado."

"Money? You are saying whoever is doing this has money."

"Money, extreme wealth and many people under his charge."

"Are they being trafficked?" He pressed on.

"No," the voice replied. "They are not alive."

"Where are they?" Sosa insisted. "Where can I find them? Is it all of them?"

"I cannot say how many, and I cannot say where you will find them. But this is no turf war, no trafficking expedition."

"Please, tell me who I am looking for because it sounds as though you are certain."

"I only know what I have heard from others inside Rocinha. Investigator Sosa, if you want answers, you need to speak to the Americans."

The line went dead and Sosa peered at the receiver. "Wait! Who are you? What Americans?" But it was too late. The caller was gone.

"*Droga!*" "*Damn it!*" he slammed down the receiver and walked out of the booth. Sosa surveyed the area in the event he was being watched—or followed. That could never be taken for granted here. He walked back to his car and began to leave, considering what the caller said. "Americans. What do they have to do with this?"

It seemed outside the realm of possibility the AdA or any other organization would allow an American crime syndicate entry into the favela—not without substantial payment. But the caller insisted this was not the AdA, which left him with one conclusion. Only one place to go where the Americans had any law enforcement in his country. "Brasilia."

3

C ontacting the FBI's international operations in Brasilia was a bold move that would have to be carefully calculated. It was one that could bring Pedro Sosa a great deal of attention. So before he could consider this move at the behest of an anonymous source, Sosa needed something substantial on the Adriana Santos investigation. Something that would make it worthwhile for the FBI and at least allude to the notion that an American was involved.

He hesitated to include Inspector Varela for the time being. Their conversation with the Amigos dos Amigos was cordial but that was only on the surface. These were not accommodating people. Sosa's plan, then, was to focus on Adriana Santos and where she was last seen the night of her disappearance.

Rather than return to the station, Sosa opted to make a visit to the woman who had decidedly changed his outlook on what had become a sad state of affairs in his beloved city. He drove to the woman's home deep inside the favela where it would be all too easy for him to go missing within a blink of an eye. Killing a civilian officer meant nothing to the gangs who had a stranglehold on Rocinha. He knocked on the door as nightfall surrounded him.

The middle-aged woman, wearing a long dress in bare feet slowly opened the door. "Sim?" she asked.

"Eu gostaria de lhe fazer algumas perguntas sobre sua filha." *"I would like to ask you some questions about your daughter."* Sosa could already see her apprehension. It was difficult to trust anyone here, let alone the police.

"Do you have news of her?" Her eyes widened with a glint of hope.

"I am sorry. No. May I come in?"

She opened the door and allowed Sosa inside her home that was no bigger than a motel room. The walls had cracks running through them. The concrete floor was adorned only with small and shabby rugs. "Why are you here then?"

"I need to know who Adriana was with the night she disappeared and where she was last seen. Do you know?"

"Her best friend, Gabrielle, was with her. They went to a night club as she usually did on a Friday night."

Sosa continued inside, eyeing the structure that hardly seemed fit for habitation. "Do you know the name of this night club or where I might find Gabrielle?"

"You will have to speak with Gabrielle's mother. I have not heard from her. And yes, I know where she preferred to go. It was in Gávea. A place called Casa da Praia."

"I am familiar with this place. Do you have a number so that I might contact the family of Gabrielle?"

The woman jotted down the number and handed it to Sosa. "I pray she has not disappeared like my Adriana."

"So do I, Senhora. I will speak to you again as soon as I know something. But I do ask that you keep this visit between us. As I'm sure you can understand why."

"Sim." She showed him to the door. "Obrigado, senhor." *"Thank you, sir."*

"Adeus." *"Goodbye."* Sosa stepped outside as the sun vanished behind the steep hills and shadows engulfed the narrow streets. The day was at its end, but there was one place he could go. First, a call would have to be made.

As Sosa drove away from the home of Adriana Santos, he made the call to Inspector Varela from his flip phone. "Yes, sir. I ran into some trouble with my wife's car. I apologize I have not returned."

Varela laughed. "No need to apologize. She is a woman! What can you expect? Go. Do what you have to do and I will see you in the morning, Pedro. "Adeus."

Sosa brushed off Varela's comments regarding his wife because she could outsmart him on just about any occasion. However, he opted to leave that out of the conversation. He'd been given a pass and it was time to use it to his benefit.

Gávea was only a few miles away and he would be there as the club was opening for the night. It was a Monday, but in Rio, every night was a weekend night. Tourists flocked to the city this time of year, most times of the year, in actuality. It was hard to believe a paradise such as this could have a stain so large and yet utterly ignored by those who came to visit. He would be among the prosperous very soon as Gávea was flush with money.

The nightclub was along a popular block of bars and other clubs where guests spilled out onto the streets. It was a sort of Mardi Gras every night. Had he been young and rich, it would have been a place for him to be seen, but he was neither and a cop showing up here would be looked down upon and disregarded. Money bought a lot of things, including freedom to break as many laws as one wished.

With a photograph of Adriana in his hand, Sosa made his way inside the nightclub where only a few people were inside, most of whom appeared to be staff setting up for the night. The flashing lights were on and the music played loudly in the empty space.

He approached the bar. "Desculpe." *"Excuse me."*

The young man with coiffed hair, a chiseled jaw line and a slim build turned to him. "Olá. What can I do for you officer?"

Sosa held up the photo of Adriana. "Do you remember seeing this young woman in here two nights ago?"

The bartender gazed upward as if reflecting on the night in question before again studying the picture. He shook his head. "No, senhor. I cannot recall seeing this beautiful young woman. I would have remembered her."

"Are you sure? Please, have another look. It is very important." Sosa pushed the photo closer.

"I am sorry, but no. Is she in trouble?"

"She's missing. Like many others."

"Sim." The bartender nodded.

"What about an American? Do you recall seeing an American in here that night?"

"Senhor, we see many Americans."

"Of course." Sosa wanted to leave a card for him in the event he managed any recollection, but that could backfire were the wrong people to ask about this visit or if he spoke about it. "Thank you for your time." He began to leave, but not before taking note of the area. The entrance points, exits. Cameras. Someone had to have seen her. And if he could not locate Gabrielle, and it was looking like she might have suffered the same fate as her friend, then he would need to find out if any of the others on that wall had been here. Maybe then he could begin to understand what happened to them.

It was a rare occasion when Kate would find herself sitting alone at a bar, but here she was, nursing a glass of chardonnay. The exception this time was that she was waiting for a friend. This was an old friend who had seen her through some of the toughest times she had experienced as an agent, and she couldn't wait for him to arrive. It had been too long since they had seen each other. When the tap on her shoulder came, her wait was over.

"Dwight." With a smile as bright and wide as ever, she was greeted with a kiss on the cheek.

"It's so good to see you, Kate." Dwight Jameson, a stocky, square-shouldered man, had been part of her Washington Field Office days and had become as close to her as a brother. "Mind if I sit?"

"Please." She couldn't take her eyes off of him. It was like being home. "It's been too long."

"It has. How are you?" He sat down and captured her gaze. "You look beautiful as ever."

"You're too kind. I am well, thank you. And you? How are you and how is Abby?"

"Same ol' same ol' for me. Abby is doing great. In fact, we're engaged."

"That's fantastic, Dwight! When's the big day?"

"It's just going to be a small ceremony and of course, you and Nick had better be there. We're looking to have it in September."

"Oh, that's not too far away. Just a few months to plan it."

"I leave that up to my fiancé. She's incredibly organized and I feel as though I would get in the way."

"Well, I just can't believe it. Finally. I'm thrilled for you both. And things at WFO? How is Vasquez?"

"She's becoming a force to be reckoned with, that's for sure."

"She always did have that spark about her. I really need to call and check in on her."

Dwight cocked his head. He still wore his hair high and tight. He had a solid build on the outside, but he was a Teddy bear on the inside, unless one chose to cross him. "How's Nick doing?"

His tone turned serious and Kate knew why. "He's okay. He's doing what he needs to be doing to stay sober."

"Good. So tell me then, and don't get me wrong I'm happy to see you, but why am I here and he's not?"

Kate reached for his hand. "I miss you guys so much. Things are different at Quantico. I'm getting to know the team and they're great, most of them, but it isn't the same as when it was just the four of us."

"Why are you skirting the issue? What's going on?" Dwight was never one to mince words.

She was holding back and he had picked up on it. "Things went bad on a case in Boston several weeks ago. It's been resolved now, but we lost someone. An agent who was young, talented, and just got into a bad situation he couldn't see his way out of. Nick took it pretty hard. We all did."

"You said he's staying sober, so what is it? Are you afraid he'll slip because of this incident?"

"No. I don't think so. He's going to AA meetings and I do believe he may finally have it under control."

"Then what?" Dwight turned to the bartender. "Bud light. Thanks."

"Someone on our team. I'm pretty sure he knows about Nick's struggles and he's dangling it over my head to get something."

"From you?"

"Yeah. Offering to keep quiet and make sure no one else discovers that Nick's a recovering alcoholic."

"Wait a minute, are you being blackmailed, Kate? Who the hell is this guy?"

"I guess I hadn't really considered it as blackmail, but by definition, it seems to be. It doesn't matter who he is. It matters that I agreed to give him what he wants in exchange for him to keep his mouth shut about Nick."

"No. This is bullshit." Dwight shifted in his seat. "Whatever you agreed to—get out of it. If word does get out about Nick, it won't be the end of his career. I'll vouch for him. ASAC Campbell, even with their past relationship, you know he'll vouch for him. This doesn't make sense. You can't..."

"Hang on, Dwight. Just please, just calm down. It's done. I get what you're saying and maybe you're right. But with what happened in Boston, what happened back when Nick was censured. All of that mess will come up and this too? I can't risk it. I won't risk it. And the reason I asked you here is because I want your help."

"Name it. Anything."

"For obvious reasons, I can't ask any of my team for this, but I want to know how he figured it out—about Nick, I mean."

"Well, I'm gonna need a name, Kate."

"First, I need you to agree that none of this will ever see the light of day."

"Fine. I won't tell anyone you and Nick are being blackmailed. What do you need me to do?"

"His name is Noah Quinn."

"Your boss? He's the one doing this? Jesus."

"I know. But look, he wants to publish a paper and he wants to root around in my head about Hendrickson, Shalot, hell, probably a whole host of other cases I've worked. He's going to use that because he thinks he'll get some sort of breakthrough on investigative techniques or something. I don't know. I tried to tell him it was pointless, but he's insisting. So, I agreed that if he keeps his mouth shut about what he knows, then I'd spill my guts to him—for whatever that's worth."

Dwight nodded. "You want me to find out how he came to get the dirt on Nick?"

"Yes. I don't know if he was following him or us to an AA meeting, or if he overheard something, but I suspect it's the former. He's incredibly resourceful. I wouldn't put it past him to have a bug somewhere or at the very least, have a tail on me or Nick."

"Well, you'd better believe I'll find out. And when I do, that son of a bitch is going down."

"That's not what I want, Dwight. I want to know how he found out, yes. But I'll be the first to admit that he's the best profiler I've ever come across, even better than Georgia Myers and that's saying something. I can't afford to lose that training. What I want is to prove to him he can't back me into a corner and get away with it. He won't do anything to jeopardize his career so whatever you find, he'll want to keep under wraps. So, I guess I'm looking to do to him what he's trying to do to me."

"What's the end-game, here?"

"Zero-sum."

"Consider it done." Dwight tossed back his beer before peering at Kate with a smile. "Now that we got that out of the way, onto happier topics."

INVESTIGATOR PEDRO SOSA HAD NO LUCK AT THE NIGHTCLUB, which didn't come as a surprise. People were hesitant to talk to the cops given their penchant for intimidation and corruption. He returned to the station this morning in hopes of continuing his efforts to discover where these other young women had gone missing. And not all of the missing persons were young women. There were some on the wall who were older women, and some men as well. While they deserved the same justice, he had to narrow down this field and focus on the young women. They were likely to remain the most vulnerable in Rocinha. If he could crack this case, then perhaps it would open doors to finding the others. Either that, or he would be killed for his efforts.

He removed six of the photos, ones he believed were most closely related to Adriana Santos and pulled the files on each one. The scant information was embarrassing. But if he could establish a last known location of each woman, that would go a long way to building a theory about the suspect, or suspects.

"Pedro, what are you working on?" Inspector Gustavo Varela emerged from his office.

"I was looking into the other similar cases to Adriana Santos, sir. I believe if I can establish a timeline..."

"Are you sure this is the route you wish to take?"

"Why wouldn't that be, sir?"

"You understand what it could mean, should you proceed without the permission of those who issue it." Varela wouldn't even speak the name of the syndicate out of fear of reprisal in his own station.

"I am willing to accept the risk. Something must change, sir. Maybe I am the one to see that change happen."

Varela carefully regarded him. "I am not absent a heart, Pedro. Things we do here are things we must do in the current environment."

"I understand that, sir."

"I'm not sure that you do, but you will soon enough." He relaxed his stance. "That being said, come into my office. We can work on this together." Varela looked around. "Away from prying eyes."

Sosa appeared pleased and followed Varela to his office. "Thank you, sir."

"Close the door." Varela took a seat at his desk. "Show me what you have so far."

Sosa handed Varela the photos. "I believe it's possible these young women may have gone to a nightclub in Gávea. I must prove this before I move on."

Varela examined the photos. "What makes you think they were at a nightclub?"

Sosa sat down. "Sir, I must confess to you, I lied yesterday. I went to see Mrs. Santos, Adriana's mother. I asked her and she said Adriana frequented a particular night club and that her friend, Gabrielle went with her. I haven't been able to reach Gabrielle's parents..."

"You lied to me, Pedro? Why?"

"I thought it best to keep you from any involvement should consequences arise from my actions."

"I see. You were looking out for me?"

"Yes, senhor."

Varela returned his sights to the photos. "Have you yet spoken to the families of these women?"

"I believe that should be our first step."

"Then what?"

Sosa hesitated to tell him about the phone call and the warning about an American connection. But if he couldn't trust Gustavo Varela at this point, then he could trust no one and would not last long on this investigation. He was going to have to jump in with both feet, as the Americans say. "Sir, there is something I hesitated to mention."

"More lies, Pedro?"

"Not exactly. More like an omission."

"Go on."

"Yesterday, I received a message with a phone number on it. I called that number from a pay phone well away from here. I do know how the eyes and ears around here are numerous. What I was told by this cryptic caller was that this could be the work of an American or Americans."

"Is that so? This caller told you this?"

"He said we were looking in the wrong place and we should be talking to the Americans."

"Well, we can't go to the Americans with just this. There will have to be some proof of association."

"I couldn't agree more. That is why I am in search of discovering if these women were also at the nightclub. Then I will find someone who will talk. Someone who will tell me who the last person was with each of them. I will find out if it was an American."

"And when you do. What then, Pedro?"

"Then we go to Brasilia."

"The FBI?"

"Yes, sir. I think they would be interested to know if they have a group or an individual taking young Brazilian women—and either selling them—or killing them."

4

When Francisca Dias roused, she had no recollection of anything since the moment she arrived at the vast, luxurious mansion. Her final memory being of the handsome American man who asked if she wished to attend a party at the home. Now, she found herself in a locked room, her hands and feet bound and sitting on a cold tile floor. There was a blanket nearby, a sofa against the wall, and no windows.

"Socorro!" *"Help!"* She screamed at the top of her lungs, but this room appeared more like a vault. "Socorro! Socorro!" Still, no one came. Francisca had no idea of the time, or how long she had been here. It must've been the drinks. He put something in the drinks. What did he say his name was? Yes, that's right. It was Scott. And there was someone else too. She knew nothing more and had come here alone, assuming the American could be trusted. He had money and was striking in his appearance and somehow, that made her feel safe.

The door opened and the man known only as Scott entered.

He pointed to the top corner. "Camera. No one can hear you, but I can see you." He spoke in Portuguese.

"Let me go. Please, let me go." She pleaded to him. "I won't tell anyone, I swear it." Her eyes were swollen and her makeup smudged.

"I can't do that. I'm sorry. He wants you for himself and there's nothing I can do. You might as well calm down because you won't be leaving, not until he's done with you." Scott left the room, closing the thick steel door behind him.

He walked along the corridor and returned to the living room that revealed glass sliding doors which opened to a balcony that overlooked the ocean. "She's fine."

Another man, yet more handsome and dressed in tailored fashion with a sculpted jawline and sparkling white teeth rested on the fine contemporary sofa sectional. With his back turned to Scott, he gazed through the glass doors at the moonlight that danced on the lapping waves. "And you're sure no one saw you leave with her?"

"No one cared," he replied.

"That seems to be a prerequisite here, doesn't it, Scott?"

"Yes, it does. Which is why we're here. No one cares what happens to those from the favelas." He approached a console table and poured two drinks. "How long do you plan on keeping this one?"

"Depends on how cooperative she is. I would make arrangements for her to leave before dawn. That should give you enough time to appropriately dispose of her."

"Then if there's nothing else, I can ensure those arrangements are set."

"Go. I'll take care of things from here." He tossed back the rest of his bourbon and got to his feet. He set his sights on the hall that led to the room where she waited. And as soon as Scott left, he started into that hall and arrived at the door that was deceptively welcoming.

From the outside, the door appeared only to lead to another bedroom. The 4-inch-thick steel door required a code and fingerprint identification to open it. It had originally been designed as a panic room. Because for a man with his wealth and status, he was a target and especially here where crime was rampant not only from the criminal elements but from so-called law enforcement as well. They were notorious for taking bribes to turn the other cheek when crimes were committed. His crimes were no exception. Scott, his cohort in these crimes, made sure they were paid handsomely for their troubles.

So this once safe room was anything but for the women who had entered, which to date, had numbered into the teens. It was all too easy for him and he saw no end in sight unless of course, boredom set in.

He entered the room and she was there. Where else would she be? "Boa noite." *"Good evening."*

"Let me go, please!" Francisca again pleaded.

"You'll go home soon enough." He closed the door behind him.

THE FORD FIESTA THAT INTEGRATED WELL INSIDE THE favela wound through the narrow roads to the top where the verdant hillside met the end of the pavement. Scott stepped out of the car with the man who had helped him before. A local who had been well paid to prepare the bodies and drop them into the fields. He never asked questions.

"Open the hatchback and pull her out." Scott walked toward the spot where the others were buried and peeled back the top layer of soil, the leaves and branches that were used as cover and exposed the gravesite.

Francisca Dias had been a beautiful twenty-year old woman from Rocinha who, like the others, had been in search of a good time and found the devil instead. But the only ones who would miss her would be her family, and maybe friends. And when they went to the police, the report would be filed and never looked at again. Francisca would become another in a long line of unsolved missing persons because this was Rocinha. A place where people were disposable and the immoral ran the streets.

Scott tossed the soil atop the makeshift burial grounds and replaced the leafy camouflage covering. "Let's get the hell out of here. I can see the sun on the horizon." He stepped back into the rundown Ford and when his partner entered, he started the engine.

The path down the hill was rough and the car bounced over the jutting rocks and crumbling asphalt. The headlights caught the attention of a young man, not more than twenty-five who was taking his morning run through the hills. He instinctively crouched down behind a tree and watched as the Ford travelled down the road and when it was out of sight, he stood upright again. He had seen this car before and wondered why it was here. There were no homes higher in the hills, only wooded areas that were mostly inaccessible to cars.

The young man was no stranger to the ways inside the favela and if he were to show concern and inquire about the mysterious vehicle, it could mean danger for him and his family. His elderly parents were unable to work and he supported them with his meager wage working for a nearby luxury hotel. He took note of the car's description and plate before continuing up the hill to where the path ended. Upon reaching the area, he scrutinized the grounds. "What are you doing here?" he asked no one in particular. Nothing stood out to him, so he moved to higher ground and something appeared out of place. He clenched his jaw and climbed the hillside just a few more feet.

Miguel Silva was born and raised in Rocinha. He had seen it for what it once was, which was a beautiful and prosperous community. And what it had now become, which was nothing short of wicked. Bad things happened here, there was no question, but when he stopped and noticed the mound covered with loose branches and leaves, there was little doubt in his mind what lay beneath. He couldn't look. He might find his friends. But maybe he could do something about it, if he was willing to risk his life to speak out. It was in his best interest to keep quiet, but then Miguel never was one to fall in line.

PEDRO SOSA SAT IN HIS KITCHEN WITH FILES SPREAD OUT ON his dining table. It was almost four in the morning and he had done nothing but mull over the cases in search of clues.

"Pedro, why have you not gone to bed?" His wife of twelve years, Maria, shuffled into the kitchen. "It is nearly morning and you have work."

He set his sights on her. "I am working. I've been working all night. Why are you up so early, my darling?"

"Because you were not in bed. I couldn't sleep." She approached the coffee maker. "Do you want any coffee?"

"Yes, please."

She put on a pot and returned to him. "What is all this?"

"I need answers, Maria. I must know what happened to these young women. No one else seems to care."

"And what of those who run Rocinha? Will they care if you find answers?" She pulled out a chair and sat down. "I am worried something might happen if you do, Pedro. You of all people understand the way things work here. Why are you doing this now?"

"Maybe I am ashamed of who I have become. I no longer enforce the laws of our city. I enforce the laws of the lawless."

"And have you made progress on this?" She asked.

"Possibly. Varela is even in my corner, for now. If I am able to point the finger at a potential suspect, he is willing to pursue this with me." The sound of socked feet padding along the tiled floor caught Pedro's attention. "Elias, it is so early. Why are you awake, boy?"

The 6-year-old with a thick head of black hair and eyes so blue they could have been mistaken for the ocean rubbed his eyes. "I could hear you both talking."

Maria stood from the chair. "Meu filho." *"My son."* She walked into the kitchen and retrieved a bowl. "Since you are awake, would you like breakfast?"

His face lit up. "Sim, por favor." *"Yes, please."*

AGENT CAMERON FISHER STOOD IN THE DOORWAY OF Scarborough's office. He pushed his hand through his thick salty hair and leaned against the opening and when he caught the eye of his senior unit agent, he entered. "Hey, are you busy?"

"Usually. What's going on?"

"Listen, I know things have been tense around here since we got back from Boston and I just want to say that I think Cole made the right call."

"Sit down." Scarborough waited for him to take a seat. "The report came from internal investigations. I don't know how much input Cole had, but regardless, I'd like to put it behind us and move on. There are still cases that need to be examined and it's time we come together as a team."

"I couldn't agree more. In fact, the reason I'm here is because I got a call and need to head to Miami."

"Miami? What's happening there?"

"The field office has been working an investigation regarding a string of hate crimes. And now it's looking like they could be connected. They want me to take a look at the file and offer suggestions."

"Of course. Go. Do what you need to do."

Fisher appeared cautious. "There's something else I wanted to talk to you about."

Scarborough didn't respond, only waited for him to continue.

"I've been mulling this over for a while. Not sure how to broach the topic, but figured if I didn't, it would end up biting me in the ass."

"What is it, Fisher?"

"It's about Duncan. About Duncan and me, specifically. We've been seeing each other for a while."

"Really?"

"Really. I was hesitant to say anything, but if I don't, I think I could lose her and that is the last thing I want to happen. Look, I feel weird even discussing this with you, but there are protocols in place for dating a colleague and I need to make sure we're following the rules here."

"First of all, I think it's great. I mean, she could do better, but you, you hit the jackpot." Scarborough smiled.

Fisher appeared more at ease. "Don't I know it. Anyway, I needed to tell you because, well because if we need to have it noted in our personnel files, then that's what I want to do. I want to try to make this work with her."

"Sure, man. I get it. Get with HR, both of you, and do what you have to do. But I have no problem with it. I'll back you both up if necessary."

"That means a lot." He pushed up from his chair. "I'll take care of it when I get back from Miami. Should be a couple of days at the most, but I'll keep you posted."

"Okay. Hey, Fisher."

He stopped and turned back. "Yeah?"

"Thanks for coming to me. With everything that's happened, and the fact that we're all still getting to know each other, your confidence in the team means something."

Fisher nodded. "See you later, Scarborough." As he walked out of his office, he headed straight to Eva Duncan's. "Knock, knock."

"Morning. Come in." A smile spread on her lips.

"I came to let you know that I just left Scarborough's office. I told him about us."

An air of uncertainty now crossed her brow. "You did? What did he say?"

Fisher continued inside and sat down. "He gave us the

thumbs-up. Not that I had any doubt. He said we needed to get with HR and fill out some paperwork but that he would back us."

"Thank you, Cam. This is a big step for us."

"Yes, it is. I wanted to do it. I've wanted to for a while but couldn't seem to find the confidence. I guess I feared changing the way things were between us would somehow upset the balance, you know?"

"I know. But nothing's going to change. Except that we won't have to keep the secret any more. We're free now."

"I do love you, Eva." He held her gaze. "I hope you know that."

"Of course I do."

"Listen, I'm heading to Miami this afternoon, but I should be back in a couple of days. I'll call you when I arrive."

INVESTIGATOR SOSA HELD THE PHONE TO HIS EAR. "AND you're sure he was an American?" He listened as the caller verified the statement. "Thank you. No, you will not have to come here and file a report. I promise you, no one will know who you are. Obrigado. Tchau." *"Thank you, Goodbye."* Sosa turned back to the wall of missing people and for the first time felt encouraged. The caller had assured him he'd seen an American at the club around the time the missing women had been seen. The tip was anonymous, though he suspected it was the bartender. Sosa approached Varela's. "May I come in, sir?"

"Yes. What is it, Pedro?"

"Sir, I just received a phone call. The caller verified the man last seen with Adriana Santos was an American. As well as a few of the others."

Varela sat back in his chair and folded his arms across his chest. "Anonymous?"

"Yes, sir. He was afraid and I don't blame him."

"No. But how can we be sure he is telling us the truth? How do we know he isn't working for AdA and is attempting to steer our efforts away from them? How would this individual even know we are working such an investigation?"

"I have to trust he is telling the truth, whatever his reasons for doing so. Sir, we have no other leads. I spent all night in search of anything else that could connect these women to each other or anyone else. I could not."

"Can this caller provide a description of the American?"

"All he said was that he was well-dressed, slim, average height, and attractive."

"Pedro, that describes many people."

"He heard the man speak, too. He knows enough English to understand some words."

"And what did he hear this American say?" Varela persisted.

"That he wanted to take her to a party where there were other rich Americans."

"Does this anonymous caller work at the nightclub?"

"I suspect so."

Varela appeared to contemplate the information. "This isn't a lot to take to the FBI, Pedro. They might laugh in our faces and tell us to come back when we have a proper eyewitness. And if word got out that we went to Brasilia..."

"I know what's at stake, Inspector. This is all we have. We cannot wait for more of our young women to be taken. I am sure they are all dead or have been taken back to America. Please, sir.

All we have to do is talk to them—the Americans. They can decide if it is worth their time."

"And if it isn't?"

"Then we get more until it is. But can we at least try?"

Varela picked up his phone. "Close the door." He began to dial. "Olá. I wish to speak to one of your agents regarding a possible American suspect in a missing persons investigation."

Sosa sat on the edge of the chair, his eyes glued to Varela.

"I do not have a name; however, I have an anonymous tip and several missing women in our community. This is an important investigation that I believe is in your office's best interest to entertain." He eyed Sosa. "Thank you. We won't take up much of your time. We would just like to understand what position the FBI wishes to take. Yes, sir. Tomorrow, sir. We will be on the first flight. Tchau."

Sosa waited for Varela, barely able to contain his excitement. "They agreed?"

"They agreed to hear us out. Nothing more. We will have to arrange a flight to Brasilia tomorrow. But you must understand, Pedro, if we go there, people will find out. People who pay us for our loyalty."

"If we tell them it is in search of an American, they will lose interest. We can make them understand we are not in pursuit of anything they are doing."

"You might be right. Unless they are working with the Americans. In which case, we might not make a safe return."

5

I nside of 24 hours, Inspector Gustavo Varela and
Investigator Pedro Sosa were descending into the Brasilia
International Airport. The city of roughly 2.5 million was
Brazil's capital and was where the US Embassy was located.
Inside the embassy was one of several legal attaché offices that fell
under the direction of the FBI International Operations Division.
All in all, the FBI had 63 of these offices worldwide. They operated in conjunction with Interpol and other foreign law enforcement entities. This was the place where they would seek help in
locating the alleged American who was the last person seen with
at least two of the missing women from Rocinha.

The white two-story building appeared ahead and was rather
dated, likely having been built around the 1970s with a flourishing
garden surround. They arrived by taxi to meet the man with
whom Varela had conversed. Upon their entry inside the embassy,
it was Inspector Varela who led the way. "Boa tarde." "*Good
afternoon.*"

The official at the security desk, an intense thirty-something man who appeared ready to fire upon anyone who crossed him, eyed the gentlemen who were in plain-clothes. "Como posso ajudá-lo?" *"How can I help you?"*

"I speak English. We are here to see FBI Special Agent Elijah Cain." Varela held out his badge. "Civil Police Rio de Janeiro."

"One moment please." He called back to the agent. "He'll be up in a moment."

Varela nodded and turned to Sosa. "Come. We'll wait over here." He started toward a row of chairs against the wall opposite the security desk.

Sosa began to feel the weight bear down him as to the significance this meeting would have. It would change things for him and his family. And could even force him to leave the city were things to go unexpectedly bad. Sosa was already planning his escape route, but if, as the tipster implied, this was the work of an American, perhaps this American was working alone and was not in bed, as they say, with the gangs. Time would tell. And the response from the FBI was about to be revealed.

Special Agent Elijah Cain appeared from beyond the corridor and made his way to the men. His pace was succinct and purposeful. It was clear already this was a deliberate man. Perhaps it was his maturity, appearing to be in his sixties. He must've seen more than his fair share and appeared to have no problems calling out those who would question his authority. The burly man dressed in a grey suit approached them. "Inspector Varela?"

"Yes, hello. I am Gustavo Varela." He offered his hand. "Thank you for meeting with us. This is Investigator Pedro Sosa."

"Investigator Sosa. Pleasure." Cain extended a greeting to him.

"I trust your flight was uneventful?" He already started back into the corridor.

"Yes, sir. Precisely how I prefer to fly." Varela fell in line behind the agent.

"My office is just over here." Cain made his way to the office and held open the door. "Please, come in and take a seat." Once they were inside, he closed the door and walked to his desk. "So you say there is a possibility an American is involved in the disappearances of two of your citizens?"

"Forgive my broken English, but that is correct, sir," Sosa began.

"Excuse me, son, but I prefer to hear from your supervising officer." Cain set his sights on Varela. "You've come a long way for my ear, Inspector. I hope you can offer evidence to support your claim."

Sosa had just been admonished by a man who was not his superior. Not even Varela was prone to such comments. It was insulting. But if he wanted help, he would have to take it, whether or not he approved of such behavior. This was why he disliked Americans. They were bold and arrogant and to behave this way in his country? With a calming breath, he listened as Varela explained.

"While hard evidence is negligible, Agent Cain, there is reason to believe based upon an eyewitness account."

"And is this eyewitness reliable?" Cain asked.

"It is an anonymous source."

Cain dropped his head. "You're telling me you don't have an eyewitness? That all you have is what amounts to an anonymous tip. Forgive me, Inspector. The time and money involved in making this trip could have been better spent on finding a viable source for your claim. What is it you believe I can do based on an anonymous tip?"

"We have the Amigos dos Amigos behind us on this effort, Agent Cain," Varela replied.

Sosa eyed him with concern. They had no such thing. In fact, it was essentially words of warning the AdA had offered. Stay out of it was the gist. But it had accomplished what must have been Varela's goal. Cain appeared acutely interested now.

"AdA." Cain mulled over the mention of the notorious gang. "They control Rocinha. Them and their partners, the Pure Third Command."

"That is correct. And sending in Brazil's military police has done nothing but given them determination to wait it out. We are here because we need the help of the FBI, if this is indeed a series of disappearances instigated by one or more of your citizens."

"Well, if I am to take this to the men upstairs, I will need more. What can you get me that will give us definitive proof? Even our teams don't want to wade into the Rocinha waters."

"The source can be traced back." Sosa spoke up and would hold his ground against this tyrant. "And I have a description of the American. With that, and your enormous resources, I think an identification would only be one step away."

"This is one hell of a big can of worms you're asking me to open, I hope you know," Cain said.

"It is dangerous, but sir, we have so many missing young women. More than a few of which disappeared only in the last few years. I think that means something." Sosa peered at Varela who nodded for him to continue. "There is no question the dangers that lurk inside Rocinha—for all of us. But if we have a description of the American, will you help us find him?"

Cain eyed the men. "A face will only get us so far. We need a name. And if this person doesn't have a criminal record or any prints on file, that will make this much more difficult."

"Are you saying you will help, Agent Cain?" Varela asked.

"Get me what I need and I'll consider it."

THE QUAINT MOM AND POP RESTAURANT NEAR THE Quantico offices was where Kate waited. She was the first to arrive and was expecting Noah Quinn at any moment. It had been agreed their meetings would occur outside the BAU because this would be off-book to anyone else on the team. And so far, Kate had only consulted with Dwight Jameson on the matter. No one else knew of their agreement and certainly not Nick Scarborough. She was doing this for him at an untold cost to herself.

Quinn entered the restaurant and spotted her at a nearby table. A stylish man, fit and in his prime at 32 would be, under any other circumstances, attractive to Kate. In fact, she had once found him handsome a long time ago. But she knew too much about him now and had seen the ugliness inside him. She wished it hadn't been that way, but she would never forgive him for using Nick's weaknesses to get from her what he wanted.

"Sorry I'm late." Quinn sat down opposite her. "Have you ordered?"

"No."

"Good." He opened the menu.

Kate trained her sights on him. He appeared as though everything was completely normal, that this was just another day in the lives of BAU profilers. She gazed at the menu and tried to remember why she was here. This would end soon and when Dwight Jameson came back to her with evidence Quinn had been duplicitous, she would throw it right back in his face.

The waitress approached. "Hello. Are you ready to order?"

"The chicken Caesar, please," Kate said. "And an iced tea."

"And for you sir?"

"Actually, I think I'll have the same." Quinn handed the menu to her. "Thank you."

"I'll be right back with your drinks."

When she walked away, Kate began. "I hope you have pen and paper ready. I'm sure you'll be underwhelmed."

"There you go again, underestimating yourself. When this is over, Kate, you'll see I'm not the enemy here. This will benefit the both of us. I have every intention of giving you credit on this study."

"I'm sure you will, but I can't say that I'll want it." She leaned over the table, resting her elbows atop it. "Where would you like to begin?"

"Oh. Okay. I figured we'd eat first, but there's no better time than now." He retrieved a voice recorder. "You don't mind, do you?"

"Not at all."

"I understand your relationship with your father is or was somewhat strained. Can you tell me if that stems back to your discovery that you had been abducted at such a young age?"

She wanted to ask how he knew, but it didn't matter. It was likely in her personnel file somewhere. The FBI conducted all sorts of personality tests before accepting an applicant. "My father had a lot of trouble accepting what had happened to me when I was six. He held himself responsible, as you can imagine."

"Sure. That makes sense. But since you're aware of that, have you forgiven him?"

She held his gaze with contempt. "Why don't we talk about Hendrickson. He's the reason you're here, right?"

In that moment, the food arrived and she was grateful for the distraction. This was going to be harder than she thought. How could he not see how insensitive his actions were? Maybe because he'd never experienced the hardships she had faced. "We should eat first." Kate tucked into her salad and shoveled a large bite into her mouth, smiling at him in return.

THE DISAPPOINTING TRIP TO BRASILIA WAS CAPPED OFF BY the chaos that surrounded the police station back in Rio.

Varela slowed as he entered the parking lot. "Check your phone."

Sosa retrieved his phone. "No messages. No calls. What is going on here?"

"I don't know, but we'd better get in there quickly." Varela cut the engine. "Don't talk to the press. Just go inside." He stepped out of the car and made his way through the reporters. "Sem comentários!" "No comment!"

Sosa was right behind him and didn't so much as look at the reporters, fearing for his safety and that of his family's. When he followed Varela inside, the station was in the throes of similar disorder.

"What is going on?" Varela demanded as he entered.

"You didn't hear?" An officer who stood among the others

asked. "A field of bodies was found buried at the top of the hills in the favela."

Sosa marched to the Missing Persons wall. "Are any of them here? On this wall?"

"Yes, many of them," the officer replied.

"We need to go there now." Varela turned to the officer again. "You. Take us now. Who is there?"

"Policia Militar."

"They don't conduct investigations," Sosa replied.

"They are there to prevent an uprising and to protect the site. I will take you there now."

Varela's cell phone rang. "Sim." He paused while the conversation began. "We are on our way now. Thank you, senhor." He peered back at Sosa. "The commissioner will be meeting us there."

The officer escorted Varela and Sosa through the swelling crowds outside and to his patrol car. "The door is open. You should get in quickly." He eyed the crowd as they shuffled toward them.

The men slipped inside and the officer started the engine, speeding out of the lot in reverse. "Sorry."

"Don't be. Just get us there quickly," Varela replied. "When did this discovery happen?"

"While you were in the air, senhor. I don't know if anyone attempted to contact you. The Commissioner called and asked your location."

"What did you tell him?" Varela asked.

"That you were out of town."

Varela eyed Sosa through the sideview mirror before turning back. "And nothing else? You did not disclose our location?"

"No, senhor."

"Good. Who found the burial ground?"

A young man who called and asked not to be identified."

Varela nodded. "Exactly what we need, another anonymous tip. And the AdA?"

"I don't know if they are aware, but I assume so. They are never far from such things." He turned right and continued up the hillside through the narrow streets and run-down shacks until reaching the end of the road. "We will have to walk from here. The terrain is too difficult." He stopped the car and stepped out.

"Someone with a car would've had to get up that hill." Varela turned to Sosa. "Tire tracks. Take photos if you see any."

Sosa nodded as he stepped out and the three started up the hillside.

At the top was where the Commissioner waited, alongside members of Brazil's military police who were tasked with maintaining order. But what awaited them as well were two high-ranking members of the AdA, including Luiz de la Costa, whom Varela had met with only a day earlier. Everyone knew who they were, but no one would dare arrest them. It was likely the commissioner was in their pockets as well.

"Where were you when this happened, Inspector Varela?" The commissioner asked.

"I was on a personal errand, senhor. My sincerest apologies."

The commissioner pursed his lips before returning his sights to the overturned earth. "Perito Criminal," "Crime scene investigators" are on their way. We should clear everyone out so that they can do their job. This is going to be a blemish on the favela. And with so much going against us, we cannot afford to bungle the efforts. Not even them." He eyed the gang operatives hanging nearby.

Varela began, "I will ensure they will not interfere as I don't believe they wish to in any case."

Sosa had gone out on his own in search of tire tracks and how the young man who phoned in might have spotted the vehicle or the people inside it. He made his way to the grounds and peered inside where layers of dirt had already been pulled away. "Who was here? Who did this?" He asked one of the officers.

"We had to know this wasn't a hoax and began to remove the earth."

"Did anyone touch the bodies?" Sosa pressed on.

The officer shook his head.

Sosa knelt down and peered again at the body that rested on top. There were others beneath it, that much he could see. But they were only partially exposed. Once the crime scene investigators arrived, they would discover what horrors lay beneath. But at first glance, he knew who these victims were. They were the women on the wall. While he couldn't put a name to the one who appeared lifeless and mangled, he knew who she was.

He started back toward Varela. "Senhor, we will need to set up lights. Dark will arrive soon and these poor children of God cannot be expected to stay in the earth this way."

"It will be set up soon. Do you recognize them?"

"I can only see the one on the top. I don't know who she is by name, though not Adriana Santos, that I can tell. However, her body..."

"I know." Varela patted him on the back. "We will get them out tonight. However long it takes." He peered down the hill at the approaching vehicles. "I believe they are here now. We should help them get started." Varela made his way to the path below.

Sosa, however, opted for another, more dangerous route. He

looked toward the two men who stood nearby, de la Costa and another of the AdA, no doubt. And the time had come to question them. He peered back at Varela to make sure he wasn't looking because he would not allow such a bold move. But Sosa needed something to take back to that "idiota" FBI agent in Brasilia. He knew they would not get anywhere without that man's help. But this, maybe now, this would convince the agent they had an American citizen murdering innocent young women from the favela. Sosa was already convinced of it.

He made his approach to the men who wore rifles on their backs. "Perdão." *"Pardon me."* My boss, Inspector Varela," He pointed in Varela's direction. "He spoke to you regarding the likelihood these victims are a result of an American. Do you know anything about that? Anything that you could tell me?"

The men eyed each other before de la Costa spoke. "We are good for the people of Rocinha. We have provided services to them. Electricity, running water. This disgrace is not the work of our people. No matter how the policia militar frame it."

"Do you know then, anything at all about these innocent victims?"

"We are only here to make it known that the Amigos will not tolerate such violence against the people of the favela."

Sosa nodded and walked away. That was rich. These people were among the most violent gangs in all of Brazil. They didn't care who got in the crossfire. They don't care how many they killed, but it was clear he would not get an answer from them. His only chance would be to find the person who called in the location. A young man. He would ask around for this boy. Because in order to solve these crimes, he knew the Americans would have to participate. And the only way to ensure that, was to point the finger at one of their own.

6

D wight Jameson, the former colleague and close friend of Kate Reid and Nick Scarborough, sat in his car outside the apartment that belonged to Noah Quinn. His window rolled down, the warm breeze drifted inside. He didn't know the man well but disliked him thanks to what amounted to blackmail in Dwight's mind. What the man had proposed to Kate seemed beyond compare. So his job now was to figure out how Agent Quinn knew about Nick's struggles with alcohol. It was an odd feeling surveilling essentially one of his own. But he would not sit by and watch him try to destroy either or both of his friends.

The night had already settled in for its warm slumber and Dwight waited for Quinn to leave the apartment. The building was well-lit and it would be easy to spot a car leaving the parking garage from where he waited. The goal was to follow him and understand his habits. Maybe get lucky enough to see who he hangs out with. If ammunition against Kate existed, he would make sure there was ammunition against Quinn.

A car emerged from the parking structure beneath the apartment building. Dwight ducked lower into his seat, keeping his eyes above the door frame. The car in question was a 2014 silver Mercedes coupe.

"Mr. Quinn. Where might you be headed off to?" Dwight turned the engine and switched on the lights, pulling out onto the road several feet behind Quinn. He kept enough distance because this wasn't his first rodeo.

Quinn's Mercedes continued through downtown D.C. until he pulled into a spot in front of a bar. Dwight had to find a place to park nearby and by the time he did, he noticed Quinn walk inside. And he wasn't going to let him go in alone. Dwight stepped out of his vehicle and entered the bar. Quinn had only met Dwight once and that was some time ago, so he didn't feel the need to be overly furtive. However, that changed when he spotted Quinn in a booth with someone he did recognize. "You gotta be kidding me?" He darted in the opposite direction before he was seen and considered his options because the person Quinn was meeting with was very familiar with Dwight. In fact, she had worked with him for a while. "What the hell are you doing with him, Myers?"

THE SUN HAD JUST PEEKED OVER THE HORIZON WHILE PEDRO Sosa camped out near the location of what the locals had already dubbed "the killing field." It wasn't a term to be used lightly as its original meaning dated back to the 1970s Cambodian genocide. But this was no less gruesome. So far, the forensics team uncovered four bodies and they feared there were more. However, the hillside was becoming unstable and an imminent collapse of the ground was feared. The team would need to bring in equipment to stabilize the slopes and continue digging. Now they waited for identities on the bodies. But Sosa wasn't going to wait for more to be killed and perhaps buried elsewhere. Maybe another killing field already existed?

For now, he waited because he was sure the boy who called in the location, a runner, as he discovered, would continue his routine. And as the skies were brightened by the sun, his hunch was right.

A young, athletic man jogged nearby. He appeared to be keeping his distance and rightly so. The area had been taped off and the earth loosened its grip on boulders and dirt that tumbled down. So he continued well enough away, but close enough for Sosa to see.

The boy appeared to slow as he neared the area, like he was waiting for another hole to open up in front of him and display the battered remains of young women, women he probably knew. This was Pedro's chance.

He emerged from behind the thick leaves and deep green foliage of the native grounds and waited on the path ahead. When he caught sight of the runner, he held out his hands. "Está bem." "It's okay." He slowed his approach. "I'm not here to hurt you."

The runner stopped in his tracks. Miguel Silva's eyes darted back and forth as if searching for a place to run. "Polícia?"

"Sim." "Yes." Sosa displayed his badge." I just want to know if it was you who called in to tell them about the burial ground? I promise, nothing will happen to you. I am looking for the one responsible for the deaths of our beautiful young women. And I think you might know more than you've said." Sosa continued his approach, lowering his arms and pleading. "I need your help. You've been brave to do what you've done, but I need more. Will you help me?"

Miguel appeared confused and frightened. "I only saw the car."

"A car? What car?"

"It was a piece of garbage. An old Ford Fiesta. I don't know the year, but I saw the plates.

"You didn't see who was driving? Was it only one person inside?"

"Two. There were two, but I left so they wouldn't see me. That's all I know."

Sosa appeared pleased. "Is there any chance you can describe them? Either of these men you saw?"

"The driver, I think." Miguel gazed upward. "Yes, the driver. He was dark haired. Groomed well."

"Did he look like he was from Rocinha?"

"Oh no. He was dressed very well, at least his shirt. The other man, he might be from the favela. Shaggy beard, longer hair."

"But the driver. Is it possible he could be American?"

"American? I don't know. I didn't hear him speak." He hesitated a moment, but then continued. "I have seen it before. A few times before. And they didn't look like good people. They looked like the kind to bring trouble."

Sosa was losing a little steam. "You said you know the number plate? What was the color of the car?"

"White. It had rust on the back passenger wheel well. It was a hatchback. The number plate was LPM-2347. It was from Rio.

I'm sorry. That's all I know." He eyed the crime scene several feet away.

"It's okay. You have done the right thing. This will help more than you know. And no one will know we talked. You should go now. Go back to your running and don't change your routine. Thank you." Sosa patted him on the shoulder before heading back to his car farther down the hillside.

"Wait!" Miguel ran to catch up to him. "There is something else. I remember the driver held his mobile phone. I remember because it was bright, like he was using it to light his way."

A wave of relief swelled through Sosa. He knew what this could mean. Cell towers. He could ping the towers for calls in the time frame of when the kid saw the car. "This is good news. Thank you, son. Thank you."

RED AND YELLOW FLOODLIGHTS ILLUMINATED THE MANSION'S exterior. It was nestled against the hills overlooking Leblon beach, which was only a stone's throw from Ipanema and Copacabana. Inside, a celebration was underway and the DJ played dance music. Though it was 1am, people continued to arrive and the house was packed.

"Excuse me?" Scott approached with his dark hair slicked back, a thin stubbly beard and sporting a fitted button-down shirt. "I have news. Can we speak in private?"

With a cocktail at his lips, the owner of the home leaned into his associate's ear, though his eyes never left the room. "Can this wait?"

"No, it can't."

Appearing disappointed, he agreed. "Fine. Lead the way." Mason Wylder had been blessed with a magnificence reserved for mythological gods. He stood at six feet with muscles so well-defined, even beneath his form-fitted clothes, they appeared airbrushed. Radiant brown eyes and cheekbones carved like a Michelangelo sculpture, he captured the eye of everyone in the room, not just the women. He followed his associate to a quiet part of the home. Not an easy task. "What is so important? You know what this party means to me."

"I do know and I'm sorry to pull you away from your guests. I have news that a burial pit was uncovered in Rocinha yesterday. And four bodies removed."

Wylder's face turned blank. "Have they identified any of the bodies?"

"Not yet."

"And what are you going to do about this?" he asked.

"I think we should go back home now. Take a break and let things cool down. You'll be needed back at work soon anyway so maybe now is the right time."

"I'm not leaving yet. The season's only just begun. I mean, look at this place." He turned with open arms. "This is why we're here. No. You'll have to figure something out. We aren't going anywhere. Not unless or until it's absolutely necessary. No one is going to care about a few underprivileged girls from Rocinha. Christ, that entire favela is rampant with drugs and crime. The cops have enough on their plates."

"Will you at least agree to a cooling off period? A few weeks, maybe a month. You can throw more parties. Whatever else you want to do," Scott said.

"I'll consider it, though I can't make any guarantees." He

smiled. "Now if you'll excuse me, I should get back to my guests." Wylder started back into the living area.

Scott was dumbfounded. This was not the reaction he expected. But he would have to do as his boss requested and hoped he could at least keep him on a short leash for the time being. "Idiota." He started back toward the party, snatching a cocktail from a passing waiter as he did.

"Hi there." A woman wearing a silky slip dress and high-heels approached him. "I saw who you were talking to just now. Are you a friend of his?"

Scott stopped and peered at the woman. "Yes. I'm his best friend."

"Do you think maybe you could introduce me? I'd love to get his autograph."

PEDRO SOSA STARED AT HIS COMPUTER SCREEN, CLOSER THIS time, just to be sure he was seeing this right. He jotted down the phone number and opened a search engine, entering it to see its origins. "New York." A smile crawled onto his lips, widening with each moment as he realized what this meant. "America."

He shot up from his chair and rushed to Varela's office. "Senhor? Senhor? Can I speak to you please?"

"Yes, what is it, Pedro? Did you trace the number plate on the vehicle?"

Sosa entered and closed the door. "I did. It was stolen. The number plate is useless to us. However, after I spoke with the runner and he mentioned a mobile phone in the hand of the driver, I searched for calls made around the tower on the hill on the night in question. I found several numbers, but only one I was interested in. It traced back to the nearest tower in Rocinha. The number is from New York. Senhor, this is what we've been waiting for. Proof. And now we have it." He held up the piece of paper with the number scribbled on it. "We can get this to Agent Cain. He'll have no choice, but to look into this."

Varela nodded his approval. "It isn't exactly what we would have wanted, but it could be enough." He grabbed his keys and stood up. "We'll make the call to him somewhere else. Many mouths are fed by the hands of the AdA here."

Sosa followed him as they walked to the Inspector's car. Once inside, Sosa continued. "How will we keep this quiet if the FBI are involved?"

"Pedro, that is something you should have considered prior to now."

"We already told the AdA that we think we're after an American. I don't think we should expect any retribution."

"I do hope you're right. And as far as keeping this quiet, I'm not sure that will be possible. The discovery of the gravesite is already on the news. Though most will believe it to be the work of the gangs. That said, I think we may need to pay the AdA another visit. Inform them the FBI may arrive but only to investigate the possible association to an American."

Sosa agreed. "Yes, it wouldn't be wise for the gangs to insert themselves into this or harm any member of American law enforcement."

Varela chuckled. "The entire favela might suffer from drone attacks if that happened." He pulled into a market where a phone booth was near. "I'll make the call to Agent Cain. You stay here."

Sosa waited while Varela left the car. He made his way to the phone booth and plucked in several coins. These booths were becoming rarer to find and especially ones that worked. But he'd used this particular booth before for less than noble reasons. "May I speak to Special Agent Elijah Cain, please. This is Inspector Varela in Rio." He waited while the call was transferred.

"Cain here."

"Agent Cain, this is Gustavo Varela."

"Inspector. What can I do you for, sir?"

Varela surveyed the area. There appeared to be no onlookers. "I believe I have the proof you requested regarding the missing persons."

"And what might that be?" A hint of derision laced his words.

"A phone number. A call that was made in the area where the burial field was found in Rocinha."

"I am aware of this development. Go on."

"It was made the night before the discovery and the call originated from a mobile phone with an American number. Specifically, New York City."

"New York City. Well, that is interesting. Anything you discovered about the call logs? Like who the call was made to?"

"No, sir. However, I am hopeful that is where you can help. Sir, these women found in the ground at the hilltop, they were mutilated, some beheaded. It will take weeks to identify them with our resources."

"And you don't believe this has anything to do with the AdA or their compatriots?"

"I do not. I have a relationship with them. They have suggested they had no part in any of the disappearances."

"Sure."

"Agent Cain, you asked for proof. I have at least four female bodies, horribly disfigured and a phone number tracing back to someone from New York City. What more can I do? I am now begging for your help. This involves your people, not mine. And if I have to make that known publicly, I will not hesitate to do so." There was silence on the other end and Varela feared the worst.

"Give me the number and give me all the intelligence you have. I need photos of the victims as well. I have some people I can call."

"Thank you, senhor. I will send a courier with the information. I cannot entrust that my email system is not monitored."

"If it comes to light this involves an American, Varela, you're going to have to find a way to protect yourself and any of my people who offer their services. Can I count on you for that?"

"Yes, of course. I will ensure their safety."

"I'll be in touch." Cain ended the call. He pulled up from his desk. "Damn it." It was all he could do not to slam down his fist. He was pissed this appeared to embroil Americans. The PR would be a nightmare. Brazil wasn't the easiest of governments to work with in joint investigations and Rio was probably the worst thanks to their tainted police force. Safety would also be an issue. There was no way Varela could guarantee his agents' safety and he knew it. It would be up to Cain to furnish his people with arms and awareness of the area. He was going to be up to his ass in this one.

He pressed the number on his phone that rang his secretary. "Hey, can you get me the direct number for BAU 4? I need to speak to the unit chief."

"Right away, sir."

Unit Chief Cole held the phone to his ear. "You get me what you can and I'll arrange for my team to make a visit. Yes, I'll inform them of the risks and the necessary steps regarding their safety. I'll let you know when they're on their way." He ended the call and started into the corridor.

Cole approached Scarborough's office. "Can I bend your ear, Scarborough?"

"Sure. Come in. What's going on?" He set down his papers and gave Cole his full attention.

"There's been a request made by International Operations out of Brasilia."

"What's the request?"

"There's a suspect—possible suspect, who the local authorities believe could be an American based on some eyewitness testimony and a cell phone number."

"Okay. And the crime?"

"Crimes. Four bodies were discovered buried near the top of the hills at a slum in Rio. A place called Rocinha."

"I've heard of the place. Rio's been going downhill pretty much since the 2016 Olympics. Crime and violence are through the roof, not to mention the corruption."

"Exactly. This is my fear in even asking this of you and your team. But the senior agent at the US Embassy in Brasilia was asked to assist. And due to the nature of the crimes, the condition of the bodies and number of them, he called us."

Scarborough nodded. "They believe this could be an American serial killer in Rio?"

"That's right. What do you think?" Cole asked.

"It will be risky for the team. No question. Can we expect to have the appropriate accommodations as a result?"

"Of course. Between International Ops and your team, safety will be priority number one. And I'll personally get the director in on this one. The consequences of this could spread beyond anything we'd be prepared for."

"I agree."

"I suggest you consult with your team and get back with me. Today." Cole began to leave. "Oh, and one more thing. If the unsub is American, the Brazilian government will prosecute to the fullest extent of their laws. There'll be no bringing anyone back."

"I'll call a meeting with the team now and get back to you. Thank you."

Within minutes, a call went out and Scarborough headed into the conference room. Kate was already inside with Quinn. Walsh and Duncan appeared behind him.

"Where's Fisher?" Scarborough stood at the head of the table.

"Still in Miami," Duncan replied. "Should we get him on a conference call?"

"Yes. He needs to be in on this."

Duncan proceeded to make the call on the speaker phone in the center of the table.

"Fisher here."

"It's Duncan. I've got the team here and you're on speaker. Scarborough called an urgent meeting. Can you talk?"

"Give me one second. I need to get someplace a little quieter." The sound of movement was evident as he made his way to a more private location. "Okay. I'm all ears."

Scarborough leaned over the table, his elbows straight and his palms pressed against it as he remained standing. "International Ops in Brasilia needs our help on a case in Rio." He filled them in on the details. "I'm waiting on the file, but this is something within our scope of services. What I need to ask from each of you, understanding the challenges of their current environment, safety issues and the like, is this something you are okay with? Cole said we can turn it down, if need be."

"If we do that, then International Ops will have to run it alone," Quinn said. "This isn't their kind of thing. I'm not sure we have a choice."

"I agree," Kate said. "I understand the risks. It's the same risks most of our agents face on a daily basis."

"Reid's hit the nail on the head," Walsh interjected. "I'm in. When do we leave?"

"And you, Duncan?" Scarborough asked. "This has to be unanimous. This is going to be an all-hands on deck situation. We're either all in or none of us are."

"I don't have a problem with it," she replied.

"That leaves you, Fisher."

"I'll be on the next flight back and we'll leave when you're ready."

"Then we're all in agreement. I'll let Cole in on the decision and we'll go from there. Thank you. And safe travels back home, Fisher." Scarborough ended the call. "Do whatever you need to do to get ready to jump in and hit the ground running. I don't know how long we'll be there but prepare for a long stay. Any other questions?" He peered around. "I'll get back to you with flight details."

7

The unavoidable layover in Panama City tacked on an additional three hours to an already lengthy flight to Brasilia. The team had just arrived at the international airport and had deplaned. The decision was made for SSA Cameron Fisher to fly directly from Miami to Brasilia to save time. His arrival preceded theirs by a few hours and now he waited at the airport with Agent Elijah Cain to collect the rest of his colleagues.

Walking along the breezeway in the terminal, Kate turned on her cell phone. There were several missed calls and texts from Dwight Jameson. It had been a whirlwind few days getting this trip cleared by the director and the State Department, so she had put the unfortunate situation with Quinn on the back burner without informing Dwight as much. It was a decision she now regretted after viewing his attempts to reach her.

"What's going on? Did something come up?" Nick appeared to notice her studying her phone.

She pulled her eyes from the screen. "I was just checking my messages. Nothing important."

"Okay. Fisher texted me and said they were waiting for us in Baggage Claim. I know we're all exhausted, but we still need to be briefed at the Embassy before heading on a flight bound for Rio."

Kate fell back and let the others go ahead, though she maintained her pace. With the phone to her ear, she listened to the voicemails from Dwight. It was when she heard an unexpected name that she finally halted.

She immobilized abruptly, forcing other travelers to make evasive maneuvers in order to avoid a collision. "Oh my God. Georgia Myers. You told Quinn everything."

It hadn't been that Quinn was following Nick or her, but it had been his meeting with someone she would have least expected to betray them. Albeit, the woman in question had deceived Nick once before. The name Georgia Myers hadn't been a part of Kate's vocabulary for a few years now. Not since they both worked at the Washington Field Office. She had admired Georgia for her incredible talent as a profiler and she was Nick's girlfriend at the time. He loved her and might have even married her. It wasn't until Georgia betrayed Nick by sleeping with one of his former colleagues, and during an investigation, that everything fell apart. It destroyed him. It almost destroyed his career. Georgia asked to be transferred to another field office as a result. Georgia had direct knowledge of Nick's battle with alcohol. And now it seemed she had divulged that information to Noah Quinn. How he figured out who she was or what her relationship with Nick had been was a mystery. However, Quinn was no novice and only needed to follow the trail.

Upon regaining her composure, she realized she was standing

in the middle of a frenzied airport and noticed the team had already disappeared down the escalator. Kate jogged to catch up.

How could she face Quinn armed with this knowledge? They were in a foreign country whose laws were different from their own, assisting on an investigation that could force them into perilous circumstances. His sedition had already created a rift between them, and now she questioned her ability to have his back as she would the others.

"I see him. Up ahead." Eva Duncan stepped off the escalator and waved her arm.

Standing beside Fisher was Agent Elijah Cain and right away, Kate noticed he was the pragmatic type. There would be no warming up to a guy like him. In time, maybe her perception of him would change, but Kate had figured out early on that first impressions were usually right. Just as it had been with Noah Quinn. The first time she met him, he struck her as arrogant. While almost two years had passed since that time, he was no less arrogant. Perhaps even more so now than at their first meeting when he tried to charm her.

"About time you guys showed up." Fisher offered his hand to Scarborough. "How was your flight? Mine was shit, by the way. But hey, we're only an hour's time difference, right?"

"It was a long flight." Scarborough eyed the other agent. "You must be Elijah Cain. Nick Scarborough. Good to meet you."

"And you. I respect the hell out of the work you folks do over there at Quantico and I hate to get you involved in the shit show we got down here, but after seeing the crime scene photos, well, this is your bag. Not mine." Cain started toward the doors. "I have a car waiting. We should get a move on."

Levi Walsh held off until Kate approached. "Guess Cain

doesn't need to be introduced to the rest of us." He put his arm around her shoulders. "What's going on with you? You've been quiet since we got off the plane."

As much as Kate adored Levi, she couldn't confide in him about this. It already threatened to tear apart a team that was held together by a fragile trust still in its infancy. "Nothing's going on. I got behind on my calls and I was listening to voicemails. I lost track of you. That's all it was."

"Okay. You know you can come to me with anything, right?"

"I do know that."

"Good." He spotted Cain open a door to a full-size SUV. "Looks like our ride."

THE US EMBASSY APPEARED AHEAD. THE WHITE BUILDING with sharp lines was built in Brasilia when it was deemed the capital, removing that designation from Rio de Janeiro. The stunning gardens and tropical foliage offered an incredible backdrop to the building's stark white exterior.

"Any of you folks ever been down this way?" Cain pulled into the parking lot at the rear of the building.

"Not me." Scarborough peered back at the rest of the team. "Too bad this won't be a vacation." He eyed Kate briefly as they'd discussed taking a much needed vacation only recently.

"No, sir. This will not be a vacation. Unless you like wearing bullet-proof vests to the beach." Cain smiled. "All kidding aside, this case is a puzzler. I got two officers with the civil police staking their lives on the notion this is the work of some American." He stopped the SUV. "Let's head on inside and I'll give you the low down on the rest of this steaming pile of horseshit."

Inside, the security was tighter than anything Kate had seen in federal buildings at home. An x-ray machine, like the ones at airports, a scanner for bags and several armed staff flanking either side of the entrance.

"Never mind the guards with the M4 Carbines strapped to their chests. They only use them on the bad guys." Cain chuckled as he led them through to the section that housed the FBI's international operations.

"Well, I gotta tell you one thing, folks, you came at a good time of year. Damn near perfect weather in May. And you won't be sweating your nuts off in the humidity." Cain turned back. "Pardon the expression, ladies."

Kate and Eva traded glances while Eva's eyes rolled.

"This is the place. Now there's only about a dozen of us here right now. Other times there'll be more. Sometimes less. All depends on the demands of the work. I've been here for going on five years now. Things seemed to turn around for the better up until the 2016 Olympics. After that, well, shit just went downhill and hasn't reached bottom yet. Maybe with the new president they elected it'll change. Time will tell."

The attaché office itself was fairly small, unlike other field offices Kate had visited. The FBI's International Operations division was here to build relationships with local law enforcement, trade information with regard to counterterrorism, assist any US citizens and essentially act as liaisons. While they worked criminal cases, mostly relating to terrorism and international organized crime, this was a rare, if not unheard of, investigation for this office.

"In here is our conference room," Cain opened the door. "As you can see, I've prepared a dossier to brief you on the investigation as it now stands. So, if you'll all take a seat, we can get started."

THE STAFF EMPLOYED AT THE RIO DE JANEIRO CORONER'S office never suffered from boredom. In fact, so many bodies arrived on a daily basis, it wasn't unusual to see them stacked on top of one another in the hallways. With gang turf wars, military and civilian police violence and drug trafficking deaths, it was impossible to keep up with demand.

Nor was it uncommon for officers responsible for killing civilians, rightly or wrongly, to offer bribes to the doctors, who were otherwise not well-paid, to destroy evidence. And it wasn't just the cops. If a member of a gang offered a bribe, it was in the best interest of the doctor to accept it.

So when four bodies, unearthed from a shallow grave, arrived at the coroner's office, it was just like any other day. However, it was the arrival of an unexpected visitor that prompted the doctor currently examining one of the victims to take pause. "Posso te ajudar?" *"May I help you?"* He pulled away from the body with a defensive posture.

"I am here on behalf of a very wealthy and powerful individual," Scott said. "What will it take to ensure no evidence suggesting a perpetrator appears on the victims who were brought in yesterday?"

The doctor laid down his scalpel. "I see. Amigos dos Amigos?"

"No."

"Polícia?"

"No."

"Then what do I have to fear from you and your powerful boss?" The doctor replied.

Scott smiled and stepped closer before his face turned solemn. "I am here to offer you a handsome payment, however if you refuse, there will be consequences and not only to you."

The doctor held his ground, but his eyes bared his fear. "I am a doctor in search of truth. This cannot be tolerated any longer."

"This is the system in which we live, doctor. If you wish to change it, you should live elsewhere. This will be the only offer you will receive. Should I take it as a refusal?"

The doctor swallowed down his fear. "I will accept. You are American, aren't you?" He eyed Scott with distain. "I wonder who it is you are protecting? A politician? A millionaire? He must be powerful, but I will say one more thing. Someone will be held accountable for these crimes. Someday, the truth will come out."

"I will be long gone before that happens. And so will my wealthy friend."

THE BRUTALITY PERCEIVED IN THE IMAGES PLACED BEFORE Kate were nothing new to her. It seemed only a short time ago when viewing such things were revolting. Now, she had grown numb to them, just as they all had. It was a necessary mechanism to protect oneself in this line of work. Otherwise, it would drive anyone mad with grief.

Serial killers who elected decapitation as their preferred method of slaughter wasn't as uncommon as one might think, rendering that marker somewhat unremarkable. Kate required another context for the killer's motivations. "Four so far?" She leafed through the dossier.

"We suspect there could be more either in other grounds or maybe the same one. Getting heavy equipment through the confined streets and up the steep hillside has been a challenge, according to the civil police. But I would take that with a grain of salt. I need to put you all in touch with the officers who brought me this little gem, Inspector Varela and Investigator Sosa," Cain replied.

"These guys, they can be trusted?" Fisher asked. "Rumors have floated that may not be the case."

"They haven't given me a reason not to take them at their word. However, I have conducted my due diligence. These men are not saints—far from it. But the risk they're taking just by bringing this to us is extraordinary, so I have to believe they're doing this for the right reasons."

"What about phone records on this cell number they pinged?" Scarborough asked.

Cain nodded. "Yes, I'm working on getting those now, though it hasn't been easy with the telecom company here. We shouldn't bet the farm on receiving them anytime soon."

"Where do we go from here?" Walsh added. "Are these cops expecting us to take the lead, or what's the plan?"

"I'll act as the liaison between you all and the Civil Police. I'll assist with obtaining records and the like because I have the relationship with law enforcement. That said, as I mentioned before, this is going to be risky. Now, I've been assured by these men that the gang who controls the favela understands the investigation does not involve them. You would be well advised to keep it that way."

"Those guys are off-limits? Is that what you're saying? Regardless of where the evidence takes us."

"If you value your life, SSA Fisher, that is what I'm saying—yes."

Walsh searched for agreement in the faces of his cohorts. "When do we leave?"

"The sooner the better. We have a lot of ground to cover just to get you all up to speed and I'd like to get you to the crime scene before dark."

"Doesn't sound like a place we'd want to be after dark anyway," Walsh replied. "Do we have lodging?"

"You'll be staying in Gàvea. It's an affluent suburb with plenty of nice hotels. There'll be no need to worry about security there."

Kate closed the file. "Is that near Rocinha? We should be near the scene to facilitate transportation."

"Oh, believe me, Agent Reid, it's about as close as you'll want to venture. Rocinha is wedged between two of the wealthiest areas in all of Rio. Go figure." Cain gathered his things. "I've chartered a flight. It's too easy to get passenger manifests on commercial flights here and I won't chance anyone knowing when you're due to arrive. Once you're there, they'll figure it out in any case. But you'll be prepared by then. "I know I'm making this sound alarming as hell and I make no bones about it, it is. But you all are trained agents. You'll have the gear you need and the protection you need. Even the gangs in Rocinha aren't dumb enough to take down a United States federal agent. Just get in and get out and find the asshole who killed those women. There's no death penalty here, nor is there a life sentence. So, if this is one of ours, we might want to consider handling this ourselves, if you catch my drift."

THEY BOARDED THE PRIVATE JET AND WERE READY TO TAKE the flight bound for Rio. Kate sat in the window seat, second row in and stared at the runway. She was haunted by Cain's final words on the matter, *"consider handling this ourselves."* Had he seriously suggested they kill this person, whoever he was? Kate closed her eyes as the plane accelerated along the runway, raising with undulating wings that listed the small aircraft. Her pulse elevated as she inhaled deep breaths.

"You never were good at flying," Nick said.

"I was okay on the flight here, but on this small plane. It's like I can feel every little bump."

He grabbed her hand and squeezed. "It'll be okay. Trust me. We'll be fine."

She couldn't guarantee that was a true statement. It was inevitable. The truth about Nick's battle was bound to be exposed. Maybe it wouldn't matter, but the risk was too great to take that chance.

"How are you feeling about all this? The case, I mean?" Nick added.

"Cain needs help, that alone is enough to warrant being here. As for the rest, I won't lie, I have my concerns."

"I think we all do. This is new to all of us and we'll just have to do our best to look after one another."

"We need to be a team, now more than ever," Kate replied.

The captain's voice sounded through the speaker. "We'll be

descending into Rio shortly. Please buckle your safety belts and flight attendants, prepare for landing."

Kate watched the ground approach and was ready to get out of this pint-sized aircraft. Sure, it was nice inside, plush even, but not for her.

The wheels touched down and the charter jet rolled to a stop on a strip of concrete that lay between enormous hillsides and ocean shores. The afternoon sun was blinding in its brilliance and when Kate emerged, she shielded her eyes from the glare. It was the end of the second leg of this prolonged journey, but the beginning of another, more troubling expedition ahead.

Agent Cain's nostrils flared as he inhaled, and a smile played on his lips. "Ah, I do love this city." With hands pressed against his waist that revealed a protruding beer belly, he surveyed the grounds as a king might survey his lands. "There it is. Our car has arrived, ladies and gentlemen." He turned back to the team. "I know you folks must be on your last legs, but it won't be much longer now. We best get a move on."

The white Ford Expedition pulled to a stop and the agents stepped inside, leaving no space inside the substantial SUV.

"You're timing is impeccable, my friend," Cain said to the driver. "To Rocinha we go."

The driver nodded before making a u-turn to exit the airport and made his way toward the road to Rocinha.

Kate noticed the beaches in the distance. "It's really beautiful here."

"Yes ma'am, it is. There's no point in denying it," Cain said.

However, the beauty didn't last long as the driver made a few more turns and suddenly, things didn't look so beautiful anymore. They were on the outskirts of the favela and one need only gaze down the long streets to see the neglected housing structures, the graffitied walls and more powerlines than should be allowed.

"This is it, ladies and gentlemen. This is Rocinha." The driver pulled into the station parking lot.

Cain opened his door. "Thanks for the lift. It's time to rock and roll." He exited the car and made his way to the entrance waiting for the others to catch up. "Let me introduce you all to some of the locals. He opened the door and entered while the team followed behind. "Investigator Sosa. I have some people I'd like you to meet."

Pedro Sosa stood and approached the agents. "Por favor, my English is just so-so. I am Pedro Sosa." He offered his hand.

"Agent Nick Scarborough. Investigator Sosa, you'll forgive me, but I don't know any Portuguese."

Sosa grinned and spotted Varela emerge before addressing him in Portuguese. "Ah, Inspector Varela. These are the people we have been waiting for."

Varela approached with an outstretched hand. "We are glad you are here." He shook Scarborough's hand. "Agent Cain, thank you for all you have done. We have a lot to do today. I assume you have all been briefed?"

"They have," Cain replied. "We're ready to hit the ground running if you are."

Varela peered at Cain with some confusion.

"I mean, they're ready to go when you are." Cain turned to Scarborough. "Our vernacular doesn't translate well, but the Inspector here does have a pretty darn good grasp of the English language. Isn't that right, Inspector?"

"Yes, that is correct, a pretty good grasp."

"Duly noted." Scarborough returned his attention to Varela

and Sosa. "I'd like to introduce you to the rest of the team." He made the introductions before turning over the show to Cain. "I assume you'll be coming with us to the crime scene?"

"I will, indeed. However, I will leave the investigating up to you folks. You're the experts in this situation. Inspector, should we make our way out of here and show these folks what's what?"

"Sim, senhor."

8

Inside the densely populated favela of Rocinha, it was an easy task to spot an outsider. Driving along in the white unmarked SUV was synonymous with waving a big American flag and shooting off rifles in the air. It would be an impossible task to stand out any more as the SUV navigated through the dangerously narrow streets.

Investigator Sosa and Inspector Varela were in front of them in their civil police patrol car, further spotlighting the group and heightening speculation as the onlookers fixed their gazes upon the vehicles.

Walsh peered through the rear passenger window, with an awkward crinkling of his mouth, as though he suffered from embarrassment. "You ever feel like the one person wearing a costume to a party where no one else is?"

"I had no idea there were places like this in Rio," Kate said. "It looks like a third-world country."

"It is," Cain replied. "You can walk a few miles and find yourself among mansions and beachfront properties. Here, it's a different world all together." He followed Varela as they wound through the favela to the top where the bodies were discovered. "I don't want you folks staying here any longer than necessary. So, get your photos and samples and whatever else and let's get the hell out."

"You'll get no argument from me," Fisher said.

They arrived at the top where vehicle access ended.

"This is the place." Cain stepped out and climbed up the remaining several feet before reaching the cordoned off area. He was out of breath and beads of sweat formed on his brow from the physical exertion to which he was clearly not accustomed.

The others joined him among the verdant grounds where the hole that had been excavated from the hillside seemed incongruous.

Varela and Sosa appeared behind them and Varela began. "This is the place. There is another crew expected soon to finish the dig, once the grounds are stabilized."

"Do you expect to uncover more victims in this location?" Eva Duncan moved toward the burial ground.

"That would be the worst of all outcomes. I hope this is the last we will find of any victims," Varela replied.

"What about the others on your wall, Investigator Sosa?" Scarborough asked. "You have several missing persons' cases on your docket."

"If they are connected, I suspect we could find another of these killing grounds."

"We should get started," Scarborough began. "We'll document the location. Let's set up a string to get some measurements. Photograph tire tracks, footprints. You all know the drill. We've got a lot of work so let's do this before dark settles in."

Kate approached Investigator Sosa. "You mentioned an anonymous tip brought you here. How can you be sure the tipster isn't the killer?"

Sosa shrugged his shoulders and appeared confused.

"Agent Reid, I'm not sure Sosa gets your meaning." Cain approached them. "I'll translate."

He proceeded to tell Sosa what she said.

"Ah," Sosa began. "The tipster, as you call him, identified those he saw here. And then there was the mobile phone. This boy was just that. He is no killer and was simply on his morning jog, which he did daily."

Kate surveyed the grounds ahead. "This doesn't look like a running trail." She walked back to the area where the team had begun to document the scene and approached Duncan. "This site's been picked clean. I think whatever they have is in the file. I'm not sure what more we can accomplish by being here."

"We don't know what kind of evidence they discovered here and we don't know if they're withholding any from us. I know Cain trusts these people, but I'm not sure I do. I would rather be here and examine this first-hand," she replied.

Kate nodded. "Maybe I'm just looking to get out of here as quickly as we can. I'm not picking up a good vibe."

As daylight neared its end, the team was driven to the coroner's office where the four victims were held. Dr. Duarte was responsible for conducting the autopsies and waited behind the double doors ahead.

"The man in there." Cain pointed at the doors. "He's the one we need to speak to, but I wouldn't get my hopes up."

"Why is that?" Fisher asked.

"You'll see. Come on." Cain pushed through the doors and led them inside. "Looks like you two beat us to the punch," he said to Varela.

"Pedro knows a short-cut, isn't that right, Pedro?" Varela patted him on the back.

"Sim. Sim."

"This is Dr. Duarte," said Varela.

The doctor appeared not long out of medical school. He raised his gloved hands that held an instrument. "My apologies for not offering a handshake."

"Your English is very good," Duncan noted.

"Thank you. I attended medical school in Texas."

"Have you completed your autopsies on these victims?" Scarborough asked.

"I have, senhor. Unfortunately, I did not find enough forensic evidence that could be sent to a lab."

"No prints. Fibers, DNA. Nothing?" Fisher asked.

"I wish that were not the case. However, you are more than welcome to read the reports and maybe they will shed light on your investigation." He paused. "Can I ask? Why are the Americans interested in these victims?"

"I can answer that," Inspector Varela began. "A person of interest in the investigation could be an American. That is why they are here."

"I see." Dr. Duarte appeared concerned. "Well, should you

need anything more, please contact me. I will make myself available to you."

"Can we view the bodies, please?" Kate asked. "It's important for us to establish a baseline for markers on the victims."

"Certainly." Duarte approached the steel holding refrigerator and opened two of the doors. Large metal trays rolled out until they were fully extended. "Be my guest." He gestured for Kate to approach. "Is your background in forensic medicine?"

"No, I'm a profiler. I look for patterns and clues left behind that help us create certain details about the killer." Kate examined one of the victims. "Who is this?"

"I'm afraid I have not been able to establish an identity."

She turned to Sosa. "I thought one of them was Adriana Santos?"

"Sim." Sosa approached another tray. "She is here."

Quinn walked toward Kate while she observed the girl. "This one wasn't beheaded. Why some and not others? She has been strangled, though." He pointed to her bruised neck before pulling down the sheet to her legs. "Bruising here on her inner thighs suggests sexual assault." He turned to the doctor. "Did you use a rape kit?"

Duarte furrowed his brow. "No. We do not have materials like that."

Quinn shot a glance to Scarborough. "Can we get a kit here asap?"

"You'd better believe it."

Sosa turned to Inspector Varela and in their native language, began to whisper. "The doctor has been compromised."

Varela raised his hand. "Not here."

Kate, however, noticed the exchange, and so did Scarborough.

This was the red flag they should be concerned with. She knew DNA databases had been set up world-wide to process these rape kits. Brazil would absolutely have access to such technology. "I understand your limited resources, Dr. Duarte. That said, would it be acceptable for us to bring in a medical examiner to confirm your findings?"

"I think that would be wholly inappropriate, Agent Reid. This is not America and you and your team have no jurisdiction over this matter. Forgive my boldness, but these are Brazilian citizens and as such, fall under our laws."

"I believe what my colleague is suggesting," Cain began. "Is that because we have extenuating circumstances in this situation, and according to the Extradition Treaty with your country, if this is the work of an American, we would be allowed limited participation in this inquiry."

Duarte appeared agitated. "This is something that will require approval of my superiors. Until that happens, all I can give you are the reports."

"I guess that'll have to do," Fisher stepped in. "We'll take what we can get for now. Thank you very much for your cooperation."

"We sure do appreciate your time, Dr. Duarte. I'm sure we'll see you again real soon." Agent Cain led the team outside. "I told you you'd find out for yourselves. Happens every day around here."

"What the hell is going on? Do these people not want to know who's killing their citizens?" Duncan asked.

"There's an unwritten code here and in all the favelas," Varela began. "It's called the law of silence. It's what keeps you alive." He walked outside into the parking lot as the sun plunged below the horizon.

"I guess this means we're leaving," Fisher said.

Varela continued toward the vehicles as he spotted the others approach. "There is still another place I want you to see. In Gávea.

Sosa caught up to his boss. "The nightclub?"

"Yes. I need them to see the power the wealthy have around here as well as the connections inside the AdA and other groups. They will have to understand what they will be up against." He turned to Scarborough. "I think it is wise to only ask the senior agents on your team to accompany us. There are too many of you and you will be easily marked."

Scarborough and Fisher traded glances before he continued, "Fisher and I will go with you. The rest of the team can begin to analyze the crime scene photos as well as the autopsy reports. There is far more work ahead of us. We can tackle this from all sides."

Cain nodded. "I'll help get your people settled in so they can do their work. You'll be working out of your hotel rooms, I'm sorry to say. I can't risk you staying at the police station. I have you set up nearby. Inspector Varela, you take care of these gentlemen and see to it they return safely."

"Sim, senhor."

CAIN DROVE TO ONE OF THE CITY'S MOST LUXURIOUS HOTELS. Resting atop the white sands of a long stretch of beach, the hotel appeared like it belonged to another world far away from the favelas.

Walsh gazed at the splendor of the resort as they approached. "Better than the 3-star digs we're usually stuck with. I admit, though, I do feel a little guilty after what we just saw. You weren't kidding about the disparities."

"It's beautiful here and it's easy to forget all about Rocinha in a place like this. So don't feel bad. Just remember why you're here."

INSPECTOR VARELA PULLED INTO A NEARBY PARKING SPOT next door to the nightclub. "It's early yet, but I'd like to go in and give you a lay of the land. There are some important people you should be made aware of inside. Oh, and we had received another anonymous tip, we assume from someone who works here. He gave a description of a man who was supposedly seen with Adriana Santos. Sosa wasn't able to get any more information, though we suspect the call came from the bartender, who he had questioned previously."

Scarborough peered back at Fisher. "I don't mind chatting to some of the locals to get a feel for the scene."

"Right behind you." Fisher stepped out of the car and stood on the sidewalk fronting the building. "Nice place."

"It is well-known for supporting the habits of the wealthy, if you understand my meaning," Varela replied.

"I think I do." Scarborough fell in behind the inspector.

They entered the night club where it appeared at about half its capacity at the early hour of only 10pm. The team had traveled some 5,000 miles and hadn't slept in almost two days. Scarborough pushed through the urge to close his eyes.

"This is where you will find a lot of tourists, visitors. Not many locals come here, mostly because they cannot afford it," Varela said.

Sosa caught up with him and pulled him aside. "Senhor, why are we really here?"

"These Americans need to understand the hierarchy if they are to uncover the perpetrator of the crimes."

"You want them to meet with the AdA?"

"It's a start. I know one of the higher-ranking members will be here tonight, possibly de la Costa. We must satisfy the AdA that these American agents will not bring attention to them. It is the only way to ensure their safety."

Sosa nodded. "Maybe you should have told them that was the reason."

"I will—before the night is over, if they haven't come to understand that themselves." He turned to Scarborough. "Would you gentlemen like a drink?"

"Soda water for me," Scarborough replied.

"I'll take a beer."

The men sat down at the bar and turned around to face the dance floor. Several people danced and the music was louder than it needed to be for such a thin crowd.

Fisher leaned into Varela. "When does it get really busy here?"

"About another hour or so." Varela set his sights to the front door. With a nudge to Sosa, he asked. "That looks like Ramos. I was hoping for someone higher on the food chain, like de la Costa."

"Yes, it is him. Should I go?"

"No, let me do it." Varela stood from the barstool. "If you gentlemen will excuse me for a moment?" He headed toward the entrance where a wiry man, 40-something and sporting a bespoke suit had just arrived. "Senhor Ramos. Inspector Gustavo

Varela." He offered his hand. "Is Senhor de la Costa with you tonight?"

"I know who you are. Why are you here, Inspector? And why are you asking about de la Costa?"

"The crime scene I discussed with him. I wished to update him on the progress. I wasn't sure if you were aware of the situation with the Americans."

"I am aware." Ramos continued inside and was shown to a large round booth that appeared to be reserved for him.

"I relayed to Senhor de la Costa that the Americans are here only to investigate the murders because of the evidence that suggests an American culprit."

"And?" Ramos sat back in the deep booth and crossed his legs.

"In an effort to avoid any confusion for those who might see them inside Rocinha, perhaps an introduction is in order?"

Ramos smiled. "You want to be sure no one kills the Americans."

"That is a concern, Senhor."

"Bring them here. I will meet them, and you will have my word they will not be harmed."

Varela nodded. "Excuse me then. I will bring them over." He started back to the bar. "Gentlemen, I would like for you to meet someone. Someone with the power to ensure your safety while you are here."

Neither Fisher nor Scarborough were armed. They were forced to leave their weapons in the patrol car for fear of any misunderstandings. Now, Fisher felt naked and unprepared. "You want us to meet with a known gangster? Sure, why not?" He eyed his partner. "Scarborough, you game?"

"I'm game."

They followed Varela while Sosa remained at the bar alone.

"Gentlemen, I would like to introduce you to Alejo Ramos."

Ramos remained in his seat with an imperious smile on his lips. His assertion of power was not lost on either of the agents.

"I'm Special Agent Nicholas Scarborough. This is my partner, Special Agent Cameron Fisher."

"FBI." Ramos accepted Fisher's handshake but did not stand. "I feel like I am in the movies, yes? FBI, freeze!" He held both his index fingers and thumbs in the shape of guns. "Pew, pew." He laughed.

"That's us." Fisher smiled in return with humorless eyes. We're assisting on an investigation."

"Of course. Americans never cease to amaze me with their over-reaching powers." He adjusted his suit and returned to his relaxed position. "Inspector Varela says we should meet to ensure there is no confusion inside Rocinha. I say that is a wise decision. Although, I cannot say you will be completely safe from harm. There are many people inside the favela. I do not control them all. However, now that we have met face to face, you will not be in put in a situation which you cannot get out of. I give you my word."

"Thank you. Your cooperation is appreciated," Scarborough let slide the jab against Americans because, well, he wasn't armed, and he was in a foreign country speaking to a powerful drug trafficker. Not the time to split hairs.

"Sit down, please. You are making my neck sore. We should drink to our alliance." He snapped his fingers and a waiter appeared. "Tequila shots for everyone. Yes?"

Scarborough's heart pounded in his chest. He glanced to Fisher who appeared unfazed, but then, he wasn't the one with the problem. His mind raced to find a way out, any excuse would do, but he couldn't think of a single legitimate reason to reject the offer without raising concerns. When the waiter returned with the shots, he reached for one with a forced smile and held it between his fingers. Surely, his anxiety was on full display.

Ramos raised his shot glass. "To my new FBI friends." He tossed it back.

Scarborough's mouth dried in an instant. He watched Fisher and Varela throw back their shots. He was the only one left and Ramos appeared to take note.

"Do you not enjoy tequila, Special Agent Nicholas Scarborough?"

Fisher's expression hardened as he stared at his boss.

"I love it." He tossed it back.

9

_____

Silver trays holding empty plates and crumpled napkins lay atop the large table in the meeting room set up at the luxury resort. The sun was set to rise in a matter of hours and a team going on 2 days without sleep had just finished scrubbing the autopsy reports and other pertinent files obtained to date.

"I don't know about you folks, but I have got to catch some shut-eye." Cain yawned and raised his arms in an exaggerated stretch. "I have no idea how the hell you all are still functioning. We ought to call it a night."

"I'm not going anywhere until we hear from Fisher and Scarborough. They've been radio silent for too long," Duncan said.

Kate had worried about this very topic, though she was reluctant to voice her concerns due, in no small part, to Quinn's retaliatory efforts.

Walsh retrieved his phone. "We need to hear from them before we break up for the night." But before he dialed, the two senior agents entered the room. "Well, it's about time you two showed up. You two have any idea of the time?"

"Sorry, Dad," Fisher replied.

Cain scrutinized them. "Looks to me like you boys had a few too many and lost track of the time. I do hope you accomplished something besides catching a buzz."

Inspector Varela entered behind them. "These two did well tonight. I introduced them to an important member of the AdA. They did partake in a few drinks that were offered but I wouldn't say it was a choice on their part. Trust me when I tell you, this will make things go more smoothly for the investigation."

Kate swallowed down the rising tide of emotions. Almost a year of sobriety flushed down the drain. Her heart sank and it didn't matter if he did it for the right reasons. Making matters worse was that she felt Quinn's eyes on her, as if he knew as well. She refused to acknowledge him.

"No reason not to catch some rest now that you're all back. We'll reconvene first thing in the morning." Cain rose from the chair. "Glad you boys made it back in one piece. The paperwork alone would've been a nightmare." He patted them on the back and chuckled as he walked out the door.

"Thank you, Inspector, for bringing them back safely. Goodnight." Kate walked toward Nick. "We should go."

Quinn's eyes followed her every step, his ears open for her every word. She was careful not to say a one as she escorted Nick into the hall.

Silence consumed them as they walked along the lengthy corridor toward their room. Kate unlocked the door allowing Nick inside first where he dropped to the edge of the bed. She approached him and raised his right leg to remove his shoe.

"I don't need your help. I'm not that drunk for God's sake." His head sank and a heavy sigh escaped him. "I'm sorry." He whispered. "I'm so sorry, Kate. I let you down."

She joined him on the bed and wiped away a stray tear from her cheek. "What happened?"

"I didn't have a choice." He averted his eyes.

"Why didn't you have a choice, Nick? You always have a choice."

"You weren't there. I was two feet away from a notorious drug trafficker and a member of a deadly gang. He offered us drinks. I didn't feel it would be safe for me to refuse."

"How many?"

He rubbed his face and finally turned to her. "I don't know. A lot. Five, six maybe. Fisher had at least that much, too."

"Cameron isn't an alcoholic. You are. Did you see the way Quinn looked at you—at me—when you arrived?"

"Kate, I didn't believe I had a choice. Now you can accept that, or you can be pissed off at me. I'm already pissed at myself. You know it won't happen again. You know that."

She pushed off the bed and walked into the bathroom to change. Upon her return, Nick was sprawled on the bed, asleep and fully dressed. This hadn't even been on her radar, worrying about whether Nick would fall off the wagon. Not even an inkling this could happen and certainly not here. But here she was.

A blanket lay at the foot of the bed and as she pulled it over him, a twinge of guilt flittered in her stomach. She hadn't been there. Nor had she known the circumstances. But a thought lingered in her mind she couldn't help but ponder. Could he be trusted not to let it happen again?

Mason Wylder stood up from the sofa in only his boxer shorts and padded to the glass doors fronting the balcony of his mansion in Gávea. The moment he opened them, the breeze rolled with salty air until it pressed against his bare skin. Tiny goosebumps arose but only for a moment. That was when a mild sting pierced his right arm, and with some surprise he eyed the scratch that had scabbed over. He recalled how the scratch came to be.

"May I get you a coffee, sir?"

Mason turned. "Yes, please. Thank you, Dominic." He resumed his gaze into the deep waters and inhaled a cleansing breath.

Dominic soon returned with his coffee. "Here you are, sir."

"Thank you. Could you also bring me a bandage?"

"Right away, sir."

Mason walked back inside, leaving open the doors to allow fresh air in the home that only hours earlier had been inundated with the stench of liquor and vomit and sex. He resumed his morning ritual of slouching on the sofa with a coffee in one hand and his phone in the other, scrolling through his social media. He had people to maintain his posts and pictures and things of that nature. Personally, he never liked interacting with the general public in such a way, but he knew it was how things were done, and he needed to stay relevant.

"Good morning, Mason." Scott appeared with a bagel and coffee. "Don't forget you have an interview with a local journalist in an hour."

"Shit. You're right. I should get cleaned up." Still half-naked and getting in a quick scratch of his balls, he continued toward the rear of the home when he stopped on a dime. A piece of jewelry lay on the tile floor in the hall. He picked it up and studied it closely. "Who does this belong to?"

Scott appeared only mildly interested. "I don't know."

"Get rid of it. Now." Mason was quickly reminded of how he acquired the scratch on his arm. This bracelet. "If there's anything else left behind, I suggest you make it disappear before the reporter arrives."

"I will." Scott urgently recruited the housekeeping staff to scour the home and clean it without delay. He checked the time and noted the reporter was due to arrive within a few minutes and walked up the stairs. He spotted his employer. "Mason, it's almost time."

At the top of the steps, Mason buttoned his white shirt and tucked it into his slim-fitting black trousers. "I'm coming. Get Dominic to bring in some drinks, would you? I want to make this reporter as comfortable as possible." The doorbell rang. "Right on time."

Scott stepped back down the staircase and opened the front door. "Good morning, Mr. Wylder is waiting for you. Please, come in."

The young reporter put on a bright white smile and flicked back her thick caramel-colored hair. Her 4-inch heels clicked on the marble floor as she walked inside. "Thank you. I am Rosella Ortiz with the Rio Gazeta."

"Your English is really good, Ms. Ortiz. You can call me Scott. I'll show you to the living room."

"With the number of American tourists we see, it is best if one speaks the language. However, outside of the large cities, you would struggle to find any English speakers."

"Have a seat. Mr. Wylder will be down in a moment."

"I'm right here." Mason appeared from the kitchen holding a tray of drinks and snacks. "I thought I should offer my guest some refreshments." He placed it on the coffee table. "Thank you, Scott. I think I can handle it from here."

Scott took his leave while Mason poured a glass of iced tea. "I hope you like iced tea. It's sort of an American thing." He handed her the glass.

"Thank you." She sipped on the drink before returning it to the table and retrieved a voice recorder from her carrier bag. "You don't mind, do you?"

"Not at all."

"Excellent. I'm here with Mr. Mason Wylder, the American actor who calls Rio home, at least in high season. Isn't that right, Mr. Wylder?"

"Please, call me Mason. Yes, I come here in our summer to enjoy your beautiful winter weather. New York can be unbearable this time of year, with the humidity and heat. I'd much rather spend my time here when I'm not shooting the series."

"Speaking of that, when will you start production on the next season?"

Mason took a sip of his drink. "Well, I..."

"Excuse me, Mr. Wylder, but your arm seems to be bleeding," Rosella said.

"What's that?" He peered at his arm where a thin red line soaked through his shirt. "Oh. Excuse me, Ms. Ortiz. Would you mind if I go take care of this?"

"Not at all."

Mason walked into the powder room and removed his shirt to examine the stain. His eyes turned black and his lips curled into a scowl. "Stupid fucking bitch. Look what you did!"

DISSECTING THE EVENTS OF LAST NIGHT WASN'T SOMETHING Kate had the luxury of doing now in the light of a new day. She needed to steer clear of any other thoughts but the investigation. A sharp mind was necessary to see the clues no one else could, so she walked along the quiet beach as the sun rose to give her that critical perspective.

Nevertheless, her nerves were threadbare, and sleep last night only came in fits and spurts. As she walked along the shore, digging her toes in the wet sand, she gazed out at the ocean and watched the waves lap against the shore. It was serene and felt almost like home, San Diego, that was. Even if that hadn't been her home in a long time.

The short-lived, but reviving walk had to come to an end and Kate headed to the boardwalk and from there, it was only steps back to the hotel. She returned to the room and opened the door to find Nick getting dressed.

He set his sights on her with noted relief. "Where were you? I was worried."

"I didn't see any missed calls on my cell." Kate closed the door and reached for her laptop bag. "I took a walk along the beach."

"Alone?"

"Yes. Alone. It was fine."

Nick faced her squarely and clasped her shoulders. "It won't happen again, Kate. I swear it. If you'd been there. If you'd seen the man, you would have known I had no alternative. Fisher saw it too. I don't know what more I can say. I have a job to do and in order to keep all of us safe, this was a necessary evil. Inspector Varela told us what those people, the Amigos dos whatever, what they're capable of. They won't hesitate to kill any one of us."

"Then why aren't we looking into them if they're so obviously killers?" Kate pulled away from his tenuous grip.

"Varela said they already confronted the syndicate and they denied any involvement. In fact, they denied even knowing about it. And his partner, Investigator Sosa got that anonymous tip saying it was an American."

"Then Cain will need to provide us with the call logs from the number that was traced back to the tower ASAP." She gathered her files. "We should go to the meeting room. Everyone's probably waiting for us."

She started out the door, leaving Nick behind, and walked ahead. Her anger was misplaced and while she recognized that, she still needed time to process what had happened.

Inside the meeting room, Quinn was the only one who had so far shown up.

"Good morning." Kate entered and made her way to one of the chairs at the table. A breakfast spread had already arrived and come to think of it, she was hungry and in need of coffee.

"Morning. Looks you and I are the only ones up and about." He sipped on a cup of coffee.

"Where did you get that?"

"There's a room back there. I put on a pot. Feel free to dive into the bagels. The croissants are actually my favorite. How'd you sleep?"

It was hard to look at him after what he'd done, but there was little choice—for now. "I woke up early and took a walk along the beach."

"Beautiful morning for it," he replied. "You should've called me. I would've come with."

She put on an unnatural smile and retreated to the back. On her return, Quinn typed on his laptop. "Any word about our ME?"

"The request was denied, unfortunately."

"Denied? Why?" Kate sat down.

"Because we aren't in Kansas anymore."

"We all saw those reports last night. They were a joke. Incomplete, no definitive conclusions. How are we supposed to find what they so clearly missed?"

"We aren't. Looks like we'll have to rely on good old fashioned police work."

Kate retrieved her files and placed them on the table. "Does anyone else know about this?"

"Don't know if anyone's checked their emails yet. That's how I found out. Probably in your inbox too."

Kate loaded up her laptop and waited for the email to arrive.

"Hey, um, you must be pretty upset about last night," Quinn said.

She shot him a look. "What's that?"

"I mean, about you know, Scarborough and what he and Fisher were doing last night."

"It's my understanding that they were securing our safety with the help of Inspector Varela. Is there something else you're referring to?"

"I guess not." He returned to his laptop but stopped and looked at Kate again. "I don't blame you."

"For what, Quinn?"

"For hating me right now."

She smirked and shook her head. "I don't hate you. In fact, I don't have any feelings for you one way or another. So, how about we get back to work."

MASON WYLDER RETURNED TO THE LIVING ROOM WHERE THE journalist waited. "Please forgive the interruption. Where were we?"

"You're sure you're all right?" she asked.

"Yes, I'm fine, Rosella." He sat back down. "Let's continue."

"Of course." She pressed record again. "I guess I should ask, how did you get that nasty cut on your arm?"

"This? Oh, it happened last night. I was walking along the back of the house in search of a cell phone a guest said he dropped from the balcony. I think it was the grasses back there."

"Ah yes, I see. So, I understand this upcoming season could possibly be your last. What can you tell me about that?"

"Well, you know, it's been an incredible six year run, but as the saying goes, 'all good things must come to an end.'"

"Will you stay in New York when you're finished taping?"

"I don't know. I might take a hiatus. I haven't quite figured out what the future holds for me."

"You have a few more months with us here in our beautiful city. What are your plans?"

"Well, as usual, I'll be soaking up the sun and enjoying the time off. I have toyed with the idea of penning my memoir, if I find the time." Mason chuckled.

"I can't thank you enough for taking a moment or two away

from your sunbathing," Rosella replied. "I'll let you know when this goes to print. Thank you for your time, Mr. Wylder."

"I'll show you out." Mason led the reporter to the door. "I look forward to reading the piece. Have a lovely day, Ms. Ortiz." He waited for her to leave and closed the door.

The smile on his face vanished and he marched to the safe room. After keying in the passcode, he pushed open the heavy steel door. "How dare you? Do you have any idea what you almost cost me?"

A young woman whose face was stained with tears was bound and gagged and shackled to the floor. She shook her head as her eyes locked onto his.

He approached her and with the back of his hand, struck her face. "Answer me!"

She cried harder while he shoved his right arm in her face, pointing at the scratch.

"You'll pay for this. I'll make you scream for your life." He walked out and slammed the door behind him. A deep breath in through his nose and he stood firmly in the middle of the hallway. "Scott? Scott, where the hell are you?" When there was no answer, he texted him on the phone. *"Safe room. NOW."*

Scott jogged along the corridor. "Sorry, man, I didn't know you were finished. Where's the reporter?"

"Gone. Make sure the house is empty tonight. I have business to take care of." Mason started to walk away and raising his voice slightly, he continued. "Make sure you get Pete lined up too. You both are going to have your work cut out for you tonight."

10

In the middle of an international investigation that had the potential to rock the delicate diplomatic relations between the two countries, Kate tried to suppress the distractions that gnawed at her. Noah Quinn and his attempt to blackmail her. Nick falling off the wagon and not knowing if he would do it again. Her mind reeled. She would be of no use to anyone if her focus didn't return. For now, however, the door to the conference room opened. The rest of the team was here to wrestle her thoughts back to where they belonged.

"We were about to send in the cops." Quinn smiled as though they were in the midst of an ordinary day.

"Jet lag." Fisher headed straight for the back room. "Anyone else want a coffee?"

Duncan peered around at the nodding heads. "Looks like everyone's a taker. Let me come help you."

Walsh must've picked up on Kate's anxiety as he sat next to her. "How long have you two been here?"

"Not long. Quinn was here before me. I went for a walk on the beach to clear my head."

"I don't know if you've seen the email." Quinn opened the file on his laptop and turned it outward. "Our request for the M.E. was denied."

"What?" Scarborough marched toward him and eyed the screen. "What the hell is this?"

Fisher returned holding two mugs with Duncan holding two more. "If I had a guess, I'd say the Rio Coroner's office put the kibosh on our request. That shouldn't come as a surprise. The doctor wasn't on board with the idea in the first place, but we had to give it a shot. It is their country and their investigation."

"Good morning." Inspector Varela entered the meeting room. "I can see by the look on your faces you already know about the denied request."

"Do we have any recourse?" Kate asked.

"I wish I could say yes, but you do not. I'm sorry." Varela appeared to think on the matter. "There could be a way around this, but it won't be easy, nor will it be safe."

"What else is new?" Walsh replied. "If it gets us what we need, I have no problems doing what needs to be done."

"Now just hold on a second." Scarborough raised his hand. "What are we talking about here?"

Varela peered at the group who had gathered around the table. "It could be possible to find a way to get you access. You collect your samples and vamos lá—leave." He eyed the elite team who appeared to consider the idea. "I am expecting the call logs to the tower today. It is possible you will find what you need there. However, we should consider alternatives such as this."

"I don't see as we have another choice." Walsh eyed Scarborough. "You're the head honcho. We need to get this ball rolling. What do you say?"

"If it has to be this way, then I'll be the one to do it." He turned to Varela. "How soon can you make this happen?"

"You're not doing this alone, that's for damn sure," Fisher replied. "We'll both go."

"I can make it happen tonight."

"Then let's do it," Scarborough replied. "Fisher and I will need to do recon and get with you on the logistics. Will we have Investigator Sosa at our disposal today?"

"Whatever it is you need, Agent Scarborough."

"Let's round him up. I'd like to have him take Reid and Quinn back to the crime scene to pore over it one more time. We were losing daylight yesterday and we might find something new this morning." He turned to Walsh. "You and Duncan will parse the call logs when they arrive, if that works for you?"

"You got it, boss," Walsh replied.

KATE STUDIED THE FILES AS INVESTIGATOR SOSA DROVE TO the crime scene once again. "Thank you for bringing us out here, Officer Sosa."

"Sorry, my English isn't good. Please, call me Pedro."

"Okay, Pedro. Thank you."

As he arrived at the scene, or as close as was accessible by car, Kate stepped out. "I'll bring my phone in case we need Google Translate." She smiled at him.

Quinn followed them out, though he hadn't spoken for the

entirety of the short drive. "What are you hoping to find this morning that we didn't find yesterday, Reid?"

"I don't know, Quinn. I guess I'll know it when I see it." She pushed past him. "Pedro, are there any other footpaths around here?"

"Sim. I mean, yes. Follow me." He started up the slope to the right of the initial site.

Quinn appeared reluctant but followed them anyway.

"Do you think it's possible there exists another burial ground, Pedro?" Kate asked.

"I believe so, yes. There are many missing women."

They approached another clearing about a quarter of a mile away. Quinn shoved his hands in his pockets. "This seems almost too remote. If there were more victims here, someone would've had to carry them up this hill."

Kate couldn't bear to concede to him, but he might be right on this one. She turned to Sosa. "Too far?"

Sosa peered at the ground. "Dig here?" He shook his head. "Not too far." He returned to his car that was at least 100 yards away and retrieved a shovel. And on his return, he smiled and held it up. "A Boy Scout? Always prepared?"

"Yes, like a Boy Scout." Kate moved in as Sosa tucked the shovel into the ground.

"Why here though?" Quinn asked. "I see no indication of any freshly turned soil. No obvious footprints. Am I missing something?"

"You want to understand how I operate? This is it. I get a feeling. A hunch. Whatever you want to call it. Look, I don't know if we'll find anything here. What I'm more interested in is seeing if anyone comes near. If anyone is watching us. That's what I care about maybe even more than finding something."

Quinn nodded. "Yeah. That's a good call, Reid."

Sosa appeared uninterested in their conversation as he turned over the soft earth. Whether he realized Kate's intent remained unknown, but it appeared he was fully vested in the idea there could be more bodies here.

"You mind if I look around while you start?" She asked him.

"Ah. Okay. I'll dig more," Sosa replied.

She turned to Quinn. "I'm going to go check things out. You mind staying here with him?"

"I'm not sure it's a good idea for you to go out there by yourself."

"Now you're concerned about me?" She scoffed. "I'm armed. I'll be fine." Kate walked away and didn't look back.

Sosa stopped digging for a moment and shifted his sights to Quinn. *"Irritado?"* He pointed toward Kate.

"Yes. Irritated."

Kate trudged through the dense greenery beneath the shadows of the lush overhanging trees. She reached another small clearing near the edge of a cliff and on looking down, the ocean came into full view. And over her shoulder, Christ the Redeemer sat high atop Corcovado mountain, looming large over the City of God.

While the view was awe-inspiring, her point in this escapade was to watch for onlookers. It was approaching mid-day and she had seen no one nearby. Below, the streets were cluttered with what appeared at this distance to be little ants scurrying about in circles. "What am I doing out here?" She started back toward the area and stopped on a dime. "Hello."

A young boy, not older than ten, stood near and fixed his gaze upon her.

"Are you here alone?" She peered around him in search of an adult but didn't see one. "Are you lost?" It was clear he didn't understand her. "Come with me." She waved her arm and started toward the site again. "Come?"

The boy shook his head and darted back from where ever he came. Kate watched as the boy seemed familiar with every inch of the path and hillside as he leapt down it. He was not lost. But then why was he there?

She headed in the direction of where the boy had returned in search of people. Climbing several feet down and still no signs of life. The boy was gone. And if she didn't stop now, it was likely she would find herself lost. A quick check of her cell phone. "No signal." She could go no farther. It was a lost cause and time for her to return.

"You okay?" Quinn approached her. "Were you talking to someone?"

"Just myself." She continued toward Sosa. "Anything?"

"No." He shook his head.

"Okay. Let's go back." She let Sosa take the lead and fell in behind Quinn. One last look at the place because she still believed it held a secret. There was a reason the killer chose this spot.

"Reid?" Quinn reached the car and held open the door.

"Yeah." She took a few steps and stumbled to the ground. "Shit!"

"Jesus, are you okay?" Quinn jogged toward her.

What she had tripped over was the reason she chose to return here. It was her hunch and it hadn't let her down after all. "Oh my God."

"Don't move, Kate. I'll help you up." As Quinn approached, he stopped dead. "What the hell?"

"Investigator Sosa?" she yelled. "Pedro? Come quick!"

Pedro figured out something had happened and rushed to them. "Meu Deus." *"My God."*

Kate remained on the ground, her eyes fixed on the object. "If this is the head, where's the body?"

"He should've been here by now." Duncan set her sights on the door to the meeting room where she and Walsh waited. "We can't sit here and do nothing."

And as if on command, the inspector entered. "I have them. I have the call logs from the tower."

"Were your ears burning?" Walsh smiled but noted the look of confusion on Varela's face. "Never mind. We were getting worried. Now maybe we can get somewhere." He retrieved the papers from Varela and proceeded to punch in commands on his laptop. "We can cross-reference these numbers and locations as well as determine how often they were called."

"That will help us to identify other persons in contact with the mysterious caller and where the calls originated. If we're lucky, we can reconstruct a timeline and determine how often and when calls were made from that location," Duncan replied.

"Is there anything else, then, I can assist you with?" Varela asked.

"Thank you, no. This will take some time," Duncan replied.

"Then I will work to arrange efforts for Agents Fisher and

Scarborough. Please contact me if you need anything at all." With a brief nod, Varela showed himself out.

"Did you spot the fact that the majority of the calls on these logs came from Rio numbers? We'll be able to track them too," Duncan said.

"I think that was the reason for the delay," Walsh began. "Varela is a smart man. He knows how to survive. If any of these logs point to his own, he's already vetted them, no doubt."

"As long as these calls aren't whitewashed. The last thing we need is inaccurate data sending us on a wild goose chase." Duncan opened the database known as DIVS, the data integration and visualization system. This new and innovative program was recently enhanced to include geospatial tools and cross-refer-encing of data. "You want to place bets on if any of the calls around the time frame in question trace back to a registered cell and not a burner?"

Walsh laughed. "I don't think I'd like my odds. If the one we're searching for is an American, and by looking at these records, I see a handful of calls with US area codes, then it's unlikely he's acting alone. This thing is fifteen pages long. I would suggest we start with the US numbers first. It'll be much easier for us to send that intel back to our folks and try to get us a name. That's what we really need."

ATOP THE HILLS OF ROCINHA, STANDING IN THE SHADOW OF its sheer cliffs, Kate wiped blood from her shoe. "This feels too planned," she said. "Like we were meant to find this head." Kate pulled upright and set her sights to Quinn. "The others were buried. Why not this one? And where is the rest of her?"

"You're the one who decided to take a stroll. You're the one who found it. I don't know. It doesn't seem planned to me. You said you saw a boy earlier. People must come up here. It could've been any one of them who uncovered it."

"Maybe someone who wanted it to be found, but couldn't be the one to discover it," she replied. "No one around here wants to talk so this could have been the only way to make a statement." She eyed Pedro Sosa who stood at the front of his patrol car on his phone.

"Should we proceed to dig in this location?" Sosa asked Varela as he acknowledged Kate.

"This could be the perfect timing we need."

Sosa's brow furrowed. "What do you mean, sir?"

"I mean, if we can get the coroner and his team out there to remove the remains you and the agents found, then maybe we can use that as the distraction we need. It could provide Agents Scarborough and Fisher enough of a lull in the activity at the coroner's office that will allow them to sneak in and retrieve evidence."

"I understand. Should I call the coroner then?"

"Yes. Please inform me when they've arrived. That is when I will have them slip inside."

"Sim, senhor." Sosa ended the call and approached the agents. "I am to have the coroner come now. We wait."

"Perfect," Kate replied. "While we're waiting, do I have your permission to photograph the exposed remains?"

"Of course."

She nodded to Quinn and both returned to the location where the severed head had been unearthed.

"Good call. In the event Fisher and Scarborough don't get what we need, we will," Quinn said.

Kate hovered over the remains. "Do you have a swab kit handy?"

"No," Quinn chuckled. "That would've come in useful right about now." He turned back to Sosa. "You think he has anything that would suffice?"

"Maybe." Kate walked back to Sosa. "Excuse me, Pedro, do you have any forensics kits on hand? Um, swab?" She used a gesture showing her swabbing her cheek. "Prints?" She displayed the underside of her fingertips.

"Ah. Yes. Prints." He smiled and returned to his car to retrieve the kit.

"Thank God."

"This?" He held out a box and opened it.

"Jackpot." Kate smiled. "Yes. Thank you." She took the box from him and walked back to the location where Quinn waited. "This will have to do for now."

"Looks like he's got a fingerprint kit. Sample holders." He looked at her. "We can try to pull fibers. I don't see a swab."

"No. Which means we won't get any DNA samples, but fibers and prints will do wonders."

11

The sun had fallen behind the cliffs. The tepid air now felt stifling in the midst of rising concern by not only the federal agents, but by one of Rio's own, a man Kate believed could be trusted. But the hour had long since passed that the coroner should have arrived. "Should we call again?" Kate gestured with her phone to Investigator Sosa. "Why aren't they here yet?"

He shook his head and shrugged. "I will try again." Sosa made another call while the agents waited nearby.

"I don't like this, Quinn." Distress built in the pit of Kate's stomach as she fixed her gaze on Sosa. "We've been here for two hours. It's time we call our own people."

It seemed she wasn't the only one to grasp the warning signs. "Maybe. Yeah. Our people don't know we're here." Quinn impulsively placed his hand on his sidearm.

She turned her back from Sosa's view and dialed Nick. "Come on. Answer." A wave of relief swept over her when he picked up.

"Kate?"

"Hey, Quinn and I are out here at the..." She peered at her phone. "What the hell?"

"What' wrong?" Quinn moved in. "He didn't answer?"

"I think I got cut off. I'll try again." She dialed the number. "Shit. I lost the signal. Do you have one?"

He peered at his phone. "No. Did you tell him where we were?"

"I was cut off too quickly."

"We need to leave. Now." Quinn started back toward Sosa. "Investigator Sosa, we can't wait any longer."

The echo of gunfire ricocheted off the hills. Sosa, with his sights fixed on Quinn, fell where he stood.

"Take cover!" Quinn dropped low and found shelter behind Sosa's patrol car. "Reid, get down!"

Kate crouched low and stepped toward him. "What the hell is going on?" Her eyes shot a glance at Sosa.

His chest spilled blood. Color drained from his face and his eyes blinked slowly as he turned to her. "Run."

Kate started toward him. "We're not leaving you."

"Get in the car now!" Quinn said. "He's gone, Kate." "And we're about to be if we don't get the hell out of here."

Sosa winced. "Go. You must go."

"I'm so sorry." Kate retreated with her weapon trained on anything that moved as she made her way to Quinn and the car. "We've been set up. Varela must've turned. We have to warn Scarborough."

"What we have to do right now is save our asses and figure a way out of here," Quinn said. "We need to get in the car and drive.

I'll go first and jump into the driver's seat. I'll cover you while you get in the back. When you're in, stay the hell down!"

"What about Sosa?"

"We can't do anything for him." He raised his head a little and another shot was fired. "Fuck! We need to work fast. On my count. One, two, three." Quinn darted to his left toward the driver's side, low and fast, until he opened the door and jumped in.

"Keys." Kate eyed Sosa. "I have to get the keys." She lurched toward Sosa's body. "Oh God, I'm so sorry."

"Reid?" Quinn shouted from inside the car. "What are you...?"

Another shot rang out and struck the car's rear bumper. Kate had mere seconds to find the keys and take cover again. Her hands felt around Sosa's pants pockets. She thrust her right hand into one of them and yanked the keys out. The elation, however, was short lived. She still had to get back to the car. With a deep breath, she sprinted to the rear passenger side and pulled open the door. A bullet struck the door just as she jumped inside. "Drive!" She tossed the keys to Quinn.

They fell to the floorboard and he rummaged to find them. "Shit!" His hands frantically searched when another bullet struck the passenger side. An instinctive flinch and he shouted. "Stay down, Reid!"

"Start the car!" she yelled from the backseat, her arms thrust over her head.

"Got 'em!" He fumbled for just a second before finding the right key and inserting it. He turned over the engine and spun the tires, and the patrol car flew down dirt road. Bump after bump felt like the wheels would fly off, but he held firm.

Multiple shots were fired. The rear window exploded. Kate still laid low in the passenger seat. "Get us the hell out of here!"

"I'm trying!" Quinn recoiled with each gun shot while somehow maintaining control of the car along the brutal path. "Do you have a signal yet?" He shouted.

Kate reached for her phone in her front pocket. "Not yet!"

A car appeared behind them seemingly from out of nowhere. Quinn spotted it in the rear view. "They're behind us. Jesus, Kate. I don't know if we're going to make it out of here. I don't know how many more are waiting."

They were in a war zone. Kate couldn't negotiate her way out of this one. There would be no reasoning. There would be only running. And for the first time in a long time, she feared for her life. And for Quinn's.

INSIDE THE FAVELA'S STATIONHOUSE, SCARBOROUGH STARED at his phone. "What the hell happened?"

Fisher, who had returned from speaking with other officers, approached him. "What's wrong?"

"That was Reid. I must've gotten cut off."

"Try her back."

He tried again, but a busy dial tone sounded. "I'm not getting through at all now." His concern grew. "Do we know where they are? Has anyone heard from them?"

"I'm sure they're in the hills in Rocinha. She'll try again when she gets another signal." Fisher peered through the window. "I think that's Inspector Varela pulling in now. We're losing daylight here and we need to get a plan together for getting into the coroner's office."

"Right. I'll try her again later." He slipped his phone into his pocket.

Varela made his way inside. "I'm sorry for the delay. I returned as quickly as I could."

"And the call logs?" Fisher asked.

"In the hands of your agents."

"Good. So what's the plan, Inspector?" Fisher added. "As you can see, I'd like to move quickly. We both would. We need to get back to our team."

"Have you spoken to your agents who are with Investigator Sosa?" He asked.

"We tried," Scarborough said. "Unfortunately, the signal was dropped. I'll try again soon. Do you have an update from him?"

"This is a common problem in Rocinha. Mobile phone service is very poor. I, too, have been unable to reach my officer. No need to worry. Sosa knows what he is doing. I have no doubt your people will be in touch as soon as possible." Varela headed toward his office. "For our part, I have a plan in place."

QUINN DROVE AT BREAKNECK SPEEDS UNTIL THEY REACHED the decaying streets of the favela. The gunfire ceased and Kate felt safe enough to sit up from the backseat. "For God's sake, what the hell is going on, Quinn? We were almost killed."

"I wish I knew. I'll tell you one thing, though, whatever assurances were given to our team leaders by the gangs who control this shithole just flew out the goddam window." He turned at the end of the road that led to the exit. "I just want to get the hell out of here. Please tell me you have a signal now?"

Kate eyed her phone. "Yes!" She dialed Nick again and the line rang. Her heart pounded, not knowing if she was too late to warn him about Varela.

"There you are." Nick answered. "I tried to call you back…"

There was no time for chitchat and Kate interrupted, "Where are you?"

"Just heading into a meeting with Varela. What's wrong? Are you okay?"

"No. Don't go in with him. Nick, you and Fisher need to leave now."

"What?"

"Just go. Please. Sosa's dead. I'm with Quinn. We just left Rocinha."

Nick was silent on the line for a moment. "Go straight to the hotel. Call Cain."

The line went dead and she screamed into her phone. "Nick? Nick?"

"Are they at the station?" Quinn asked.

"Yes. He said they were walking into a meeting with Varela. He told us to go to the hotel and contact Agent Cain. Then he hung up."

"Christ."

"We can't go to the hotel, Quinn," Kate pleaded. "Please. You have to go the station. It's less than a mile from here."

"How do we know Varela is the problem?"

"We don't for certain, but we have to know our people are safe. I'm not sure any of us is safe anymore."

"I won't argue that point." Quinn made another turn and continued until they spotted the station. "You have a plan or are we shooting from the hip?"

"I don't think Varela is going to gun down two federal agents inside his own station. If he is behind Sosa's death, he'll know the minute we walk inside that we figured it out. I'm pretty sure we weren't supposed to make it out of there alive." Kate pondered an idea. "There are two entrances. We park at a distance and go on foot to the rear entrance."

"They're armed too, and we're outnumbered at least 3 to 1."

"What choice do we have?" Kate replied.

He stopped a block away and shifted the patrol car into park. With a glance over his shoulder, he studied Kate. "We'll have no choice but to take down anyone who tries to stop us. We have no idea who Varela has in his pocket. Then we get our people out. You ready?"

"I'm ready." She stepped out onto the side of the road while Quinn joined her.

The streets were lined with small drainage channels on either side. No sidewalks. They walked next to the buildings fronting the road. The station was only feet away now.

"I see only a few patrol cars. That bodes well for us." Quinn stopped and grabbed Kate's arm. "Whatever happens once we're inside, just worry about yourself, okay? Don't play the hero."

She wanted to offer a scathing retort, but this wasn't the time. Quinn had all but certified his cowardice. In the face of danger, this was his reaction; to look out for yourself. "I know what to do."

They approached the rear entrance and Quinn pulled on the door handle. "Shit. It's locked."

The plan was flaming out and Kate had to find another solution. "It's pretty damn quiet around here. I don't know if Varela planned it that way or not. But our only choice is to go around to the front."

They reached the main entrance to the station. It was still eerily quiet and Kate couldn't shake the idea this was another setup. Although it was already dark, there should have been more activity in the area. It was as if others had been warned to keep their distance.

"I'll go in first. Stay close and ready your weapon." With his sidearm aimed ahead, Quinn pushed through the door.

The bullpen was vacant. Kate was only steps behind and on spotting the empty room, she experienced minor relief. Maybe they wouldn't be outnumbered after all. But where were her teammates? She tapped on Quinn's shoulder and pointed to a closed door. "Varela's office."

He nodded and they continued to the door in stealth. As they approached, Quinn stopped her. "Let me." He reached for the door handle and turned. "Don't move!"

Scarborough and Fisher leaped into action, both reaching for their weapons before recognizing who stood before them. Quinn trained his gun on Varela who sat behind his desk while Kate entered with her weapon drawn and pointing at Varela's head.

They weren't the only ones ready for a battle. Varela had his gun pointed right back at Quinn.

"Put down your gun, Inspector," Reid demanded.

"Reid, what the fuck are you doing?" Fisher said.

"I told you to go to the hotel." Scarborough turned his gun on Varela. "I know about Investigator Sosa."

"Wait? What? Did I miss something, here?" Fisher asked.

"Was it the AdA?" Scarborough added. "I have to assume they threatened you or why would you have let them kill one of your own?"

"You don't know what you've unleashed," Varela refused to

disarm. "I tried. I tried to convince the gangs you would not interfere. They didn't believe me. And now I've lost a good man."

"We came here to help you capture a killer. An American killer. You asked for our help," Scarborough said.

"That is what I cared about too, until I got the call. They are holding my wife hostage until you leave."

"I can't fucking believe this." Fisher jumped up from his chair. "You sacrificed your own man for these people?"

"For my wife, Agent Fisher." Varela peered at the four who held firm their weapons. "I cannot take out all of you, but I can get at least one. Is that what we want right now?"

"You can't be trusted," Scarborough said. "Did you tell them we were going to the coroner's office? You had no intentions of allowing us to get out of there alive, did you?"

"I can fix this, but please help me get my wife to safety. I wanted none of this. Pedro Sosa was a good man. A fine husband and father. I will have to bear the responsibility for his murder."

"We drove out of Rocinha in a hail of bullets and you want us to trust you now?" Kate asked. She hadn't revealed that to Scarborough and she could feel the burn of his stare.

"We're here to find a killer. We will find him and if that means taking down any member of the so-called Amigos dos Amigos, then so be it. We have work to do and someone's going to have to take care of him." She pointed to Varela.

"Wait. Just hold on a second," Scarborough said. "We need him. He's our only link to the AdA." He turned his attention to Varela. "I want the American. And you're going to help us get him."

❧

Mason Wylder stood on his balcony overlooking the ocean as the sun lowered over the western horizon. The fiery sky mingled with the rolling waters to craft a stunning canvas. The day had drawn to a close and there was work to be done. He turned from nature's portrait and walked inside where his assistant and closest confidant waited for orders.

"I have news that could end up being a problem for us." Scott held out a glass of malt scotch poured atop two ice cubes. "You might want this first. An officer was murdered in Rocinha today. The civil police are investigating and there is talk the military police might intervene. Word has it the gangs were responsible."

"That could present a problem for us, yes. Has anyone found the rest of them yet?"

"The only ones discovered were the ones already taken to the coroner. And I've handled that situation," Scott replied.

"Then how should we handle our current guest? We might be forced to keep her until this blows over." He sipped on his drink.

"Mason, things have become extremely complicated. I haven't been able to confirm this yet, but I've heard the FBI is here. Supposedly offering their expertise on the ones found in the hills. This might be the right time to go home."

"Wouldn't that only raise suspicions?"

"You haven't done anything that would cause suspicions to be raised in the first place. Not yet," Scott began. "This is the best position for us to be in right now. We have the upper hand."

Mason turned away from Scott and again peered through the glass doors. "Let me go to the club. I'm expected there and if I don't show, that might make others apprehensive." He turned back and downed the remainder of his drink. "However, I won't disagree with you. Tomorrow we will go home."

"Thank you. Okay. I'll make sure the jet is ready." He turned to leave.

"Scott?"

"Yes?"

"There's one other thing. I'm going to need you to scrub that reporter."

"I'm sorry? What?"

"You heard me. She saw something she shouldn't have seen and in light of the current situation, it would be in our best interest to see to it nothing goes to print. And that she doesn't resurface. I have enough on my plate, so she is yours to handle."

"She has a spot on the 10pm news," Scott pleaded. "They're going to notice when she doesn't show up. Look, she doesn't know anything."

"We're leaving tomorrow anyway. I don't see the problem here. This is something that needs to be handled. And, forgive me if I'm wrong, but I thought I hired you to handle them."

12

It was Agent Cain's footsteps and subsequent push through the doors of the meeting room that caused Eva Duncan and Levi Walsh to jolt to attention.

"We need to pack up and get the hell out of here," Cain said. "And I mean, like now."

"What happened? Is everyone okay?" Walsh asked.

"You're not safe here. Not anymore. I've set up a safehouse for you and your team. They're already there. And now you need to be too."

"Okay, hold up here. I'm going to need to speak to Scarborough," Walsh replied.

"You can, once I get you to the safehouse. Look, I don't have time to explain. Suffice it to say, you've been led down a rabbit hole and I'm here to bail you out."

Duncan shut down her laptop and thrust it into her computer bag. "I knew this was too easy. Just answer me this, is everyone okay? Is the team safe?"

"Yes. For now. I'll explain when we get into the car." Cain gathered files and placed them in a stack. "You can believe me now or not. But if not, then you'll likely find yourself at the mercy of the AdA in the next few hours."

Walsh walked toward her. "Keep packing. I'm going to call Scarborough." He set his sights again to Cain. "You need to let me confirm this with my boss or we aren't going anywhere with you."

"If you insist, but I suggest you do it on a secure line." Cain handed over his cell phone. "Here. Make the call."

Walsh retrieved the phone and dialed Scarborough's number. The line rang.

"Cain, you have them?" Scarborough answered.

"What the hell's going on, man? It's Walsh. Where are you?"

"Christ. You and Duncan need to get out of there. We've been compromised. Cain has us set up someplace safe and we're all here. Except you two. Please, there's no time to waste."

"Fine. But you're going to need to fess up when we get there."

"I will. Just come. Now." Scarborough ended the call.

"Happy now?" Cain held out his hand. "Can I have my phone back?"

Walsh returned the phone. "We'll go, but what about the stuff in our rooms?"

"I've got people in there now packing up everyone's things. This has turned into a giant shit show and I've had to get my own team involved."

Walsh threw his laptop bag over his shoulder. "Duncan, you ready to haul ass out of here?"

"I'm ready."

"Good. Let's move." Cain led the way out of the hotel and to his car parked alongside the entrance. "Get in." He returned to the driver's side and started the engine,

Walsh ensured Duncan was inside and set his sights on Cain. "Now you've got us. Where are we going and why?"

"Pedro Sosa's been murdered. And your colleagues were almost taken down too. Looks like Inspector Varela isn't the stand-up guy I thought he was."

"Reid and Quinn, they're okay?" Duncan asked.

"They managed to drive out of Rocinha unscathed."

"Jesus. What the hell happened?" Walsh said.

Cain eyed him. "Rio happened."

KATE PEERED THROUGH THE WINDOW AT THE LONG DRIVEWAY to beyond what she could see now in the dark of night. "Head-lights." She dropped the blinds and turned her attention to the others in the living room. "That's Cain with Levi and Eva."

Scarborough pulled open the blinds briefly as if to confirm Kate's statement. "Thank God. At least we can get going now. I want to get down there as soon as possible."

"If I don't make contact with them soon, they're going to wonder what happened." Varela was seated with his hands bound and Fisher's gun pointed at his head. "Is it necessary to have a gun on me the entire time? I have agreed to your demands."

"You almost got my people killed today," Fisher said. "So yes, it's necessary. I don't trust you. And if Scarborough didn't believe you were a necessary component to this operation, I would've seen to it you were buried alongside those women."

"You must feel very powerful, Agent Fisher. Americans." He chuckled. "You have no idea how the rest of the world operates."

A knock on the door sounded, followed by a voice. "It's Cain. I'm coming in." He inserted his key in the lock and opened the door. "I've got the rest of your folks here. Safe and sound."

Fisher marched toward Duncan and wrapped his arms around her. "Thank God you're safe."

"I'm here too." Walsh opened his arms. "Don't I get a hug?"

"I'm glad you're here too, man." Fisher returned a manly embrace. "Things have gone south in a hurry and we're up shit creek right now."

"I figured." Walsh turned to Scarborough. "What's the plan, boss?"

But before he could answer, Fisher jumped in, waving his gun at Varela. "This guy here sacrificed his own man today and almost sacrificed two of ours. So now he's gonna help us out. Scarborough and I are still going to the coroner's office. We're going to get those samples from the initial victims found in the hills and then we're going to the nightclub where word has it, we'll find American's there. Maybe our guy."

"Wait, you two have already been to that club," Walsh said. "If any members of the AdA are there, we're screwed. I'll be the first to volunteer my services."

"No." Kate moved in. "I'll go. No offense, but all you guys scream American federal agents. I can get his attention."

"Reid's right," Duncan said. "But you aren't going alone. It'll be you and me."

"You want me to send both of you in there?" Scarborough asked.

"Is there something wrong with that?" Duncan replied. "We both have field agent experience. We know what we're doing."

"I didn't say you didn't know what you're doing. But here, in a foreign country, all bets are off." Scarborough turned to Cain. "What are your thoughts?"

"I gotta agree with the ladies. You aren't going to catch that bee without some honey. Pardon me, ladies, if I offend, but it's the truth."

"We know. And that's why it should be us." Kate looked to Duncan. "We can narrow down our field of eligible suspects while they go to the coroner's office and get what we need there."

"There's one other thing," Quinn began. "Reid managed to trip over a severed head on the hillside. Luckily, Sosa had a forensics kit on him before he was gunned down. We were able to use what he had in that kit. I have the samples." He patted his laptop bag.

"You found a head? Why are we just now hearing about this?" Fisher asked.

"Sorry. We were pretty busy running for our lives today and making sure you two weren't killed in the process," Quinn replied. "Must've slipped our minds." At this, he winked at Kate.

His insinuation that they shared some sort of comradery was nauseating, but he had a point. Kate began, "The only thing better would be if I could whip out the head from my laptop bag right now. Unfortunately, we didn't have time to retrieve it amid the gunfire. So, can we get something lined up so Duncan and I can go do our jobs?"

~

Cain arrived a few blocks from the nightclub and parked curbside. "You ladies ready?"

Kate and Eva were in the backseat and Kate began, "We're ready."

"You remember the plan?" Walsh asked. "Cain and I will hang back here. You two go inside, check things out and see if you can spot a man who most closely resembles the description we received from Sosa's tipster. Don't engage. Come back and we'll follow him. Any questions?"

"No, sir," Kate replied.

The women stepped out of the car, dressed in nightclub attire and stood on the narrow sidewalk.

"Ready when you are." Duncan tugged on her too-short dress.

"I feel like we stand out, but for all the wrong reasons." Kate said. "Look, if we see this guy, you really want to walk away from him, like Walsh says to?" She turned to the car and with a nod, started ahead.

Duncan kept up. "That's a loaded question. All we have is a generic description from an anonymous source relayed to us by a cop who's now dead. And all we know is that this source saw him driving up near the burial grounds."

"And your point?" Kate grinned.

"Unless Fisher and Scarborough get the samples we need..." Duncan started.

"And the killer left behind DNA, which would have to make him a pretty careless killer."

"Exactly. So to answer your question, I don't know what I'll do until it happens." Duncan pointed ahead. "That's the club. I guess we'll play it by ear."

They made their way to the club entrance where a bouncer

stood guard. "Evening ladies. Go right in. You're early. Must be new around here. The club doesn't start getting busy for another hour."

"Oh, we know," Duncan said. "It's our chance to scope out a good spot." She laughed. "Have a good night."

"You too," he replied.

"Smooth," Kate said. "I'll let you do the talking."

They approached the bar and Duncan spoke. "Vodka cranberry, please." She turned to Kate. "What do you want?"

"I'll have the same."

"Two." She said to the bartender. "So, when's the real party start?" she asked him.

"About midnight. Are you American?"

"Yes."

"We get a lot of Americans. I was born in Rio."

"Your English is better than mine." Duncan was flirting and she was good at it.

"You can't work here until you speak good English. I mean, speak English well." He smiled as he made the drinks.

"So, you say you get a lot of us here. Any regulars?"

"Too many to count." He placed their drinks in front of her. "Tab?"

"No. Cash." Duncan handed over the money. "Thank you. Cheers." She offered Kate her drink. "Sounds like we won't be the only Americans here tonight."

"We're only interested in one. Here's to hoping he shows up." Kate raised her glass.

∼

Fisher gazed out through the windshield from the passenger's seat of Varela's patrol car. "Lights are on. I thought you said no one would be here?"

"I said not many would be here," Varela replied. "You'll only find a few people inside, mostly in the lab."

"Okay." Scarborough shut off the engine. "You'll be coming inside with us. And if I get a whiff of something going bad, you'll be the one to pay the price." He stepped out of the car walked to the rear passenger seat.

Varela remained bound at his hands and Scarborough pulled him out. "You're going to have to untie me. I won't be much help inside otherwise."

The agents traded glances, both seeming to come to an agreement before Scarborough cut the zip ties.

"I'm not the enemy, Agent Scarborough. I did what I did out of fear for my family's safety."

"You didn't seem overly concerned about your officer's safety. He's dead on some hillside right now."

"That is right. But if you don't let me contact them, they will kill my wife."

"You help us now and we'll help you out later," Fisher said. "That's the deal." He continued toward the entrance.

Varela stopped dead. "No. It cannot wait. I won't go in unless you let me call them."

"Who is it that you're afraid of, Varela?" Scarborough asked. "The AdA? The man I met? It didn't seem like you were afraid of him last night. Somehow, I don't think you're being completely honest about this situation. For a man who fears for his wife's safety, again, you don't seem very concerned."

"He's stalling," Fisher said. "We don't have time for this." He pulled Varela by the arm.

"Okay. Wait." Varela stopped again.

"They don't have my wife. I no longer have a wife, which is why I've done what I've done. I have nothing left to lose."

"Except for your own people," Fisher pronounced.

"It wasn't supposed to happen like that. Pedro wasn't supposed to die. It was a scare tactic. That's all."

"It got pretty damn far out of hand, wouldn't you say, Inspector?" Scarborough asked. "Why try to scare us? You said yourself this was an American. Why ask for our help then allow this to happen?"

"It wasn't the gangs. This goes far beyond them. They were not the ones who opened fire on your team and killed Pedro. It was the government. They don't want you here. The military police were the ones. I had to tell them where your people were. And it was an accident that Pedro Sosa was killed."

"Why? Why would they care if we were here to track down a supposed American killer?" Fisher pressed on.

"The attention it draws to the favelas. The bad publicity about the murders. Because there are far more than those you know about. Everyone knows it. They just don't want you to know it too."

"I really don't give a shit about what you people do down here. If an American is here doing the killing, that's what I care about." Fisher pulled him along again. "Get us inside now. We're done listening to you."

They arrived at the doors and Fisher began. "Get us in."

"I don't know if they will be here, the military police. That is why I hesitate." Varela pressed the button on the intercom just outside the entrance. "É Varela. Abra a porta." *"It's Varela. Open the door."*

The buzzer sounded and the door clicked open. "Gentlemen. This is what you asked for." Varela gestured for them to enter.

The lobby was illuminated with red emergency exit lighting only and the corridor leading to the autopsy rooms was sparsely lit as well.

"I told you not many would be here," Varela said. "We'll need to go to the back to where the bodies are."

Scarborough held a forensic kit that Cain had given him. Fingernail clippings, DNA swabs and hair samples. That was what they needed, then they would get the hell out of there. "Back here. I remember from earlier." He scanned the area and made sure no one was around while he opened the door to the room where Adriana Santos lay on a metal slab.

"Scarborough, we have company." Fisher peered through the small window in the door. "Someone's coming." He retrieved his weapon and eyed the man in the white coat as he walked past the door. "Never mind. He's gone. Let's get this over with."

Scarborough pulled out the cabinet where the girl lay. "She's gone." He whipped around to Varela. "She's fucking gone. Where did they take her?"

"I told you, Agent Scarborough. No one wants you here. They will not make it easy for you. We should go. Now. Before it's too late."

It took about two hours, but the club now brimmed with party-goers as the clock struck midnight. The bartender was spot on, Americans appeared to be in abundance, and they did tend to stand out among the locals. Mostly, it was because they flaunted their wealth.

However, the one the agents had hoped to find resembled far too many of the men here. The description was so general that it would be impossible to know for sure if they had the right one, short of questioning them. That probably wouldn't go over well.

Kate leaned into Eva's ear. "I never realized how similar they all looked. Short beards, gelled hair, all in black. It's like they have the same design consultant. Anyone stick out to you?"

"Not really. They look like a bunch of lemmings to me. Christ, I'm glad I'm not single."

"I'm with you on that." Kate surveyed the floor until her eyes landed on one man who stood outside the crowd. "Hey, isn't he the guy from that TV show? Oh, what the hell is the name of it?"

Duncan squinted her eyes. "Yeah, you know, I think it is. Wow. I didn't expect to see a celebrity. Can't think of his name though. He's on that show on the cable channel. I can't remember which. Not that I get much of a chance to watch TV."

"You think we should ask for an autograph?" Kate laughed.

"Sure."

"I was joking."

Duncan placed her drink on the bar top. "I wasn't. Besides, we look like wall flowers just standing here like this. We need to mingle so we don't look like the cops we are."

"Sure. Why not?" Kate followed her.

Duncan opened a path through the packed dance floor until

they reached the other side. She smiled and approached him. "Hi. I'm sorry to bother you. My friend and I here love your show."

Mason Wylder smiled. "You're American."

"You're very perceptive. We're on a girls' vacation," she replied.

"Very cool. You are a stunner, aren't you?" He exuded charm and laid it on thick, like he was performing just for her.

Duncan retrieved a cocktail napkin that was tucked in her cleavage. "Do you think I could trouble you for an autograph?"

"It would be my pleasure." He reached for the napkin and retrieved a pen from his pocket. "What's your name?"

"Eva Duncan."

"That's a beautiful name, Eva." He scribbled on the napkin, then kissed it. "Here you go." He turned to Kate. "Can I sign something for you too, miss?"

"Uh, I don't actually have anything."

"That's okay, this one will do." Duncan attempted to salvage the deal.

What's your name, sweetheart?" He asked Kate.

"Kate Reid."

"Another beautiful name. I do hope you both have a lovely evening. It was a pleasure to meet you."

"Thank you so much." Duncan pulled on Kate's arm and led her back to the bar. "I still don't remember his name. What's it say on the napkin?"

Kate squinted to read the handwriting. "Geez. He writes like a doctor. It was weird that he kissed the napkin, right? I think it says Wylder. M-something Wylder."

"Mason Wylder. That's right." Duncan raised her hands. "He's on that cop show. I remember now."

"Interesting, but we should probably keep our eyes out for the man with dark hair, blue eyes and a five o'clock shadow." As Kate gazed out into the crowd, she replied. "Yeah, I just described every man in here."

"Not Mason Wylder," Duncan pointed out. "His eyes were brown. I noticed that much."

"Is that all you noticed?" She smiled. "I don't know. I think this is as good as it's going to get. I'm not sure who we think we'll find, but maybe it's time to call it."

"Apart from meeting Mason Wylder, this was a bust." Duncan started to leave.

Kate followed her and as they reached the exit, a man entered and nearly collided with her. "Excuse me, sir. I'm so sorry."

"No problem." He smiled and carried on.

Kate reached for Duncan's shoulders and pulled her to a stop. "Did you see that man?"

"Who? The guy you bumped into?"

"Yes," Kate replied.

Duncan seemed to pick up on her implication. "No. Do you think?"

"He's American. Matches the description, down to the blue eyes. Let's wait and see what he does and who he talks to. What do we have to lose?"

"If you got a feeling, I'm all in." Duncan kept her eye on the man they had just encountered. "He's going to talk to the actor."

"A fan?" Kate asked.

"Not from the looks of it. They're having words and I'm not sure they're good ones."

"Maybe he's not the guy we're looking for after all. He probably works for Wylder or something," Kate said.

Duncan held her gaze. "Hold on now. Why rule him out?"

Kate appeared somewhat bewildered. "Well, because he's with the actor."

"And your point?"

13

In the north zone of the city, in the bairro known as Tiajuca, lay a modest middle-class residential home tucked behind tropical foliage. This was where Noah Quinn waited alone. The hour approached 2am and none of the agents had returned.

Every minute, he opened the blinds and revealed only darkness. "Damn it. Where the hell is everyone?" He paced the small living room, his arms folded and eyes cast to the ground. Regardless of what Reid thought of him, he wasn't a spiteful man. She'd turned everyone against him. That was what was happening now. And to think, he helped save her life today. "This is the thanks I get." He never wanted any of this to happen. She just wouldn't do what he asked. She's his damn subordinate, for Pete's sake and she refused to help him—to help each other. They could've been a great team and Reid screwed it up. None of this was his fault.

Quinn reached for his phone. "You better answer the damn phone. Don't leave me alone in this God-forsaken city." Within a single ring, Fisher picked up. "Where the hell are you guys?"

"On our way back. The bodies are gone, man. They're gone. Someone knew we were coming."

"Varela?" Quinn asked. "He must've leaked it."

"He's not who we thought he was, that's for sure. Look, we'll be there shortly. Just hang tight and we'll fill you in on our return. Have you heard from the others?"

"No," Quinn replied.

"I'll put a call into Cain then. They should have been back by now. That's all we need," Fisher said. "This whole thing is fubar and I think the time's come for us to leave this country before one of us gets killed."

Duncan negotiated among the swollen throngs inside the nightclub and maintained a line of sight with Kate and their target, the man who was talking to the actor, Mason Wylder. The last-ditch effort to walk out of there with something tangible led them to make the move, regardless of unforeseen dangers.

Kate looked on as her cohort pushed through the drunken dancers with handsy men grappling as she passed them by. The target was still within her purview and the dark-haired stranger still spoke to the actor with obvious agitation. She retrieved her cell phone and snapped pictures of the man and his apparent companion, Mason Wylder.

A man who appeared inebriated slammed into her. "Desculpe, desculpe." *"Sorry, sorry."*

"Shit." Kate dropped her phone and began to search the floor to retrieve it, but the drunkard stumbled around and she heard a crackling beneath his feet. "My phone!" She squatted to retrieve it after the final, crushing blow. The screen was shattered and pixe-lated. "No." She pulled back up and realized she'd lost sight of Duncan. Panic rose in the pit of her stomach as her eyes shot back and forth, all around the club. "Duncan?" Amid the smiling, drunk faces of the people around her, she'd lost her and the man who collided with her was gone.

Kate pushed and shoved her way through the club in search of her teammate. Her phone was destroyed. It wouldn't turn on. She had no way to communicate with anyone. But she wasn't going to leave without Duncan. Her elbows flew and pissed off people yelled at her. She didn't care and barreled her way through the floor until she made it the spot where she last saw Duncan. "Eva? Eva, where are you?" Her voice could not rise above the loud techno-music. She stood in place, turning and peering everywhere when a hand touched her shoulder. Kate spun around. "Oh my God. There you are."

The look on Duncan's face was nothing short of fear. "We need to go. Now." She grabbed Kate's hand and pulled her toward the exit.

"I couldn't find you. Where did you go?" Kate pleaded.

"We need to get to the car and leave." Duncan pushed through the front doors.

They could breathe again in the refreshing night air versus the stifling sweaty bouquet inside. Kate's pulse settled now that they were outside and Duncan was okay. "I see them. Just ahead." She caught Cain's eyes and he started the engine anticipating their arrival.

The two quick-stepped in their high-heels like manic speed walkers until they reached the car.

"Get in." Duncan held the door, her gaze shifting everywhere, before slipping in after Kate. "We need to go back to the house before someone sees us all together."

Walsh kept his eyes glued to the vicinity of the club. "Are you being followed?"

Cain didn't hesitate to shove the gear shift into Drive and speed away from there.

"I don't think so, but there were a lot of eyes on us inside," Duncan replied. "Are you okay?" She asked Kate.

"Someone ran into me. I dropped my phone and then he stepped on it. It's shattered. I'm pretty sure it was done on purpose because as soon as I picked it back up, I lost sight of you and the man who crashed into me."

"Last I saw was him running into you. That was when someone pulled me away."

"Who?" Cain asked.

"Some asshole who tried to dance with me and when I managed to get away from the creeper, I lost visual with Reid. They were watching us. I think they knew who we were."

"But do you know who 'they' were?" Walsh peered into the rearview mirror. "Who did you see before all of this went down?"

"We split up," Duncan began. "We saw a man who resembled the description, and he was talking to an actor we both had met a little earlier in the evening."

"Splitting up was your first mistake," Cain said. "You two should know better than that. Especially since you're both unarmed."

"We didn't think we had a choice," Kate replied. "I think the point of concern is that as soon as we split up, they saw me taking pictures. And that was the end of it."

"The actor. I'm sure his people thought you were paparazzi," Walsh added.

"It's possible. I hope that's all it was." Kate turned to Duncan. "Did you get any pictures?"

She held up her phone. "I did."

QUINN SPOTTED THE HEADLIGHTS APPROACH. "FINALLY." HE unlocked the front door and stood with it open as the others stepped out of the car. "Looks like they're all in one piece."

"Then luck was on our side tonight." Fisher stood next to Quinn when he spotted Duncan. "Glad you're all back and in one piece."

"The one piece thing being the key phrase." Duncan walked inside. "We're fine. When did you and Scarborough arrive?"

"Twenty minutes ago, maybe. Not long."

"I see you're still holding onto our guest." Duncan nodded to Varela.

"Things didn't go as we planned, thanks to him."

Quinn closed the door after Walsh entered and the rest were inside. "Well?"

Varela remained stone-faced. "It wasn't supposed to go like this. I promise you. They got spooked and it went badly from there."

"Who's they?" Walsh asked.

"He tells us the government." Scarborough placed his hand on Kate's shoulder. "Everything okay?"

She nodded.

"Local? National? Who wants us gone and why if we're in search of an American?" Walsh added.

"Too much attention, according to this one." Fisher thumbed to Varela. "No one expected to find a burial ground with Rocinha women inside. No one knew what to expect and now they're afraid."

"But afraid of what? We have no authority here," Scarborough insisted. "Even if it's one of our citizens, it would be up to Brazil to decide to prosecute. Something isn't adding up. And the time's come for you to talk."

Varela appeared defeated. "As I've already told you, it's the government. Rio government. They were afraid the gangs would use you, maybe take you hostage and then that would mean America's law enforcement would intervene."

"But you said an agreement was reached with the gangs," Quinn began. "That Scarborough and Fisher all but solidified it the other night. I don't think that's the real reason." He marched toward Varela. "And if you don't get to the truth, there's a whole lot we can do to make all of this go away. Including you."

"That's enough," Scarborough held Quinn off.

"I was almost killed today. And you sure as hell don't seem to give a shit. Maybe it's what you want, huh? Get me out of the way?"

"Quinn, what's going on with you?" Fisher asked. "Are you insane? None of us wants anything to happen to you or any member of this team."

"I'm not so sure about that," he replied. "Maybe you should talk to Reid."

"What?" Scarborough moved closer with menacing intent. "What did you say?"

"Nothing. It's nothing. I'm just tired of this shit and we need to leave this crooked city."

"If anyone cares, Duncan and I have something that might interest you," Kate held up her damaged cell phone.

"What happened?" Scarborough asked.

"They were watching us," she began. "Duncan was at one end of the club and I stood at the other. Some guy ran into me when I started taking picture of a person of interest. I dropped my phone. He smashed it with his foot. It was no accident."

"What happened with you?" Fisher asked Duncan.

"I'm fine. Things didn't go quite as we had planned. But my phone survived and we found a man who could be a possible match to Sosa's description." She showed him the pictures.

"It's tough to see in the low light, but I suppose I can see some similarities," Fisher replied.

"It was dark inside and I had my flash off." Duncan turned to Kate. "We think they knew who we were and that we were taking pictures."

"I keep hearing a lot of 'they.' Who exactly are they?" Scarborough said.

"It's possible the folks the ladies were photographing thought they were paparazzi. It was some actor, right?" Cain asked.

"Yep. We weren't taking pictures of him, but a man next to him. He was the one who resembled the description." Duncan pointed to the screen. "He was talking to the actor and that's when things went to shit and we left."

"An American actor?" Quinn asked.

"Yes. I don't know who the guy was he was talking to. An assistant maybe? But we weren't as covert as we should've been.

But I still think it's worth looking into this guy. Otherwise, we were out there for nothing," Duncan replied.

"What about you? Did you get the samples?" Kate asked Scarborough.

"The bodies were gone." He glanced to Varela. "And we're pretty sure he told someone we were coming. So we got absolutely nothing. No evidence. No bodies."

"We do have a head." Kate turned to Quinn. "Samples from it, anyway."

"The question is, how are we going to get those samples out of here and to our labs?" Walsh asked. "If what Varela says is true and the local government is keeping tabs on us, I'm not sure we're going to get anything out of this country. Maybe not even ourselves."

"DID YOU DESTROY IT?" SCOTT ASKED THE MAN WHO approached him.

"Yes. She won't get anything off of it. Not without some serious tech." Turned out, the man who slammed into Kate wasn't drunk after all. He stood next to Scott. "Who were they?"

"No one you should be concerned with. I'll handle things from here. You can leave." He turned away from the man and approached his employer. "Mason? We should leave. You have an early flight."

"If I must." He leaned in to whisper into a young woman's ear. "Until next time." And with a smile and a wink he followed Scott outside to the valet. "The reporter, Ms. Ortiz?"

"Taken care of. Regardless, trouble is following you. It's the right call to pack up and head home until this settles down."

"I won't argue with you this time." Mason smoothed his button-down shirt and clasped his hands at his front.

The Tesla arrived alongside the curb and the valet handed the keys to Scott. "Have a good evening, gentlemen."

Mason slipped into the passenger seat while Scott made his way behind the wheel. "The jet will be ready to leave by 5am. It's best we depart before daylight breaks. The airport will be quieter no doubt." He pulled away from the club and started toward the mansion.

"Will you be coming with me?"

"That was the plan, unless you feel I should remain here to keep an eye on things?"

"No. We should go home together," Wylder said. "We have enough people on the payroll to monitor things from here."

Scott made his way to the lavish home and pulled onto the large circular driveway. "You go in. I'll pull the car into the garage."

Wylder stepped out, a noticeable stagger in his step, and walked toward the house.

When the boss was out of sight, Scott pulled in the car and then walked around to the back of the home. A small guest house lay just over the boardwalk near the beachfront. He had left something of value inside and needed to make sure it was still there. He inserted the key and opened the door. "Good. You're still here."

Rosella Ortiz, the reporter who had interviewed Wylder a day earlier was handcuffed to the railing between the living room and kitchen. Her mouth was covered with duct tape and her shoes removed. She moaned beneath the tape as he approached.

With a swift yank, Scott pulled the tape from her lips. "I don't want you to scream. I saved your life. Now you're going to do me a favor. But should any word of our agreement see the light of day, you won't survive. Do I make myself clear?"

Her hair was mangled and her eyes puffy with black lines running down her cheeks. She nodded.

"Glad to hear it." He unlocked her cuffs and helped her to the sofa. "I had hoped it wouldn't come to this, but my employer gets a little paranoid."

"I don't know anything. I swear it. Please, let me go," Rosella said.

"Not until we hash this out. There are people here who don't belong. People who work for my government."

"Why are they here?" she asked, wiping away her tears.

"They are under the impression. Well, let's just say they were asked to come by those I understood were loyal. But I was wrong. No worries, though, that particular problem has been solved. Now is the time to give these US government officials reason to leave Rio because what they know, or what they think they know, could be incredibly damaging to my employer. Much like this conversation."

"What am I supposed to do? I have no power."

"That's where you're wrong. You have the power of the pen, or more accurately, the keyboard. You're going to let everyone know that these people, these American law enforcement people have been working to place blame for a series of murders at the feet of the Rio civil police. Given the reputation of your police, that would be an easy sell. The real problem is the attention. And it will get world-wide attention. That is what will upset many powerful people here. People who help to protect me and more importantly, my boss."

"You want me to write an article? That's it?"

"It has to be tonight. Word has to be leaked before they leave because I need a diversion. I need the focus of the police to be on them and not me. If you do this, we'll forget any of this every happened and you will be paid well for your efforts."

"Why can't you just get these powerful people to stop them from leaving? You clearly have wealth and resources."

"Because this has to come from an independent source, untraceable to me or my employer. And that source is you."

"Can I go home to do this?" She asked.

Scott considered the idea of letting her leave. "I'll have to trust you'll do as you're asked. But you'd better believe I will have people posted at your home should you decide not to hold up your end of the deal."

He stood and helped her up. "So, now that I have helped you, you will help me. And I can promise that you will not be harmed again."

She pulled on her shoes. "What kind of monster do you work for?"

"The kind that lets nothing stand in his way." He started toward the door. "I'll have someone take you home. You will contact me when it's done. If I don't hear from you within the next three hours, you will most certainly hear from me." He turned his back to leave, stopping to speak to the men at the door. "Take her home. Stay there. Call me if there are problems." Scott started back toward the main house.

Wylder was sprawled out on the sofa when he returned. "What a shock. You passed out." He made his way to Wylder's bedroom where a half-packed suitcase lay open on his bed. "Idiot." He tossed in more clothes and zipped up the bag.

On his return to the living room, he gazed through the window and spotted a car driving away. The reporter was leaving along with his men. The risk was his now and if the plan went astray, Wylder would not let it slide. He'd already demanded the reporter be taken care of, which was a polite way of saying she would be thrown off a cliff somewhere, never to resurface. However, Scott was smarter than Wylder gave him credit for. Killing her would mean the end of Wylder. Why he didn't see that was a mystery because it would only take someone looking at her schedule to figure out she was with Wylder only a day before. Sometimes Scott questioned why he let Mason make decisions at all, except he didn't want to see an end to his gravy train, so he would obey like the dog he was, with this one exception. "It's time to go." He shook Wylder's shoulder. "Mason, we need to go to the airport now."

"What? What time is it?" He pulled up and swayed as he did.

"It's time we leave. The plane won't wait." He leaned down and hoisted up Mason.

"Where are we going?"

"Home."

"Back to New York?"

"That's right. Where everything can return to normal."

14

Daylight would breach the night skies in less than an hour. Tensions flared inside the quiet residence among the team who waited for a solution, who needed a safe way out. It was Agent Elijah Cain who appeared to be the only cool head to prevail as he suggested a plan of action.

"I'm going to need you folks to come back to Brasilia with me. You'll stay at the consulate so that I can ensure your safe return home."

"We can't leave," Kate began. "There's a killer out there and we're getting close."

"Which is why you have to find safer ground." Cain peered at the others. "I've been here for a long time. I've seen this place change from a prosperous and lively city to something along the lines of a third world. The disparity between rich and poor and the sheer corruption has spread like a disease. I thought that if I brought you here, you would find whoever was responsible for killing those women."

"And that's what we're trying to do," Scarborough replied.

"Yes. But it's cost more than even I could have imagined. The time's come to pull the plug before it's too late."

"I couldn't agree more," Quinn said. "We can still work the case from Quantico. If this is an American, it won't be hard to trace him back here. Reid, you and I could've been killed today. Cain's right. It's time to cut bait."

"Maybe the solution is to divide and conquer," Fisher said.

Scarborough looked on with interest. "In what way?"

"Maybe Quinn is right. He should go home. Duncan, and Walsh should go back too. Three and Three."

"You want Reid to stay?" Quinn asked.

"Frankly, she has a nose for sniffing out clues and I don't think I'm the only one who sees that. We need her here. Duncan and Walsh should also return because they'll need our databases and our resources in order to find out if the American has ties back home, which is an almost certainty. They can use the phone records Varela gave up in order to expedite that effort. Run facial recognition on the photos to get us a name of this person of interest. There could be a way to bring him out of hiding if they can find the right ammunition."

Scarborough nodded. "And the three of us?"

"We track him down. Whoever it is, Reid, you and me, will do what we do best—track down a killer. We can work to get the only samples we have out of the country and sent back to Quantico where you three can process it with the labs. None of the political maneuvering with local law enforcement. We get down to the business of finding the son of a bitch. And with Cain's help, he might be able to provide us with the equipment we'll need. Whether it be arms, vehicles, getting a meeting with the AdA, whatever. He's got the contacts and we'll need him for that." Fisher gauged their reactions. "I think this is our best chance at catching the killer. What do you say?"

"I don't like it," Walsh began. "We're a team and we need to stay that way. This is bullshit."

"It's the best option to keep at least some of you out of harm's way. I won't disagree." Cain's attention was diverted when his cell phone buzzed. He peered at the screen. "I need to take this. Excuse me." He pulled away from the table and answered the call.

Kate waited for him to step away before beginning, "I won't argue the point that we do need help back home. If we can get what samples we have out of here, we can get them properly analyzed and that could make all the difference."

"I feel like we're abandoning you three and I don't like it." Duncan turned to Walsh. "I'm with you."

"This is a precarious situation and as the head of this team, I'll make the call." Scarborough eyed each of them. "We split up, like Fisher said. "We find the son of a bitch, then we go home."

Cain returned wearing a somber expression. "A local reporter was found dead about an hour ago."

"That's awful, and I don't mean to sound callous, but how does that concern us?" Kate asked.

"She had just submitted an article to her editor, a short time before. When she was found, she had been tortured and beheaded."

"For Christ's sake," Fisher replied. "Sounds like our killer might have decided to move up the food chain and go after higher profile people."

"You'd think that would be my primary concern," Cain contin-ued. "But it isn't. The article, according to the editor, who was the one to make the call to us, indicated several US FBI officials were in Rio searching for a killer. Except that the article speculates the FBI is here under false pretenses. That they are in fact here to help oust the local Rio government."

"A coup? We're here to instigate a coup?" Walsh laughed. "That's the most asinine thing I've ever heard. What are we, the damn CIA?"

"They're going to believe we had a hand in the reporter's death," Kate said. "It's an attempt to turn the cops here against us, but at whose direction?"

"We can't split up now. Not a chance," Walsh added.

Scarborough eyed the team. "Yes, we can. And we will. Starting tonight."

Inspector Gustavo Varela, the man the team thought could be trusted, stood ready at the plane that would carry half the BAU team back to Brasilia and then back home. It was already 8am and finagling the flight took an act of congress. Or in this case, an act of God. Cain pulled strings and now owed favors to just about everyone in Rio, but that didn't matter. His people, the FBI's elite, would get out safely. That was the only thing that mattered. The others who would remain, however, would be even more difficult to protect.

The safety of the entire mission now relied on the editor of the paper whose reporter had been brutally murdered. After some persuasion on Cain's part, yet another string he pulled, the editor agreed not to publish the article Rosella Ortiz had written that suggested the American FBI was attempting a coup. It took money and a lot of it to convince him, but he reluctantly agreed for the safety of the others, though his anger at whoever killed his reporter could not be doused. There would be reparations, and it was a guarantee Scarborough had no idea if he could fulfill.

"Okay folks, let's get you all on this plane." Cain parked next to the private plane and met Varela on the runway. "Did you take care of the pilot and the tower?"

"I did. Despite what you believe, Agent Cain, I am not the enemy. The choices I made were not made without regret."

"Look, Varela, I don't give a shit what your reasons were for letting one of your own be killed and allowing two of mine to be shot at. That said, if you want to stay on my good side and at the end of the day, that'll be the best place for you, then help these folks get out of here, without incident."

Varela nodded and approached the plane. He signaled for the door to be opened while the stairs were moved into place.

"It's time," Cain led the reluctant team toward the plane. "I know how you all must feel, but Scarborough's made the right call. There's a better chance at finding this killer by splitting up."

"You'll excuse my candor, sir," Walsh began. "But this isn't your team. I am not onboard with the decision to see us divided. That's not how we operate."

"Things are changing around here, man." Quinn pushed in front of him and started up the stairs. "Nothing's going to be the same now. Not with Scarborough at the helm." He boarded the plane.

"What the hell is going on with him?" Walsh helped Duncan onto the steps.

"I don't know, but it's not looking good for us right now. I'm with you. This isn't how we should be handling this situation. Reid is Quinn's subordinate. Scarborough's overstepped his bounds this time. And I don't think Quinn will let him off the hook for it." She stepped onto the plane and sat down near the middle, one row behind Quinn.

Walsh was the last one on and sat in the front row. "That's all of us."

A flight attendant nodded and secured the door.

Walsh peered through the window at Cain who stepped back to his car. "Good luck."

INSIDE THE YELLOW POLICE TAPE THAT CRISSCROSSED THE surrounding trees, Scarborough stood over the body of the reporter who had written the article. "She knew something." He peered at Fisher and Reid who stood nearby. "She knew something and was killed for it."

"He has formidable friends." Fisher nodded. "We aren't dealing with some kid taking a year off school to travel and decides to take out his aggressions on the locals. This person has a network and money to operate it. This killer is calculating and meticulous."

"And without remorse." Kate squatted for a closer look. "The brutality. Decapitation usually signals something deeper, religious even. Maybe we're dealing with a killer who has a God complex." She pulled back up again. "Then again, not all of them were beheaded."

"He might've run out of time on the others," Fisher replied.

"Maybe, but I'm not so sure. He's spending time with them. Seducing them first, gaining their trust. I don't know. It's too random to include it in his M.O. And with this one, who knows?

He might've wanted to send a message. Maybe she betrayed him after writing the article. She could've tried to get help. I just can't say with any certainty."

"Her editor must know what her schedule was. He has to know who she was with last. I think we need to have a word with him in person." Scarborough stepped away from the body. "In the meantime, someone needs to pick her up. We can't keep the local cops away from this for long."

"I'll contact the officer who contacted Cain. Tell him he can have his people come back," Fisher said.

"Cain must have faith in this cop. We were already burned by Varela," Kate said.

"He probably has as much faith in him as money can buy." Fisher stepped away to make the call.

"Let me reach out to Cain before we leave." Scarborough retrieved his cell and waited for the line to answer. "Are they in the air?"

"Yes. They just took off. I'm heading back with Varela to the safe house. Where are you folks?"

"At the crime scene. Fisher's calling the officer to come collect the body. We've pulled what we can from it with a kit. I don't expect the city's coroner will let us touch her after they take her into custody. Unless you can pull rank."

"That's not going to happen. I'm afraid I can't circumvent the system on this one. It'll only feed into the narrative of the article."

"But that article isn't due to be published, wasn't that the agreement?"

Cain laughed. "The only agreement that means anything here is one backed up by green paper. The editor will keep his mouth shut if we pay him well enough. And I'm working on that as we speak. That said, get what you can from the victim. It's going to have to be enough. We'll figure a way to get it out with the other samples."

Scarborough ended the call and returned to the team. "Cain's on his way back to the safehouse."

Kate pulled off her latex gloves. "What about the others?"

"They're in the air, headed back to home."

"Good. I hope that's where we'll be by this time tomorrow. I don't want to stay here any longer than necessary."

"It's what, almost 9am now?" Fisher peered at his phone. "I'd like to get up to see this editor. The sooner we find out what she was doing, the sooner we can get some answers."

"You and Reid can go. I'll stay here and wait for the officer and the coroner. I can't stomach the idea of leaving her here alone."

"I don't want to leave you out here," Fisher replied.

"You don't have a choice. I'll be fine. Go. You two get something we can use. Otherwise, we'll have stayed behind for nothing."

As THE MORNING SUN PUSHED HIGHER IN THE SKY, THE clouds vanished, and it was shaping up to be another sunny day in the city of Rio de Janeiro where it was supposed to be parties and playtime. Not murder and beheadings.

"This looks like the building." Kate peered through the windshield as Fisher drove. "The editor knows we're coming, right?"

"He knows. Cain said it was all arranged and the money is to be wired as soon as we give him the okay."

"Things certainly work differently down here."

"Yes, ma'am." Fisher pulled into the parking lot and cut the engine. "Before we go inside, I want to say something." He appeared to consider his words carefully. "You and I haven't had a chance to work together much and I'm glad to get the opportunity to get to know you better. You've been through a lot in the short time since you joined the team. And I just want to say I'm glad you're here."

"Thank you." Kate didn't really know what else to say. They were in an awkward situation. The team was split. There were tensions between her and her boss. This whole thing was turning into a calamity and nothing made sense anymore.

"Is there anything you want to say to me?" Fisher pressed on.

"I don't think so."

"Reid, I can see something's going on with you and Quinn and it's starting to spill over. I don't know what it is, but he's pretty up in arms about it. Especially Scarborough's decision to keep you here when he's the senior profiler."

"Yeah. I kind of figured that would be a sore spot. He already thinks Scarborough favors me."

"Doesn't he?"

"What am I supposed to do? I'm here to do a job and I want to find this killer. Look, I'll be honest, there are things about Quinn that I've only recently discovered. Things that shed a whole new light on him. And I don't know if we'll survive this. I mean, if the team will survive what's going on with Quinn and me."

"Yeah, I figured." Fisher exhaled. "I know Quinn pretty well and I think I can guess what's going on. The thing is, you can't let it distract you. Not here. Not now. I need you here 100 percent and so does Scarborough. We're operating at half capacity as it is.

Whatever's going on is going to have to be put on the back burner. Can you do that?"

"Absolutely. My concern is getting the three of us out of here safely and putting the killer behind bars. Whatever it takes to make that happen is what I'm willing to do."

"Good." Fisher pulled the keys from the ignition. "Then let's go inside and see what this editor has to say." He stepped out of the car and waited for Kate to join him. With sunglasses on his eyes and a toothpick between his lips, he led the way into the building. "Time to brush up on our Portuguese."

Kate grinned and followed inside.

"Good morning." Fisher appeared slightly rattled while he used his phone to try and translate for him. "Um, Bom dia."

"I speak English. Good morning," the receptionist replied. "How can I help you?"

"We're here to see your editor, Mr. Santiago." He showed his badge. "Agent Fisher, FBI."

"One moment." She dialed Santiago's line.

Fisher turned to Kate. "I'll get us started, if that's okay with you."

"Sure."

"He'll be right up to see you," The receptionist said.

Fisher nodded before patting Kate on the shoulder. "Now we wait."

15

Mason Wylder stepped out of his steamy shower and wrapped a towel around his waist. He walked atop cold, polished concrete floors in the hall of his modern high-rise apartment in Manhattan and made his way to the kitchen. The coffee was brewed and a tray of croissants lay on the Italian Statuario marble counter. He poured a cup and grabbed the flakey breakfast bread and walked toward his sliding glass door that led to the balcony. Gazing at a much different view from here, he missed the white sandy beaches of Rio and now only noticed people scurrying below and a sea of yellow cabs flooding the streets.

His cell phone rested on the coffee table and began to vibrate, capturing his attention. The time was approaching noon and he'd finally begun to feel like himself again. Back home, and mostly sober. "What's up, bro?" He chomped down on his food.

"I'm coming over. We need to talk," Scott replied.

"What about?"

"I think you know. I won't say more on the phone. I'll be there in twenty minutes."

"Whatever you say." Wylder ended the call. "I thought you might be pissed. Shit. Now I have to get dressed."

He returned to his bedroom and pulled on a dress shirt and slim-fitting grey dress pants. Wylder was known for his style and anytime he stepped out onto the streets of New York, he had to be dressed to the nines. He was hounded by paparazzi in public and he had no idea if Scott would make him leave the apartment, so he had to be prepared. The man was too paranoid. Always thinking trouble followed him. But trouble was back in Rio and Wylder was done with that for now. No one would give a shit about the girls. No one would care he went behind Scott's back and took care of the reporter because he knew Scott hadn't. Hell, if anyone should be pissed, it should be him. His most trusted friend lied and that lie could have cost him dearly.

A knock sounded on the door. "It's Scott."

Mason sauntered to the door and pulled it open. "Hey, man. What's up?"

Scott pushed his way inside. "I know what you fucking did. Do you have any idea the trouble you just created for yourself?"

"Calm down, dude. I took care of it because you didn't."

"How? How did you get to her?"

"How do you think? She was at her house for fuck's sake. And I did what I always do. She couldn't be allowed to talk to anyone. You of all people should've known that."

"I did know that and I made a deal with her. She was a popular reporter who also made TV appearances. Do you believe her murder won't be investigated?"

"I'm sure it will, but they won't find shit and you know it." He moved back into the living room. "I don't get what's the big deal? She was a loose end you were supposed to handle. I pay you a shit ton of money to handle and you didn't. I did your job for you and this is the thanks I get?"

Scott shook his head. "You know the feds are still down there. The plan was to have that article published so the civil cops would go after them. You just prevented that."

"You worry too much, my man." He patted Scott on the back. "This'll blow over. Things down there don't get solved, and this won't either. Now, it's time to get back into the swing of things. I guess I have to chill out for a while and that's cool. I think I can manage that."

"Yeah. Right. Okay." Scott still appeared incensed.

"Hey, should we get a party going for tonight?"

"Really? You just got back, and after..."

"After what? Dude, it's done. Now, are you going to set it up, or should I?

"I'll get it handled," Scott started toward the door.

"Don't' worry so much. You'll get wrinkles."

Mason Wylder sat on his couch and flipped through the channels. It was late afternoon and too early to get ready for the party his assistant was oh so eager to arrange. He was getting antsy and hated sitting around doing nothing. Sure, the flight had been long, but jet lag never affected him and his energy level rarely sank.

He needed to get out of the apartment. That's what it was. Maybe grab a few things for the party tonight? Just a few of his close friends, only about thirty or so people. Just to celebrate his return. It would help satiate his desire to be back in Rio. He had spent the past three summers there during his show's hiatus, and it had all become so easy for him. Getting away with things no one should. It was easy when cops had their hands out, looking for bribes to keep their mouths shut. And if there was one thing Wylder had a lot of, it was money. But now he had left much too early. He felt cheated and contemplated returning without Scott, but then something inside him told him not to do it. Even he had some sense sometimes.

He walked out of his apartment building and onto the streets of Uptown, feeling euphoric. The sun was shining and the weather was warm. It almost felt like Rio, except there weren't any women in bikinis roaming around the streets of Manhattan, well, maybe just a few.

Wylder made his way into a café and waited in line. People around him began to whisper. They had figured out who he was. When he made it to the front of the line, the barista smiled.

"You're Mason Wylder."

"Guilty as charged. Can I get a half-caf latte, please?"

"Of course." She began his order but stopped. "You know, I love your show."

"Thanks."

Another woman approached and tripped over a chair before stumbling into him. "I'm so sorry, Mr. Wylder."

"It's okay. Don't worry about it."

"Wow. You're even more handsome than you are on the show," she said.

"Thank you. That's sweet."

"Can I get your autograph?"

In that moment, the barista returned with his coffee. "Here you go, Mr. Wylder."

He grabbed the drink. "Thanks." And on turning back to the young woman who ran into him, he began. "Sure. Why don't we get out of their way here and go outside?" He started toward the door and held it open for her. "Let's walk around the corner before everyone starts to come up to me. It can get hectic at times." Wylder led the way. "What would you like me to sign?"

She looked around for anything to use. "Um, my shirt?"

He eyed her for a moment and felt the familiar twinge in his stomach. He swallowed hard while maintaining a pleasant smile. Inside, he was churning. He had learned when to draw the line for the past few years and this was something new. Why it was happening, he didn't quite know. But when it happened, it was overpowering. Only he wasn't in Rio anymore. He would threaten everything if he made a move here. "You know, maybe we should grab a bite to eat? You hungry?"

The girl smiled. "Yeah. Definitely." She followed him to his car.

"Hop in." Wylder slid into the driver's seat of his Porsche. When she was inside, he started the engine and gauged his surroundings. No one watched him. He'd slipped away just in time before the crowds built. "I didn't get your name."

"Jenny. Jenny Larson. I can't believe I'm in a car with Mason Wylder." She reached for her cell phone. "Can I live-stream this?"

He swatted away her phone. "No."

"Hey." She leaned into the footwell to search for it. "I can't see it."

Mason watched her while she was bent over. He quickly searched for something he could use while his pulse quickened and his mouth turned to cotton. A quick check of his location. This was still Manhattan and even side streets were busy, but he could find a secluded spot, and he had to work fast.

"Finally," she said. "Here it is."

She begun to pull back up. It was now or never. He couldn't stop the impulse driving his decisions. It was too strong. He reached into the back seat and recalled the umbrella he always left inside. That would do it. Wylder he swung hard with the umbrella in hand and struck the back of her head at the base of her neck. She collapsed in place. Slumped over her knees, her phone fell to the floor again.

"Yeah!" Wylder shouted before breaking into laughter. "Damn that felt good. But don't you worry, Jenny. There'll be lots more fun for you later. Just need to figure out where the hell we can go."

He hadn't thought it through and now he had no choice but to follow the impulse inside him. There had only been one other time he'd committed a similar act here and that was when he was just starting on the show. Before he was as famous as he was now. He'd gotten away with it then. Perhaps he had returned from Rio too soon. The thirst still raged inside him, and Wylder was arrogant. He'd gotten away with a great many horrific things. He could get away with this too.

"Mr. Santiago." Fisher offered his hand. "Thank you for agreeing to meet. I can't imagine how difficult this must be for you."

"Difficult, yes, but not unexpected." Santiago turned on his heel. "Please, follow me." He led the way to his office. "Have a seat. I must apologize for the accommodations. We are but a small newspaper."

"It's fine, thank you." Kate offered her hand. "I'm Agent Reid."

Santiago returned to his desk. "So, I understand you have left the investigation regarding the murder of my reporter in the hands of a corrupt civil police inspector. I would have expected more from the United States FBI."

"I'm afraid this is well outside our investigatory jurisdiction." Fisher adjusted in the uncomfortable chair. "That said, since our arrival here in Rio, we have faced unexpected challenges and considering we were asked to assist, as you can imagine, it has come as a bit of a surprise. We've already sent three of our team home due to safety concerns. In fact, I'm not entirely sure those of us who remain are safe."

"You are not. Make no mistake." Santiago retrieved the article and slid it across his desk to Fisher. "And if this were to be published, you would not make it out of Rio alive."

"You understand what would happen if our government was forced to intervene?" Kate said. "Which they most certainly would."

"Oh yes. I understand. And that is why I have agreed with Agent Cain not to publish this final piece of journalism that cost my reporter her life."

"Can you tell us, Mr. Santiago, who the last person was who saw or spoke with Ms. Ortiz?" Kate asked.

"Rosella frequented the popular night clubs where she received word that an American celebrity had returned for the summer. She acted on that tip without my knowledge. Although, it was something that would not normally require my approval. That is a mistake I will be forced to live with."

"You don't know who she went to see?" Fisher asked.

"I do not. It was not usually the sort of thing I kept track of. Rosella had a job to do and did it with little oversight."

Fisher pursed his lips in disappointment. "Can we view her schedule or her laptop. Anything that might give us an indication of where she went?"

"The civil police have beaten you to the punch, as you say. It has already been turned over to them in Gávea. I was not in a position to deny them. No one ever is."

"There was no cell phone found near her body," Kate said. "We would like to request her phone records."

"I will have to discuss that with the authorities. You said yourself, Agent Reid, this is no longer your investigation. Why the concern?"

"Mr. Santiago, we suspect your reporter was murdered by the same person who killed those four women discovered in the hills of Rocinha. I would assume you would want to know that for fact, especially considering the primary person of interest is suspected to be an American."

"I agreed to this meeting to discuss the article. We should come to an agreement on that."

Kate knew exactly what this man was getting at. He wanted money in return for his silence.

"What will it take, Mr. Santiago?" Fisher asked.

He wrote down a number on a piece of paper and pushed it toward Fisher.

Fisher glanced at it and turned it so Kate could see. She peered at him with disgust. "And this is the figure you presented to Agent Cain?"

"That was hours ago. This is the new figure."

"I'll need some time, but we can make this happen." He folded the paper and placed in his shirt pocket.

"Good. Then I think we are done here." Santiago stood. "Once this is settled, the article will be destroyed."

"What guarantees can you offer us that you will follow through on your end of the bargain?" Kate asked.

"Guarantees? I can offer none. My word is all you will have."

"We are done here, Mr. Santiago." Fisher pushed off the chair. "We'll get back to you as soon as possible." He started toward the door with Kate only steps behind. "Oh, and when we do find the person who killed Ms. Ortiz, we'll be sure to let everyone know how forthcoming you were with information."

The two stepped out into the corridor and made their way outside. Fisher shook his head. "Jesus. What kind of place is this?"

"I'm starting to wonder why we're even here," Kate said.

"You and me both."

Their original safehouse was deemed compromised the moment Varela ensured there were no bodies left at the coroner's office. Agent Cain was forced to relocate the team. The temporary accommodation was just ahead as he spotted the small, abandoned building on the outskirts of another favela. While Rocinha was the largest, there were others that were not as dangerous but also didn't have the infrastructure. Running water was scarce and indoor plumbing was even more so. The request from the International Ops division to set up secure satellite phones and a dedicated satellite for internet access, was granted and it was a good thing. There was no internet here either. Despite its shortcomings, this was the best place for them to remain covert in their efforts to get the vital samples out of Brazil.

Scarborough stepped out of the car and started toward the building. "This is your safe house? I'm not sure it's even safe to occupy. He peered at the crumbling exterior and boarded up windows.

"This is probably the safest place for us to be right now without holing up at the US Consulate." Cain inserted a key in the lock and opened the door.

Scarborough followed him inside and noted the interior was in worse shape. The walls revealed exposed brick, the ceiling was covered in rings left from water stains and the floor was concrete with enormous fissures running through the slab. "As long we aren't exposed."

Cain flipped a switch and two fluorescent lights flickered on. "Your team should have arrived in Brasilia by now. I want to make sure the arrangements for their flight home have been made."

"I thought the plan was to get them the samples to take with them?" Scarborough began. "How are we going to doing that?"

"We don't have that kind of time. I want them on a plane in the next couple of hours." He picked up a phone. "This is a secure line. There are people who can help us get the samples out. People who are on our side."

"CIA?"

He only responded with a nod. "They have plenty of assets who they trust and we can make a drop. After that, we'll arrange a commercial transport to move the samples along with other deliveries which will make it less likely to be inspected."

"You must believe the corruption goes all the way to the top."

"I wouldn't put it past this government. Even their former

president was charged with corruption. Trust me, Scarborough, there's no one here in law enforcement we can trust. I thought Varela could be, but clearly, I was wrong. Pedro Sosa must've been the last of his breed and now he's dead too."

"So we get out the samples with a commercial carrier and when my people get back to Quantico, they get them in their hands and to our labs."

"That's the plan. We have a lot of ground to cover so we should get started."

"What about Fisher and Reid? I want them here as soon as possible."

"They don't have secure phones."

"Cain, we need to get word to them."

"Not from here. I haven't fully vetted the location myself. You know where they are. The only way to be sure the call isn't being monitored is if you get far away from here and that would only mean wasting more time."

"They're my responsibility. I'll find a place to make the call and get them back. You do what you need to do to get these samples out of Brazil."

"The AdA and the government have eyes everywhere. I can't say for sure you won't be followed. But if this is what you need to do, then go."

Scarborough nodded and caught the keys Cain tossed him. "Thank you." He walked back out into the afternoon sun before stepping into the car. He worried for Kate. He worried for all of them, but she was at the top of his mind. She always was. There were feelings he couldn't control when it came to her. And now it had forced him to reexamine his leadership. Maybe Quinn was right. Whatever was going on between Quinn and Kate appeared to have culminated into something possibly irreparable. He began to wonder if he'd damaged not only his career, but hers as well.

Several miles along the road, Scarborough reached a part of town that appeared to be a heavy tourist spot. He realized he was near the Christ the Redeemer statue. He gazed up at the massive monument to Christ and reflected on the idea they might not make it out of here alive. And it would be his fault.

Scarborough shook off the negative vibes and retrieved his phone. He made the call to Fisher. "Where are you two?"

"Leaving the newspaper. We got jack squat. All Santiago wanted was money. He says we'll have to trust him not to publish the piece but gave us nothing in regard to where his reporter was last seen. I don't think he cared, in all honesty."

"How much?" Scarborough asked.

"Ten grand."

"Could be worse." His eyes caught sight of a row of shops across the street. One of the places appeared to be a bar. "Look, um, Cain set us up somewhere else. Safer, from what he said. I'm going to send you the location."

"Are you there now?"

"No. I had to move away because this line isn't secure and he didn't want anyone to trace me back to where we're holed up. I'll text you the coordinates. I want both of you to get there as soon as you can. Cain's working on getting our samples out of the country by tonight."

"Without the editor's cooperation, what's the plan here, boss?" Fisher asked. "Are we still going after this killer or what?"

"Let's get these samples out and have our team push them through the system. I want an ID before we consider leaving. If he's here, I want to find him."

"Then we're in agreement. We're too vested in this to give up now."

"How's Reid?" he asked.

"She held her own. I expected nothing less. I'll wait for your coordinates and we'll be there as quickly as we can. Fisher out."

Nick sent the information and exhaled as he reluctantly peered again at the hole in the wall cantina. He recalled the days in his not so distant past. Sitting in a bar during a case, becoming numb to the horrors of the death that surrounded him. He had grown so tired of the depravity that he witnessed in the killers he chased. It was the reason he wanted to go back to Quantico. But it seems it was something he could not escape. Not without giving it up all together. But Kate. She thrived in this environment. She was made for this work and maybe there would come a day when she too would grow tired, but not yet. She hadn't peaked yet. Quinn must've seen that and feared it.

Even she wouldn't be able to prevent the thoughts swimming in Nick's mind as he gazed forth, his mouth watering with desire for a drink. "Not now. There isn't time," he said to himself. But there was. It would only take a moment to relieve his anxiety and the pull was strong.

16

The plane touched down on a remote runway shorn from the dense green terrain. Controlled by the FBI's International Operations, the airstrip was a designated landing zone for clandestine operations and was also utilized by the CIA.

Levi Walsh peered through the window of the plane. He noticed a man who leaned against an old minivan that was parked at the edge of the runway. The man's arms were folded and his legs crossed as he watched the plane roll to a stop. "I'll bet a dollar to a dime he's CIA."

Duncan viewed him from her window. "No way am I taking that bet. Suppose he's our ride?" Duncan asked.

Walsh eyed the front of the plane as the flight attendant approached. "Any idea who the man out there is?"

"I'm sorry, sir. I don't know. The captain will come out and speak to you all." She returned to her seat.

The captain soon emerged from the cockpit. "Senhors,

Senhora, I have been asked to relay to you that you are to exit the plane and immediately enter the vehicle that awaits you. The man outside is an American and will be taking you from here." He turned the handle and opened the exit door as a staircase arrived. "Please, you must hurry."

"You heard the man." Walsh stood in the aisle, hunched over in the small aircraft. "Duncan, let's go. You too, Quinn, you're next." And then it was his turn. Walsh looked back at the captain. "Thank you. I hope your efforts weren't in vain."

"So do I, sir. Goodbye and good luck to you all."

Eva Duncan stepped off the staircase and hurried toward the gentleman next to the minivan. "It might be a good idea for you to tell me who you are before I get inside."

"Bryce Lambert. I can only tell you that I'm on your side. Please, you need to get in." He pulled open the sliding passenger door.

Quinn and Walsh jogged to catch up to her when Walsh began. "You're one of the good guys, right?"

"That's what they tell me," Lambert replied. "It's time to go."

With the agents inside, Lambert pulled away from the plane and exited the private airport. Walsh sat next to him and looked in the back row at Quinn and Duncan. They appeared to reach a silent consensus and Walsh nodded. "Lambert—CIA Officer Lambert, I assume? I want to thank you for your help, but it's imperative I get word to the rest of our team."

Lambert kept his eyes on the road ahead. "Word's reached them already."

"Uh huh. Where are we headed to then?" Quinn asked.

"To another airstrip where another plane is waiting to take you back to the States."

Again, we are grateful you're facilitating this effort, but we'd feel a whole lot better talking to our agent in charge who is still in Rio. I think that's going to need to happen before we get in the air again. I don't suppose you have a phone we can use?" Walsh said.

"Here," Lambert tossed him his cell phone. "It's secure. Make the call, but unless whoever you're calling is on a secure line, you'll be putting them at risk."

Walsh glared at the man. "CIA or not, we aren't getting on that plane unless we talk to our people. So either you make that happen, or we'll all be sitting on that runway for a long time."

Lambert snatched his phone again and dialed a number. "Get Cain on a secure line and have him contact me ASAP. I got some stubborn ass FBI agents preventing me from getting my job done." He ended the call and turned back to Walsh. "Happy now?"

"Very."

SCARBOROUGH PUSHED THROUGH THE DOORS OF THE CANTINA and walked outside to his car—Cain's car, actually. His eyes watered from the glare of the setting sun and he realized that at least an hour, maybe longer, must've passed. "Shit." He slipped into the driver's seat and started the car. When he retrieved his phone from his pocket, he noticed several missed calls. Cain, no doubt, wondering what the hell had happened to him and if he was still alive. Then he noticed the time. Three drinks in an hour. That's how long he'd been inside. The voicemail notification light flashed on his phone. He knew he had to check it, he just didn't want to. With his phone to his ear, he listened.

"Where the hell are you, Scarborough? Your people are here

and you're not. The rest of your team is in Brasilia and are refusing to leave without talking to you first. Get your ass back here. Don't make me come find you. I swear, if you're dead I'm gonna be pissed."

Yep. Cain was pissed. "Damn it." Three drinks for a man who'd been sober for a year until blowing it the other night had hit him hard. He knew he shouldn't be driving and was now o for two in poor decisions this week. He slammed the gear into reverse and pulled out, whipping the car ahead and making his way toward the new safe house. "She won't forgive me for this."

Scarborough felt like he'd made a wrong turn somewhere and now couldn't remember the way back. While he'd felt more clear-headed; roaming this city alone as an FBI agent was his third bad decision. Any more and he might not make it back at all. He was going to have to call Cain for help.

"It's me. I got lost. I need help getting back," He said as he held his phone to his ear.

"Where are you? Give me some sort idea," Cain replied.

Scarborough surveyed the area in search of a landmark or road marker. "I see a sign ahead. Hang on." He squinted for a better view. "Says Bem vindo a Los Guava."

"Are you shitting me? Get the hell out of there, Scarborough. You do not want to be there," Cain replied. "Make a U-turn. I'm going to track your cell signal and help you back."

"Are Agents Reid and Fisher with you? Are they safe?" Scarborough pleaded.

"They're safe. Now we need to get you safe. What the hell took you so long? I told you to get back as soon as possible."

"I got lost. Really...lost." His face masked in shame.

"I've locked the signal. I'm tracking your whereabouts on my computer. Jeez, you really did go adrift."

While Cain relayed instructions on how to get back to the safe house, Kate listened and eyed the monitor. Something had gone wrong. Nick wouldn't just get lost like that. Not now when their lives were at stake.

Fisher must've picked up on her apprehension. "Are you okay? Cain will get him back here. He'll be fine. It's easy to get turned around in a strange place."

"Yeah, I know. He's been lost before and has found his way home. I just didn't expect it to happen again." Her words conveyed a deeper meaning than Fisher could know.

"Is there something you want to say, Reid? It's just me here."

She held his gaze for a moment, considering his request. "No. I'm just worried for him. I want him back here."

Cain continued to guide Scarborough. "You should be pulling onto the street now."

"I'm here. I'll see you in a minute."

Cain ended the call and switched off the monitor. "Well, that was fun. You two good?"

"Fine," Kate said. "Thank you for bringing him back."

"It's my fault for sending him out. It's easy to get lost here. I don't blame him. I just don't know why the hell he took so long. He should've been back here well before you."

Kate had an inkling. "I guess we'll have to ask him about that."

Cain pulled open the door and revealed an orange sky as the sun crawled toward the west. "Glad you finally decided to join us, Scarborough. Your people in Brasilia are refusing to leave without hearing from you first. I suggest you get on the horn with them and get them the hell on that plane. Assuming it's still there waiting for them."

"Who's with them?" Scarborough walked inside and cast a brief glance to Kate but quickly shied away.

"A CIA operative. His name's Lambert. He's waiting." Cain held out his phone. "Make the call."

"I'll tell you, man, I thought we'd seen the last of you." Fisher offered his hand. "Glad you're back."

"Me, too."

The word "guilty" might as well have been engraved on his forehead from the way he looked. Kate was well-versed in the many faces of Nick Scarborough, but it seemed unfathomable for this to be happening now. Giving him the benefit of the doubt again was a notion that she couldn't swallow this time. How or where he got booze, she didn't know, but that wasn't the part that mattered. What mattered was that he let down the team in the worst possible way. Absolution was well outside her province right now.

"Copy that. Keep in touch and we'll do the same." Walsh handed the phone back to Lambert. "We'll be getting on that plane now." He eyed Quinn and Duncan. "They're safe and in a better location. The samples are going to trail us by only a day or so, if all goes to plan."

"Nothing's gone to plan so far," Quinn said. "And now we're leaving half our team behind. This is a bad call and you both know it." He started up the stairs to the plane.

Walsh held back Duncan for a moment. "He's made his position clear. And I'll be honest with you, I don't like this either, but our job is to support those we're leaving behind, whether or not it was the right call."

"I agree. The rest will have to sort itself out when this is over. I won't abandon them, regardless of what Quinn thinks was the right thing to do." Duncan boarded the plane.

As Walsh entered the aircraft, he realized Lambert wasn't onboard and returned to the door. "Hey." He spotted the CIA operative still on the runway. "You're not coming?"

"No, sir. I'll be staying here to assist Cain."

"Thank you." Walsh returned to his seat and secured his belt. "It'll just be us from here on out. Lambert's staying behind for backup."

"They'll need him more than we do," Quinn replied.

MASON WYLDER DROVE INTO THE GARAGE OF HIS $10million upper east side home. The single car structure was below street grade and was surrounded by block walls. Cameras bordered his property, but no one occupied the home at present since he'd only just returned from Rio and had released his staff for the summer. Located in a quiet New York suburb, this was his third home, the one he bought solely for family who rarely visited anyway. He was alone with the young woman who had only wanted his autograph and now floated in and out of consciousness in the passenger seat of his car.

He hadn't always acted out in this way, but money changed him. It gave him power and influence—opportunity. It awakened something in him that had been dormant. His fetishes always lay toward the sadistic, but with money, he could fulfill that desire in any way he saw fit. Up to this point, he had been so very careful not to let it spill over here and now that it had, he was left with no choice but to finish the task. And it didn't bother him one bit.

The humidity was stifling and especially in the garage where there were no windows to the outside. "It's time to go now, sweetheart." He stepped out of the car and walked to the passenger side. "Wake up, now. We aren't finished yet." He reached beneath her legs and hoisted her from his car.

There were things he understood about the legal system and how easy it was to find even the most remote pieces of evidence. He wasn't stupid. After all, he worked on a crime drama television show. They had advisors who knew a lot. He'd learned a lot from them. There were things he could do to protect himself. Plastic, gloves, protecting everything around the scene. It was all he had to do and he felt confident he could do it without Scott's help. Oh yes, his assistant would be very unhappy if he knew what Mason was doing right now.

"How about we go to the gym?" The home gym was on the basement level and only steps from the garage. "Are you awake yet?"

She was rousing into consciousness and at any moment would flail and it would become difficult to control her. He had to get her inside. She was light and petite and carrying her was like carrying a child. Inside the gym, a yoga mat lay before him and he placed her there. She was beginning to struggle now as her senses returned.

"Calm down, honey. This will only hurt for a minute." In his back pocket, he retrieved a Swiss Army knife and pulled out the blade. With his knees pinning down her arms and his full weight on her stomach, he smiled. "You're so pretty." And with a swift clean lash, he sliced her throat.

K<small>ATE LOOKED ON AS A KNOCK SOUNDED ON THE DOOR AT</small> their new and supposedly safer lodging, though at this point, that seemed frighteningly laughable. "Is that him? The CIA officer?"

"If it isn't, we're all in trouble." Cain approached the door and squinted through the fisheye lens before pulling it open. "Glad to see you made it out of Brasilia safely. I appreciate you helping us out here."

CIA officer Bryce Lambert entered. "Seems like I'm always bailing you people out." He gazed at the others. "You all must be what's left of BAU?" He approached Fisher. "I'm Bryce Lambert."

"Cameron Fisher. Glad to have you here." They exchanged a greeting.

"That must make you Kate Reid?"

"Yes, sir. Thanks for offering your services." She took his hand.

"I'm Nicholas Scarborough. I want you to know how much I appreciate you getting my team out safely."

"My pleasure, Scarborough." He shook Nick's hand before turning back to Cain. "But it's Elijah you should thank. He told us what you all have been up against since your arrival. I'm sorry it's been so difficult, but that's Brazil for you."

"How long have you been posted here?" Fisher asked.

"About six years. I've seen it go from good to great to shit. We're deep in the excrement now." He turned toward the makeshift kitchen, which was really just a bar fridge and a microwave set atop a folding table. "Hey, you guys got anything good to drink? I could really use a beer."

"No beer, just water." Cain retrieved a bottle for him. "Sorry."

"This'll do, for now." He chugged it half way down. "What about these forensic samples you want me to slip out of the country?"

Cain walked to another folding table and grabbed the case. "Right here. You think you can get these on commercial transit tonight?"

Lambert eyed the time. "It'll be tight, but I think I can do it. The port isn't far from here and I have people who will meet me to make the handoff." He peered at Scarborough. "What are your plans after that?"

"We'll get them to our people at Quantico and they'll rush it through the labs. We're hoping for a match to the unsub we believe is responsible and track him down while he's still here."

"And if you don't get an ID?" Lambert asked.

"Then we stay until we do. We've come too far to quit now. Our people have been threatened, shot at and now we're in hiding. We aren't letting him get away with it. We'll find the American and bring him to justice and if we take down some government officials, then all the better," Scarborough replied.

"Whoa, now. Hold up." Lambert raised his hands in defense. "I'm going to have to stop you right there. If you find anything that leads to the government authorities here in any way, you're going to have to let it go. This can't involve them."

"It already does," Kate said.

"Oh, I get that. But we're talking a major situation if you start indicting their people. I'm afraid I can't let that happen. You want to find and catch an American killer here, more power to you. But you won't be taking any officials down with you."

"We're risking our lives to stop a killer roaming free in Rio. We assume he's an American. Then we're forced to fight an uphill battle to escape the authorities and we have zero recourse against them and their corruption? Fisher asked.

"You hit the nail on the head, my FBI friend."

"What the hell are we doing here then, Scarborough? They don't give a shit about the dead women, they don't give a shit about anything here. Even Varela let his own man get killed to protect himself. What chance do we stand of finding this asshole? What's the goddam point?"

Kate stepped in. "The point is, it's our job. I don't care where we are, or what the risks are, that's what we're here to do. And I'm not leaving until it's done."

"Then let's stop pussyfooting around," Cain said. "Get these samples on a plane and let's get this show on the road."

17

Inside the safehouse, individual cots lined the walls and were made up with a small pillow and a light blanket on each one. It was better than sleeping on the floor, if only a little. Kate hadn't expected to sleep well in any case, and the makeshift beds made that all the more difficult. Then again, her mind reeled with a host of other troubling thoughts as she lay awake while listening to the men around her sleep soundly.

The only comforting thought was of her team returning to Quantico, safe and sound. Though she had been left to wonder if Quinn would use the division as a tool to wedge between them. Kate set her sights on Nick in the cot next to her. She was devastated and beyond angry. He put himself in peril and it could have resulted in putting all of them in peril.

The longer she lay even this near to him, the more her skin crawled until finally, Kate sat up. She padded quietly to a back exit that led to a small, fenced in patio. She needed air.

As she gazed into the night sky, staring at the stars, the door behind her opened.

"What are you doing out here?" Nick asked. "He closed the door behind him.

She studied him. He appeared still half-asleep, but the words were at the tip of her tongue and could not be contained. "I know you were drinking." Her tone was matter-of-fact, but there was no mistaking its bite.

He stood in silence.

"I know you were drinking and that was why you got lost and why you were late. Do you have any idea what would've happened if you'd been harmed? What it would have done not only to this investigation, but to the relationship between Brazil and the US? A federal agent? Jesus. How could you be so incredibly selfish?"

"You're right. I screwed up. I don't have an excuse and I wouldn't insult you with one. I wanted a drink and I had one. I had three, if I'm being honest. Not my finest moment."

"Not your finest moment?"

"What more can I say, Kate? I had the shots the other night and it messed me up. I wanted more and I was absolutely selfish. I had more. You think I'm not pissed at myself?"

She tried to find calm in the rising tide of anger that swelled in her stomach. "Maybe you should go back home. Get out of this place. Go to a meeting. And then you can help the rest of the team."

"You think I'm going to leave you here alone?"

"I won't be alone. Fisher and Cain will be here and we've got Lambert to help now. Nick, I'm afraid you'll put us all in danger. I want you to go." All Kate wanted to do right now was leave; jump on a plane and go home herself. Instead, her eyes shot daggers at Nick and he appeared defenseless.

"I won't leave you, and I won't screw this up again. I swear it. You have to believe me. This case is too important. You're too important. I want all of us to get back home alive."

"You slipped and you know the only thing that will help you get back up is to go home. Go to your meetings. Clear your head and get the hell back on the job."

"No." He held her gaze. "I won't leave you here. I can control this and you're going to need to trust me on that."

"Trust you?" She took a step back in disbelief. "Isn't that what I've done for the past two years while you were pulling your shit together? I followed you to Quantico. I've trusted you since the very beginning even when I didn't have a reason to. I can't trust you right now. Not with my life or with Fisher's or Cain's or anyone here."

"Look. After we get the results and we can identify this prick, we can use Cain's resources to track down the killer. Then we can go home. We're so close, Kate. I promise you that when this is over, I will do whatever you want to fix this. I want to fix this. It's on me and I take full responsibility."

She studied him again. "You have no idea what I've put on the line for you. If your screwup costs us here, I'll never forgive you." Kate walked back inside.

IN THE MIDDLE OF THE DAY AT A TRENDY EATERY IN Manhattan's upper west side, Scott waited for his boss. They were supposed to go together to the studio for a table read of the season premiere episode set to begin filming in a matter of weeks. Mason's early return from his summer hiatus was what prompted the expedited table read and Scott thought it would be the best thing for him. It generally took a few weeks for Mason to return to normal—his normal.

With the trip having been cut short, Scott's concern grew that Mason might not have been ready or willing to get back to work. And that his alter ego might still prevail. While the despicable actions were already inexcusable, Scott looked the other way because he was well-paid to do so. It seemed he had no moral compass either.

Scott pulled up in his chair when he spotted Mason's arrival. He surveyed the restaurant and the nearby street, wondering if he was the only one to notice Mason's rather haggard appearance. He stood up and waved him over. Upon Mason's approach, Scott began, "You look like shit. Sit down."

Mason pulled out a chair and dropped into it with an aloofness that was even more alarming. His shirt was untucked and his face sported stubble, which wasn't his style.

Scott leaned over the table and lowered his tone. "What the hell is wrong with you? Have you looked in a mirror?"

Mason examined his finger nails. "Not recently."

"You should. Where have you been?"

"Working on some things." He picked up the glass of water in front of him. "Speaking of... I'm going to need you to stop by the house on Grovers and do some clean up."

Scott's face turned deadpan. "What are you talking about? Where's your housekeeper?"

"Not something the housekeeper should handle."

"For fuck's sake. What did you do, man?"

"Nothing you haven't dealt with before. What's the big deal?"

"The big deal is you're supposed to go in for a table read today. Are you kidding me with this shit? I mean, look at you." He pulled back. "You look like a walking turd. You can't go to the studio like that."

"Then we'll both go back to my house, you can call whoever it is you call in these situations and I'll get cleaned up. No big deal."

Scott eyed him. "There's no coming back from this."

"What are you talking about? We take care of this just like the rest and move the fuck on. I don't see why you're getting so bent out of shape."

Scott had just figured it out. He'd played with the devil and now he was about to get burned. To hide something like this here was going to take a lot of money and help from people one should only ask as a last resort. Scary and dangerous people that might actually be scarier and more dangerous than the man sitting in front of him.

"How much time do we have?" Scott peered at his phone. "You have to be at the studio in two hours."

"Don't worry, there's extra money in it for you. I get it's an inconvenience."

Scott stood up and dropped two twenties on the table for the drinks. "An inconvenience. Sure. We're leaving. Let's go before anyone recognizes you." He waited for Mason and started ahead of him, almost shielding him from those walking nearby. "Get in the car." He opened the door and slammed it shut after Mason stepped inside. Scott slipped into the driver's seat and keyed the ignition. "Where is this problem right now?"

"In the gym."

"Well, at least you thought about the mess it would leave." He pulled away.

"See? I got your back, dude. You're stressing way too much."

Scott remained silent as he drove back to Mason's townhouse and pulled onto the driveway. He cut the engine and peered at him. "Get inside and get changed."

Mason stepped out and keyed in the code to open the garage door. The door rolled up and revealed a gleaming garage with coated floors and a Ferrari inside. He made his way toward the house and entered.

Scott was only steps behind him and lowered the garage door from the inside. He inhaled a breath before making his way to the basement, preparing for the unknown. "Oh Jeez!" He covered his mouth, holding back his gag reflex. He was no stranger to the carnage Mason usually left in his wake, but this was a whole new level of degeneracy. "What the hell did you do in here?" He stepped inside the gym and stared at the blood-splattered walls and while the floor had been covered in plastic, it wasn't enough to contain the spillage. The sloppiness of the kill was going to make this infinitely harder to manage.

He approached the body and searched for the head that lay only a few feet away. Scott picked up his phone and for a moment, considered calling the police, but the moment passed. He had to protect himself as much as he had to protect Wylder. So he hovered over the head of the victim and held his phone to his ear. There was a fixer he knew who belonged to a dangerous group of people. It was a last resort and it would cost him. "Wait. What the?" He moved closer to the head and crouched for a better look. There was something familiar about this woman, even in this condition, he sensed he knew her. He continued to study the victim, trying to place her when his eyes widened and he pulled back up. "No. No way. This can't be happening." He shot a look to the door, ready to bolt into the main house and take Wylder by the shoulders and scream in his face. Instead, he could only stare at her. He knew her. Lots of people knew her. This woman was the niece of a prominent Broadway director. She'd been beheaded and defiled and lay bloodless inside the home of the famous actor, Mason Wylder.

Levi Walsh waited at Customs inside Reagan National Airport ready to sign for the case containing the samples that had just arrived. It had been well-packaged and should have survived the journey. He and the others had only arrived back in D.C. yesterday which meant Cain had to pull some serious strings to get the shipment here so quickly.

He attempted to contact Scarborough earlier, but didn't get through, which was alarming. All he could do now was wait until he picked up the samples and return to Quantico to make the call on a secure line.

The idea that half the team was in Rio on their own gnawed at him. It was the only thing on which he and Quinn agreed. They should have all returned together, but what was done was done.

A man in a U.S. Customs uniform approached the table where Walsh waited. "Mr. Levi Walsh?"

"That's me." He retrieved his driver's license and handed it to the Customs agent.

"Just sign this for me here, please and I'll let you be on your way." He held out a clipboard with papers attached.

Walsh signed the document.

"Here you go, sir. Have a good day."

"Thank you." Walsh picked up the small black metal case and started toward the exit of the airport.

It would take nearly an hour in traffic to reach Quantico, but the case had been preserved with ice packs. If he ever felt like a covert operative, now was certainly the time. It was a strange feeling because he was supposed to be hunting killers, not subverting governments. That was the CIA's job. But whatever he needed to do needed to be done quickly. Getting the rest of his team home was his first priority, even above capturing a killer.

Walsh arrived at Quantico and headed into the laboratories where he was scheduled to meet with an old and trusted friend who would help him keep this off-book until the results were in. The investigation had been scrapped according to the Brazilian government and he didn't want any trail left behind. "I appreciate you handling this discreetly." Walsh handed the case to the lab tech. "Please only contact me directly when the results are in. And of course..."

"You want it rushed," he replied.

"Yes. It's a matter of life and death for those on our side."

"I'll take care of it. You have my word."

And with a nod and a handshake, the case was now in the hands of Quantico's finest technician. Walsh could walk away with the knowledge that the tests would be completed as soon as humanly possible and they could move forward with the case, whether the Brazilian government wanted to or not.

Upon his return to the BAU offices, Walsh approached Unit Chief Cole who was in his plush corner office. "Knock. Knock."

Cole peered up from his computer. "Walsh. Come in. What news to you have for me?"

He entered and closed the door before sitting down across from Cole. "I handed over the samples to the lab. We might know something tomorrow. He's running the tests as quickly as he can."

"That's good news. Have you informed Scarborough yet?"

"I was waiting to return to reach him on a secure line."

"Good idea." Cole pulled up in his chair and folded his arms against his chest. "I don't agree with what Scarborough's done, but he's the team leader. And if he feels this was the way to go, I have to let him see it through."

"I understand that, sir. Sometimes we do things we don't want to do, but if we can identify him here, they'll be there to pick him up."

"What if it turns out he's not an American? Or there is no match?" Cole asked.

"Then they'll have no choice except to walk away, but I don't think that'll happen, sir. I think we'll find something. Whoever did this was extremely careless. He was being protected by crooked cops and figured he could get away with anything, including murder. That will be his downfall."

"There's something I need to ask you, Levi, and I want you to be completely honest with me." Cole paused a moment. "Have you noticed tensions between Scarborough and Quinn?"

Walsh appeared to consider his reply. "There have been some, but then again, we've been in the middle of a deadly serious game and there's bound to be tension."

"But it's more than that, isn't it? Even Scarborough has alluded to it. Quinn's kept mum about it, so I haven't pushed the issue, but

I won't have this team fracture. What can we do to nip this in the bud?"

"I've known Quinn for longer than I've known Scarborough," Walsh began. "They have distinct personalities and I think it's going to take time for them to see eye to eye. There are things about Quinn, which I'm sure you're already aware, that can make it difficult to work with him. He is an ambitious man. Not that that's a bad thing, but it can rub people the wrong way. And I think it rubs Scarborough the wrong way. And maybe Reid too."

"Is their relationship becoming an issue? Scarborough's and Reid's?"

"Not for me. Not for anyone else that I'm aware of."

"Not even Quinn?" Cole replied.

"Maybe. Look, sir, I understand it's your responsibility to see to it we're one cohesive unit, and I do believe we will get there, in time. But right now, I just want to get the three remaining team members home without incident. And with Agent Cain and his CIA buddy, I think we'll get there, but I need to be on my toes. I'd like to go do that, now, sir, with all due respect."

Cole nodded. "You're right. We'll deal with all this when they return. Go. Call Scarborough and see to it they're updated on your progress. And keep me posted."

18

Even the sunshine and blue skies couldn't make Rocinha appear desirable. It was a dilapidated slum that the government largely ignored because it was under the control of ruthless gangs. And this was where Agent Cain stopped the car—at the crossroads of Rocinha's entrance.

"I'm not sure I'm fully on board with this, Scarborough. Talking to these people might just get you killed."

"I don't see another way. Not right now and not until we get the labs back. Walsh said to expect them in another 24 hours. Well, you'll excuse me if I'd like to try to get some answers sooner than that."

Fisher, who was in the back seat with Kate began, "I have to agree with you on that one, boss."

"Same here," Kate started. "You've already established a rapport—sort of, so I think this is our best option."

"Fair enough. I know when I'm in the minority. Who's going in?" Cain peered at the three of them.

"I am." Scarborough opened the door. "He knows me."

"Uh, I was with you too. They know me," Fisher replied.

"Stay here. If we team up on them, I think we'll be asking for trouble. I go in there alone and they're going to see I'm no threat."

Kate wanted to disagree with him on that point but wouldn't because he was right. "Be careful." Regardless of how angry she was with him right now, she still loved him and the idea he could be hurt or killed sent her nerves on end.

"I'll be okay. I know what I'm doing." He stepped out of the car and made his way on foot to the known location of one of the AdA buildings. Varela, so far, was still cooperating, if not reluctantly, because he knew what would happen if any agents were murdered in Rio. The hellfire of the US government would be unleased upon the city and even he didn't want that.

He turned the corner and disappeared from view of the others waiting in the car. Nick was on his own and it was the way he wanted it right now. His shoulders weighed heavily with the burden of his mistakes from yesterday and he wanted to not only make it up to Kate but prove to himself he wasn't a screw up like he appeared.

The building was just ahead and as he stood in front of it, he knocked on the glass door. From the back, he noticed a large, angry looking man approach. Must have been one of the gang members seeing as the man had an AK47 strapped to his chest. Nick was unarmed.

The door opened. "O que você quer?" *"What do you want?"*

Nick didn't understand him, but it sounded like a question. "Senhor Ramos?"

The man eyed him. "Americano?"

"Yes." He followed with a nod.

The door closed and the man disappeared beyond the corridor. However, Scarborough didn't wait for long. Another friendly looking gentleman appeared with a big gun and sporting a heavy beard. He waved for Scarborough to follow.

"Gracias."

"That's Spanish. The word you want is Obrigado," the bearded man replied.

"Sorry." He walked inside.

"Follow me." The man led the way to another back room where he opened yet another door in this maze and spoke in Portuguese to the man behind the desk.

It was Ramos. He'd made it this far and there was no turning back now. "Mr. Ramos, thank you for seeing me."

"FBI Agent Nicholas Scarborough, please sit down. I'm curious as to why you are here. It is not a safe place for you to be, senhor."

"I understand that more than you know. I'm here because I want to talk to you about Inspector Gustavo Varela and his investigator Pedro Sosa."

"I am aware. Investigator Sosa has recently perished. That is unfortunate. But what can I do about that?"

"I think Mr. Sosa might have been murdered by people who work for you. Maybe as a favor for the Rio civil police?"

"Be careful of your accusations, Agent Scarborough. They might get you in trouble."

"Unfortunately, I had agents with him at the time of his death and their lives were also in danger. Can you tell me what you know about that?"

He laughed. "I know nothing more than you. Why are you here? Only to lob allegations?"

"I'm here to get to the truth."

"This is Rio. There is no truth here. Only money and power and lies."

"I understand that you indicated to Varela you and your people had nothing to do with the deaths of those women found in the shallow grave at the top of Rocinha. And if that is the case, and I choose to believe you, then you must know who is responsible. You're a smart man, Mr. Ramos. I imagine nothing happens here that you aren't aware of. I want to leave Rio with my people, and the American who committed the atrocities. I'm sure that would benefit you and the people of Rocinha if we could capture this monster." Scarborough understood that the man with whom he was speaking was also a monster except he was one who didn't get his own hands dirty, in all likelihood. Now he was asking the gangster to go a step further and give up the American who probably paid him for his silence.

"What can you offer me?" Ramos replied.

"More than whoever is paying you to bury this, so to speak. I can assure you, I have the support of my government behind me and if an American is responsible, we will bring him to justice."

"American justice. Only for the wealthy, sim?"

"I won't argue with you there. But as far as I'm concerned, I don't care who has the money, I want this man. I want him alive to face trial. Here or in my country. I don't care."

"Okay, Special Agent Nicholas Scarborough, but I want something else in return, besides money."

"Name it."

"I want Varela gone."

❧

THREE FOLDING TABLES HAD BEEN PUSHED TOGETHER TO create a large one that would hold the cast of the television show starring Mason Wylder. It was time to read the season premiere episode and he felt invigorated to be back at work, even if it was earlier than he anticipated.

"Welcome back, everyone." The showrunner stood at the head of the table. "And to you, Mason, for cutting short your summer plans to join us. We appreciate that." He instigated a round of applause.

Wylder soaked up the attention and bowed to his colleagues. "Glad to be back."

"Good. Then we should get started. You'll see your scripts are in front of you and this will just be a quick and dirty read-through so you all can go back to enjoying the beautiful hot and sticky New York summer day."

Wylder picked up his script and felt his phone vibrate in his shirt pocket. He retrieved it to find a text message from Scott. *"It's taken care of."*

"Uh, Mason, no phones," the showrunner said.

"Sorry." He slipped the phone back in his pocket and felt better than ever. It was his opening line and so the read began.

With few interruptions, the table read was finished after about an hour. As Wylder stood up to leave, he spotted Scott in the doorway. "You'll all excuse me for a moment?"

"We're finished for today, Mason. You can go on home if you'd like," the showrunner said.

Wylder nodded and walked toward the entrance. "Hey. We just wrapped up. You want to grab a drink or something?"

Scott eyed him as he placed his hand on his shoulder. "Look, man. We need to talk. And not here."

"Fine. We'll grab a drink then. Come on." Wylder started into the hall and turned when Scott wasn't following. "Dude? You coming or what?"

With some reluctance, Scott followed him outside toward his car and stopped him. "Do you have any idea who that was?"

"Who what was?" He clicked open the car doors.

"Jesus. I knew you were crazy, but this is batshit crazy. We're going back to my place. Now."

"Fine. Whatever." He stepped into his car and waited for Scott to return to his. "What crawled up your ass?" Wylder peered through the windshield before pressing the ignition to start his Mercedes. And just as though today was like every other day, Wylder followed Scott back to his high-rise apartment, which was just a stone's throw from his own.

Upon arrival, Scott inserted his key in the apartment door. "Just get inside." He held open the door while Mason entered, closing it behind him. "What the hell is wrong with you, man? You don't take risks like this. Do you have any idea what you've done?"

The apartment was much smaller and far less grand than Mason's. Scott's taste was more subdued as well, teetering between traditional and contemporary. Still, the place cost him over $8,000 a month.

Mason made his way into the kitchen and grabbed a beer from the fridge. "Want one?"

"No. I don't want one."

"Suit yourself." He twisted off the top and tossed half of it back. "Okay, what were you saying?"

"Look, we aren't in Rio anymore. You get that, right? There's no one here you can buy. No one who will look the other way, you understand?"

"Oh, I get it. This is about the girl. Yeah, I know, man. I got a little crazy. Shit won't happen again. Not here. I get it."

"I don't think you do, man. Do you know who she was? Does your brain comprehend who that girl was?"

Mason's face twisted and his lips raised into a menacing smile. His eyes blackened and his cheeks flushed. "I don't think you want to be talking to me like this, bro. I did what I did. It's done and it won't happen again. That's all you need to know. Understand? I don't give a flying fuck who she was. She's gone now. You took care of her. That's what you need to remember. I'm the one who calls the shots, unless you forgot where you get your paycheck from." He stepped to within inches of Scott. "So this conversation is over. Do what the fuck I pay you to do and we won't have any more problems."

Scott watched as Mason's smile turned genuine, his face returned to its normal color and his eyes were brown again. He was Mason Wylder again. But what Scott had just witnessed meant that he had fallen deep into another dimension and he wasn't coming out again. It was either continue to cover up and hide and lie for Wylder or find himself dead. And if Wylder had a hand in it, it would be the worst kind of dead. "Okay. I said it was taken care of and it is. Problem solved." He backed up several steps.

Wylder appeared almost jovial in a stark and troubling about-face. "Good. Now are we going to go out or what?"

HE'D BEEN IN THERE FOR TOO LONG. KATE FIXED HER EYES ON the road Nick had traveled and still there was no sign of his return.

It had been nearly an hour. "We should get in there. I'm sorry, but I can't sit here and not know what the hell is happening."

"Just give it a little more time, Reid," Fisher said. "I get these guys are dangerous criminals, but they'd be crazy to do anything to a federal agent. You're going to have to trust that Scarborough knows what he's doing. I figured that wouldn't be that hard for you to do, all things considered."

"What?" She whipped back. "What's that supposed to mean?"

"Nothing. I didn't mean anything by it. You're starting to freak out, Reid and you need to reel it in, okay?"

"Besides." Cain pointed at the road ahead. "There's your boy now."

Relief swept through her at the sight of Nick, unharmed and heading their way. "Thank God." She turned back to Fisher. "I'm sorry. I was just feeling, well..."

"I get it. You're allowed to worry. But as you can see, he's still in one piece."

Nick opened the door and slipped into the back seat. "So, we're going to need to get Inspector Varela the hell out of Rio and the sooner the better. Once we do that, they'll tell us who paid them off."

"Wait." Cain peered at him. "Where are we supposed to send Varela and why?"

"Well, the plan was that we were supposed to kill him. And that's what they think we're going to do. But I say, get him into our protection until this is over."

"Then what?" Fisher began. "Release him to those guys?"

"Say we do that," Cain added. "They're going to give us a name?"

"That's what they're telling me."

"And you believe them?" Fisher asked.

"What else are we doing here, then, man? We need answers. And I know they have them. They just want something in return. Same as everyone else." Scarborough turned to Cain. "We should leave now."

Cain started the engine and pulled out, heading back toward the safehouse. "How soon are we supposed to vacate the inspector?"

"As soon as we can," Nick replied.

"And they aren't going to want proof we took care of their problem?" Kate asked.

"I'll give them proof and we'll get Varela to cooperate. Either that, or we turn him over to the military police and let them deal with him. They're the ones everyone around here really worries about."

"Is there no other way?" asked Kate.

"I don't think so. These are not people who are easily reasoned with."

"Alrighty then," Cain said. "We'll get Varela out of here and give them proof we've taken care of the problem. But then we'd better get some damn answers."

"I can only do what they ask and hope for the best," Scarborough replied.

"So what are we supposed to do in the meantime?" Fisher asked. "Sit on our thumbs?"

"We can do more than that. We can track down one of Rosella Ortiz's co-workers," Kate said. "Someone has to know where she was before she was killed. If her editor won't talk, then maybe another might, without wanting a fat check at the end of it."

"Okay. You and I will do that," Fisher looked to Scarborough.

"You and Cain can handle Varela. We'll reconvene at the house and go from there."

"Sounds like a plan," Nick said. "You'll need a car. We'll have to go to the safehouse anyway so you can pick it up. Then Cain and I can take care of business." He peered at Kate. "You're good with that, Reid?"

"I'm good." She worried that now they were making deals with drug kingpins. It was bad enough they had to hunt down killers, colluding with drug lords was a whole other level of bad.

THE THREE MEMBERS OF THE TEAM COULD DO NOTHING MORE than to wait for the results to come back for the samples that had been smuggled out of Brazil. They were paralyzed while the others risked their lives thousands of miles away.

Quinn pressed his thumb inside the palm of his hand, a nervous tick, as he sat in the chair across from Walsh's desk. "Is there anything more we can do to expedite these labs?"

Walsh pressed a button on his phone. "Hey, Duncan, you have a minute?"

"Be right there."

"I'd like to get her in on this," Walsh said.

A moment later, Duncan arrived. "Hey. Tell me you have some good news."

"No news, actually. Have a seat," Walsh began. "Listen, that night you and Reid were at the club."

"What about it?"

"You met Mason Wylder there, is that right?"

"Sure did. He gave me his autograph too on a napkin. And I

thought it was really weird because I guess he must think pretty highly of himself, but he kissed it before handing it over."

"Wait, he kissed the napkin?" The dawn of an idea masked Quinn's face. "Please tell me you still have it."

"I packed it. Probably sitting on my dresser or something. Why?"

"You saw him talking to the man you believed was a close match to the tipster's description?" Quinn asked. "And from that moment on, you and Reid started taking pictures and then the heavy-weights moved in and caused problems for you both."

"That's right."

"We're going to need that napkin just as soon as you can get it to us," Quinn replied. "I could be way off target here, but given that association, there's a chance, a minuscule chance, that he could be involved in the murders of those women, or..."

Walsh jumped in. "He's the murderer himself."

19

The building that housed the Rio newspaper where Fisher and Kate had been the previous day fell into view once again. This time, they arrived in effort to home in on a co-worker of Ms. Ortiz's. Someone who knew where she had been on the day of her disappearance and why.

"Who is it you say we're looking for?" Fisher asked as he pulled the car to a stop.

Kate flipped through copies of the daily paper. "According to the majority of these bylines, we want a man by the name of Phillippe Villanueva. He appears in multiple articles and co-wrote a few with Rosella Ortiz. Here's what he looks like." Kate held up the paper where a small thumbnail sized image of the reporter was posted next to one of the articles.

"Anyone else on that list we can approach in the event we strike out with that one?" Fisher asked.

"There are two others who don't appear as frequently, and we can talk to all three if need be."

"We might just need to do that." Fisher peered at the small, flat-roofed structure painted a bright blue. "I don't know what time these people around here knock off, but it's getting close to 5pm. If we don't see anyone leaving in the next hour, we're going to have to go in."

"The editor, Santiago, will probably have us kicked out," Kate said.

"Oh, I have no doubt, since we're not here to dole out cash, but if we can catch sight of any of Rosella's co-workers, we might get one of them to talk. Surely, they must be upset by the loss."

"Hang on. I see some people leaving." Kate studied the door as it swung open. Several people filed out. "Nope. No sign of Villanueva."

"Just hold your horses. Looks like we got ourselves a few stragglers." Fisher pointed ahead. "Who've we got there?"

Kate examined the image on the newspaper and looked at the man who had just stepped out. "I think that could be our guy. Should we approach him now?"

"Let's wait until he separates himself from the rest and see where he goes."

They both watched as the man waved goodbye to his colleagues and started toward the parking lot.

"Now." Fisher opened the door.

Kate followed him and both made their way to the man.

"Excuse me?" Fisher jogged toward him. "Uh, I mean, Desculpe?"

At this, the man stopped and looked at them. He appeared confused but waited for them to catch up.

"Inglês?" Fisher asked.

"Yes."

"Here's to small miracles. Can we talk to you about Rosella Ortiz? She was a colleague of yours, is that right?"

"Who are you?" He asked before turning to Kate. "And you? Both American?"

"We are," Fisher began. "We're trying to find the truth about Rosella's murder. We want to give her justice."

"You do understand that you are in Rio? Justice here comes at a steep price."

Kate moved in. "Listen, you don't have any reason to trust us. I understand that. But we are here because there is an American who has come here to hurt your people. And we believe he may have hurt Rosella. We have spoken to your editor to no avail. We're hoping you might not be so inclined to turn your back on her."

His expression revealed that he might actually consider this request. "If I take you at your word. If I agree to help, I cannot be named in any investigation or anything relating to her or to this newspaper. If I am, I will be killed."

Fisher nodded. "We understand. Is there someplace you'd like to go to discuss this further?"

The reporter peered back at the building. "Yes. I cannot afford to be seen here with you. Follow me." He continued into the parking lot and toward his car.

Fisher led Kate back to their car. "What do you think?" He opened the passenger door for her.

"I think he wants to help, but I also think he understands what's at stake if he does."

CIA Officer Bryce Lambert flicked away his cigarette as he stood outside the safehouse and spotted Cain and Scarborough pulling onto the driveway. He walked back inside and looked at Varela. "Today's your lucky day, Inspector."

Varela appeared exhausted. "Do I get to go home now?"

Lambert laughed. "Not a chance, my man. What you get to do though is to get the hell out of here and out of my hair." He peered through the curtains. "Your ride is pulling up now." He made his way to the door and pulled it open. "I was wondering when you'd be showing up. I see you're both still alive. Things must've gone well with the AdA?"

"Well enough." Scarborough walked inside and spotted Varela. "You on the other hand. I'm not so sure about you."

Cain entered and closed the door behind him. "How's he been for you?"

"Fine," Lambert replied. "Nary a peep. So, you mentioned taking him with you? When is that going to take place? No offense, but I got shit to do. Shit that don't involve you folks or him."

"I think we're ready to take him off your hands," Cain said. "And I don't think we'll be needing anything from you good folks in the interim. At least, not until we're ready to leave."

"And when might that be?" Lambert asked.

"Best guess? Tomorrow."

"You want me to line it up?"

"Give me this afternoon. I'll be in touch tonight." Cain offered his hand. "Thanks, brother. You bailed us out and we won't forget it."

"We're all here for the same reasons. Or so they tell me." Lambert grabbed his things. "You know where I'll be and I'll wait to hear from you tonight. Don't make me track your asses down if I don't hear from you, yeah?" He started toward the door. "Scarborough, pleasure. Good luck to you and your team."

"Thank you." Scarborough returned his greeting. "We'll be in touch."

"Yep." Lambert walked outside.

"Guess that leaves us to deal with you." Cain sat down on the cot next to Varela. "This isn't how we would've wanted things to go, but you didn't leave us much choice."

"I thought Americans always chose the high road, like in the movies. Always doing the right thing." Varela traded glances with the men. "Where are we going now?"

"You get to go hide out someplace else for a while." Scarborough said. "The only thing is, we'll be needing a favor from you."

"A favor?" Varela asked. "And what favor is that?"

"Well, see we made an agreement with the AdA," Scarborough began. "They want you dead. And, I don't really have a problem with that seeing how you almost had my people killed and Mr. Sosa died on your command, so, I'm good with that. Except Agent Cain here says we can't do that. So, we need to make it look like you're dead. But you'll be safe and sound far away from here."

"You want me to play dead. Is that what you're asking me?"

"Bingo. If you don't, we'll have no choice but to hand you over to them and they can do the dirty work. We figured this was the best way for you to help us out and keep you alive." Scarborough eyed Cain. "And we'd better act on this now."

FISHER SLOWED THE CAR AS THE REPORTER, VILLANUEVA, pulled to a stop in front of a café inside the favela called Jacarez-inho, in Rio's north zone. "Why is he stopping here? This place hardly looks secluded."

"I think he wants us to be seen," Kate replied. "It would play into the narrative written in the article that US agents were trying to subvert the government."

"Somehow, I think you could be right." Fisher stopped only feet behind him and turned off the engine. "You have your weapon?"

"Never leave home without it." She tapped her hip and opened the car door to step outside. "He's waiting for us."

Fisher joined her on the narrow sidewalk, and both approached him.

"This is the place?" He asked.

"It is. My parents own this café. It's about the safest place I know of." He led them inside. "Mãe. Pai." Villanueva opened his arms to greet his parents.

They began to speak Portuguese, leaving Fisher and Kate to wonder and hope that what was being said wouldn't cause them any trouble.

"We might've been wrong about him after all," Kate said. "Assuming he isn't ratting us out right now. Probably should've tried to learn the language before coming here."

"Yeah, sure, with all our spare time. Let's hear him out and get back to the others. I don't know about you but I'm itching to get the hell out of this country."

"Follow me." Villanueva led them to a table. "You'd better order something or my mother will think you're insulting her."

"Uh, okay. I'll have a coffee and a sandwich," Fisher said.

"Same here," Kate replied.

"Good." He turned to his mother again and ordered for them. "Now we can get down to business. What is it that you think I know and how can I help you find the person who killed one of my dearest friends?"

This was sounding more positive. Perhaps he was on the side of justice and after swimming upstream from the moment they stepped into this country, things were looking up.

Kate sipped on her coffee before being the first to enter into this foray. "Did you happen to have access to or know anyone who had access to Rosella's email or calendar?"

"I didn't have access to it. If anyone did, it would've been our editor. But as you're here, I imagine you didn't get very far with him. Not that I am surprised by this."

"Did she stay in contact with you on a regular basis?" Fisher asked. "Had you received any text messages from her on the day she went missing?"

He retrieved his cell phone and scrolled through the messages. His brow furrowed and he exhaled a deep breath.

Kate and Fisher traded glances again. They may have overestimated him after all, but then the reporter's tone changed.

"Wait a minute." He continued to study his phone. "This is from her. Looks like it was sent the day before she was killed." He handed the phone to Fisher. "What do you think about this?"

Fisher peered at it. "Sorry, you mind translating?"

"Of course." Villanueva looked at the message again. "Will have to postpone our lunch tomorrow. Need to send out an article as quickly as possible."

"Do you think it was the article about us?" Kate asked him.

"Possibly." He turned to Villanueva. "Nothing from her after this?"

"No. It was sent late. I don't even think I saw it until the next morning. And by then, of course..."

"She didn't mention at all who she was meeting with?" Kate asked.

"What you see there is everything I know. Of course, there is another you could ask. A friend of hers. The two often hit the clubs and then she would do her writeups. There's a good chance she would know where Rosella went that day. A very good chance. I'll give you the information."

"Do we have time for this?" Kate asked Fisher.

"We'll have to make time." He turned back to the reporter. "I hope we can trust you and that you aren't sending us down a path with no return."

At this, Villanueva leaned in and turned serious. "I am first and foremost, a journalist. And not like the ones you have in America now who only seek to post sound bites and who are intent on sowing division. I seek justice, the same as my colleagues. The same as Rosella. She might have been an entertainment reporter, but she was a journalist. And I want justice for her. Speak to this woman here," He held out his phone again. "She will give you the answers you seek. I'm sorry I couldn't do more."

"This will do for now." Fisher stood. "Thank you for your help. Reid, we'd better track her down."

"You'll find her at the Los Palmas resort. That is where she works. Be sure to give her my name. She will speak to you."

~

In the midst of the abundant woodland, Varela sat up from the ground and brushed the dirt and leaves from his shirt. "Are you sure this is absolutely necessary?"

"Yes," Cain began. "Now lay back down so I can finish taking pictures. Oh, and, Scarborough, put a little more blood him. It's drying too quickly."

"Got it." Scarborough squirted more of the ketchup on his forehead. "Now just lay back down and be still. It's either this, or the real thing. You decide."

Varela eyed him with contempt before surrendering.

"Good. Okay. Let's get a few more shots and that should be enough to convince the AdA he's dead." Cain snapped several more pictures. "We're done here, Varela. You can get up now."

"Now what?" Scarborough said.

"We get him out of town." Cain started back toward the vehicle. "Varela, get a move on, would you? The plane won't wait for the likes of you."

Scarborough helped him off the ground. "Come on. We're doing this for your own good."

"You keep telling yourself that, Agent Scarborough. You do not know these men. These gangsters. They are not in the business of keeping their word. You will find that out soon enough." He pulled away his arm and walked to the car on his own before slipping into the back seat.

Scarborough joined Cain in the front and waited for him to start the engine. "Is everything ready to go?"

"It is. We've got about a two-hour drive from here. Once we get him on the plane, we'll reconvene at the safe house."

"And the pictures?"

"It's best you deliver them in person tomorrow first thing," Cain replied.

"And if Fisher and Reid have new information, along with whatever we get from the AdA, we might actually find this asshole and then get to go home."

Varela pulled up in the backseat. "I wouldn't count on that, Agent Scarborough. In fact, I'd be surprised if you left this country alive. Any of you."

Noah Quinn stood with his arms folded as he waited for the lab technician to sign-off on the results that had finally come. "Well?"

"You're going to have to give me a minute. I need absolute certainty. Maybe it would be best if you returned to your office. I'll be a little while."

Quinn shook his head. "Fine. Yeah. Sorry. I'm anxious. Call me when you're finished." He started to leave.

"You know I will." The lab tech returned to his computer.

Quinn stopped in Walsh's office. "He's almost there. Has Duncan returned with the napkin?"

"She texted me and said she'd be here shortly. I'd like to put a call into Scarborough and see how things are going there. I haven't heard from them all afternoon."

"I think he'd call if he needed to or had the opportunity. I'm not sure it's best for us to initiate contact."

With the phone at his ear, Walsh lowered it again and cocked his head. "What is it about him that you don't like?"

Quinn ambled his way to a chair and sat down. "It's not that I don't like the guy, I just don't think he's suited for this position."

"That's a bold assertion. Do you think you're better suited? Is that what I'm hearing?"

"Not at all."

"And you're sure this has nothing to do with Reid? Seems things have turned a little cold between you two."

Quinn shook his head. "She's stubborn. Doesn't see what's right in front of her."

"And what is right in front of her? You?" Walsh appeared concerned. "Are there possibly some feelings involved there?"

"No. That's not at all what this is about. Look, I just think Scarborough has made some bad calls. And Cole seems to be on his side 100 percent."

"Then why does it bother you?"

Quinn paused for a moment. "Because he's holding her back."

"Who? Reid?"

"Yeah. Reid. He's holding her back. She knows it. I know it. And she won't do a damn thing about it."

"By the sounds of things, you've decided to force the issue. Reid seems convinced of it. Is that true? Cause I'll tell you one thing, Quinn, what we got going on here with all of us is a team trying to find its legs. And you're knocking them out from under us. Something's gotta give. And I think it's going to have to come from you."

Duncan severed the rising tension on her return. "I got it. Here's the napkin. I don't know if we'll get anything from it. I've seen stranger things happen, but I say it's worth a shot."

At that moment, Quinn's phone rang. "It's the lab." He answered. "You have the results? Hang on, I'm going to put you on speaker. I'm here with the rest of the team." He pressed the speaker button. "Go head."

"We did pull DNA off the samples you provided. However, there is no match in the system."

"That's no surprise. The good news is you pulled DNA," Walsh said. "But we might have something that could match what you've just pulled."

"And that is?" The tech asked over the speaker.

"How good are you at retrieving DNA from a napkin?"

20

The last refuge in a city seemingly hellbent on ensuring the destruction of US federal agents was where Cain and Scarborough had returned. The abandoned structure hardly suitable for occupancy lay inside a suburban community that hid its own objectives.

Cain returned the phone to his pocket and sat down on the cot. "Lambert says Varela is safely on the plane."

"Now we have to play off like we killed him." Scarborough checked the time. "I should reach out to my team before we head back to Rocinha." He picked up the landline. "This line is still secured?"

"I'm no amateur, Scarborough. It's secure." He walked to the small refrigerator. "You want some water?"

"Yeah. Thanks." Nick waited while the line rang. "Hey, Walsh. I'm glad you answered. Please tell me you have the results?"

Scarborough listened as Walsh relayed the news that they had retrieved DNA, but there was no match to anyone in ViCap, the Violent Criminal Apprehension Program. But he added the napkin could be the lynch pin. "I was hoping for something more definitive. You might not have enough on that napkin to get anything."

"That's what the lab tech said, but he said it was worth a shot. What have we got to lose? There was another interesting development. A case was just entered into ViCAP by the NYPD. A woman who went missing a few days ago. When Duncan ran the parameters to find a match on our sample, it popped up as a new entry. She initially disregarded it but, well, now that we suspect Mason Wylder could also be involved, she opted to take a look, in the off-chance. Here's the kicker. You won't believe who the last person was who saw her."

"Who?"

"Mason Wylder. He was at a café in Manhattan which just so happens to have been the last place the woman was seen alive.

"Mason Wylder has returned from Rio?" Scarborough asked. "When did this happen?"

"Don't know. If Duncan hadn't seen that NYPD report, I'm not sure we'd know now, but he's here, Scarborough. He left Rio. What do you suppose that means?"

"It means I might've made a deal with the devil and didn't need to." How much longer until we know for sure on this napkin? I don't want to cut bait here until we are 100 percent certain there's a match to the samples we provided and this napkin," Scarborough said.

"The tech says he'll have something soon. I don't know what that means. But I trust he's busting his ass for us on this one."

"Okay. Cain and I have taken care of things on our end. We're waiting for Reid and Fisher to return, which should be any time now. We'll stick to the plan until we hear otherwise from you."

"Okay. Hey, be safe. All of you."

"You know we will. Talk later." Scarborough ended the call.

Cain peered through the window. "I think the rest of your people have returned."

"Good timing." Scarborough returned to the cot and dropped down. "We might've just been handed a reason to go home. Regardless of what the AdA has."

Cain opened the door. "Welcome back. Come on in and join the party."

"Looks more like a wake in here than a party." Fisher walked inside. "Good thing we come bearing news."

Scarborough perked up.

"Reid, you want to let them in on what we found?"

Cain closed the door. "Please do, Reid."

"So, our first meeting was a little bit of a bust. The guy was a friend, but he didn't know anything." Kate continued inside.

"Right. But after that. Tell them what happened." Fisher appeared as delighted as a child tattling on his sibling.

"He gave us the name of one of Rosella's closest friends. We went to her work and she was willing to talk."

Scarborough stood up. "What did she say?" A thunderous noise rang out and a window exploded, sending shards flying through the room. He instinctively ducked, throwing his arms over his head. "Jesus!"

Cain ducked and pulled Kate down with him.

Scarborough's eyes widened as he set his sights on the shattered window with curtains that now hung in tatters. "Fisher! Get down! Kate? Are you okay?"

"I'm okay. What the hell is..."

The sound that followed was unmistakable this time. Gunfire. The front door splintered, and beams of light shone through the bullet holes. Shells clinked and clattered as the they fell to the ground.

"We need to get the hell out of here!" Cain reached for his cell and pressed a button. "Lambert! We need help! We got people firing on us left and right and I need to get these people out of here!"

"I'll send backup now. Stay put!"

Cain dropped his phone into his pocket. "Lambert's sending people, but I don't know how much time we'll have. We need to find a way out of here."

"How many are out there?" Fisher asked, still low to the ground.

"Hell if I know. You want to look?"

More shots pinged against the concrete exterior with one making it through the broken window and ricocheting off the refrigerator.

"Holy hell!" Scarborough said. "We're going to have to hold them off."

"Who's out there?" Kate asked.

"Varela had to get word to someone. There's no other way," Cain said.

"Unless we were followed," Fisher said.

"No. Not a chance," Kate replied.

"We can dick around here and figure out why we're being shot at, or we can find a solution for how we can vacate these premises," Cain said. "I vote for the latter."

"Scarborough, you and I will have to provide cover so Cain

can take Reid and get to the car. We'll have to catch up with them," Fisher said.

"No way. We all go or none of us goes," Kate said.

"Nice try, Reid. But you aren't calling the shots here." Cain pulled her arm. "In five. You boys better be ready."

With Cain's countdown, Kate had to be ready whether she wanted to or not. "Goddamn it! I need to stay with my team!"

In unison, Fisher and Scarborough replied, "Go!"

While Kate wanted to be offended for their overprotective prejudice, after all, she had done her share of joining in shootouts, she had to consider the idea that they were senior to her. "Fine."

"Five!" Cain pulled her along while they both remained crouched down. "Let's go, Reid. Pick up the pace!"

She trailed him outside amid the barrage of bullets and felt as though they'd just gone from the frying pan into the fire. Some relief came at the sound of returning fire from inside the house as Fisher and Scarborough provided cover so they could reach the car.

Cain jumped in and Reid leaped into the back seat. "They'd better get their asses out here cause as soon as they hear this car running, all bets are off."

"I see them! I see them! Start the car now!" Kate said.

Cain fired up the engine. "Come on boys. Come on."

Fisher and Scarborough reached the car and jumped inside. Scarborough was in the back with Kate.

"Thank God," Kate said.

"We ain't in the clear yet." Cain slammed the car into reverse. "Keep your heads down, folks!" He pressed his foot on the gas and the tires spun.

The hail of bullets followed them. Rapid fire weapons sprayed the car from every direction.

"Go! Go! Go!" Fisher tucked his head between his legs.

"Don't you worry about it, son. I'll get us clear." Cain raced out of the driveway and shoved the car into Drive. Smoke billowed from the tires. "Hold on to your britches!"

IT HAD BEEN OVER AN HOUR SINCE THEY MADE THEIR harrowing escape and no word on who sang about the location of the safe house, though it was impossible to believe it was anyone other than Varela.

"Where the hell are you?" Lambert screamed at Cain through the phone.

"Still driving. Did your people find anything there?"

"No. The assailants were gone before we got here. Your safe-house is shot all to hell, though."

Cain checked on the safety of his passengers before continuing. "Where's Varela?"

"In our custody in Brasilia. We've got our people interrogating him now to find out if he was responsible," Lambert replied. "I think it's time for you to get out of there and for the BAU team to go back home."

"I don't know if I'll get buy off on that. There's still a killer out there and these folks won't be keen to leave until he's found."

"Then they'll be risking their lives. You need to talk some sense into them. I don't know how much more I can do to help. It's a different ballgame here and I think you and I are the only ones who realize that."

"Let me see what I can do. I'll be in touch." Cain ended the call.

"I already know what you're about to say," Kate began. "And I think this time, you might be right." She looked at her colleagues for agreement. "What we found today, Fisher and I, I'm starting to believe we've overlooked the obvious. Mason Wylder. Rosella Ortiz's friend said she was going to interview someone that day. Someone famous. That can't be a coincidence."

"That would explain things," Scarborough replied.

"What do you mean?" She pressed on.

"Just before all hell broke loose when you two returned, I was on the phone with Walsh. Mason Wylder is back in New York. I don't know when he left or why. But here's the thing, there's a missing persons' report from the NYPD and Wylder was in the location of where the victim was last seen."

"ARE YOU KIDDING ME?" FISHER ASKED.

"It's still a longshot to jump to the conclusion Wylder is the killer. We have zero evidence," Scarborough replied. "Except for one thing that could tie all this together."

Kate nodded. "The napkin."

"What?" Fisher asked.

"The night we met Mason Wylder. He autographed, then kissed a napkin and gave it to Duncan."

"You got it," Scarborough replied.

"Lambert's insisting it's time to pull the plug on these shenanigans. Sounds like he's right," Cain replied.

∾

INSIDE THE MANHATTAN APARTMENT OF MASON WYLDER, light from a setting sun reflected through the windows and cast a purple and orange haze across the modern interior. He sat on his sofa with a scotch in hand and pressed the remote control of his television in search of news.

The words of his closest and only confident reverberated and concern gnawed at him about the director's niece. How was he to know who she was? It was her fault for harassing him for a signature. But now, he believed his behavior might jeopardize the lifestyle in which he enjoyed virtual impunity. These small moments of lucidity didn't last long, and he recognized their transient nature, though could do nothing about it.

"And in other news, the niece of a prominent Broadway director has been missing for over 24 hours. The director, along with the young woman's parents, have pleaded for her safe return. This is Marc Aguilar, News10 live."

"This could be a problem," Wylder opined. The question now was, should he return to Brazil where he could continue to bribe the officials until this blew over? Of course, how would he explain his absence from the set? The job kept him in the public eye and he desired fame almost more than he desired to kill.

Without the job, the money would vanish quickly and so would his lavish lifestyle. No. These were not viable options. Perhaps the only solution would be to keep his head down and stick to the set and home. No more parties because he recognized his weaknesses. All of this would bring elation to Scott, no doubt. Then perhaps in a few months people would forget about the girl. They always did.

Wylder picked up his phone. "It's me. You might be right about keeping my head down." He could hear the relief in Scott's tone. "I'm sure this will blow over. Things can get back to normal. I'll see you tomorrow." He ended the call and stood from the sofa. After turning off the television, he walked toward the corridor and made a right down the lengthy hall until reaching the room adjacent to his bedroom. While not as sound-proof or sophisticated as the killing room in Rio, it was sufficiently equipped to do what was necessary. He unlocked the door and walked inside.

A richly upholstered wide chair rested beneath a window. On that chair, a woman whose mouth was taped shut and whose hands and feet were cuffed, appeared fearful of his presence. "I'm really sorry about this, but I think I made a mistake." He crouched to meet her and placed his hands atop the arm rests.

Her reddened eyes revealed a glint of hope.

Wylder rubbed his smooth chin. "I have seen the unintentional results of my actions, but I don't suppose I can set you free."

She vehemently shook her head and her muffled words formed. "No. No. I won't say anything."

"You are lying," He used his index finger to remove the strands of hair that clung to her face. "I really wish I'd come to this conclusion just a few hours earlier. My friend left me alone for just a little while and look what I did—again. But there you were, looking lovely. You've been a lot of fun, really. There's just too much at stake here. I wasn't thinking clearly. Not like I am now."

He pulled up. 'Maybe I should sleep on it. Weigh my options before coming to a decision. Yes. That's what I should do."

Her eyes closed and her shoulders dropped.

"Oh, don't worry. I'm giving you another chance to live." He started to leave but stopped short and turned on his heel. He inhaled deeply and as if smelling a sweet rose and smiled. "I mean, you're here anyway, right?" Wylder returned and removed the tape from her mouth. "Maybe just one last time."

∼

A KNOCK SOUNDED ON WYLDER'S DOOR AND HE ROLLED OVER in his bed to check the time. It was barely sunrise and he had been awake most of the night. He sat up and pulled on his shorts before walking to the door.

"It's Scott." The voice sounded through the door.

Wylder pulled it open. "Good. You're here."

Scott slowly eyed Wylder's appearance, noting every drop of blood, every pink vein of it that covered his undershirt, his face, his forearms. "What the hell did you do?"

"You'd better come in. Don't want the neighbors to see."

Scott appeared reluctant but walked inside anyway. "I thought. I thought this was the end."

"It was. It is. I swear it. No more, you have my word." He held up his bloodied palm. "It's just, well, she was here and I thought, I can't let her go. That would be suicide, right? So just this one last thing and now we're all finished. We'll take care of this and go about our business, I promise."

"You're fucking insane."

Wylder appeared confused. "Of course I am. It took you this long to realize it? I thought you were smarter than that."

Scott was only a handful of those who knew of Mason's habit. The rest were in Rio. But he had left no evidence behind. Not that he was aware of. No trails. He'd worked exceptionally hard to cover them up for his boss who paid him hundreds of thousands of dollars to clean up his messes. But now as he peered at Wylder's empty eyes, his bloodied clothes and hair and face, a sinking feeling bore down on him. He wasn't going to make it out of this unscathed after all.

"Come. I'll make some coffee." Wylder started into the kitchen. "I should get cleaned up first, but I'm desperate for some caffeine. It's been a long night. But you're here now and we can wrap this up."

"I—I can't help you. I don't know how to fix this. Mason, it's over." The look of resignation and defeat masked his face. His own death warrant had just been signed. Maybe that didn't matter because life in prison didn't seem like a great alternative.

"Sure you can. Don't be ridiculous. Fix it like you always do. You'll handle it. You don't really have a choice." Wylder pushed a coffee mug toward him along the counter. "Drink this, you'll feel better."

Scott peered at the cup that was imprinted with Mason's bloodied fingers.

Mason held firm his confidant's gaze. "Just drink it. Look, man, it is what it is. Either you do this, or you die."

21

The labs inside Quantico were a bevy of computers scrolling lines of what would appear to an outsider as inexplicable code. Centrifuges spun and microscopes displayed their findings across large screens. They received requests for analysis from across the country. This was where law enforcement went when there was nothing left to find. This was where the three agents who had already made it home arrived with a last-ditch effort in hopes of a hail Mary.

"I'll try, but I won't lie, it's a long shot." The lab tech with gloved hands viewed the specimen from the Ziplock bag. The napkin with which Mason Wylder so willingly offered up his DNA.

"Better than no shot." Walsh eyed the time. "Can you get us something by tonight?"

"You know I'll do my best." The technician turned his chair toward his computer.

Walsh peered at the others. "Let's go. Let him do what he needs to do." He started back into the corridors.

"Our people have risked their lives more than once and we still have nothing to show for it," Duncan said.

"That's not entirely true," Quinn said. "Scarborough said the AdA had a name for him, didn't he?"

"He did, but they were left with no choice but to flee before he could meet with them again. They suspect it was Varela who gave up their position bearing in mind he was the only one who knew where they were. I can't say I'm not happy about that result. I think those gangs were just stringing them along, and I think it would've ended badly for Scarborough. No. It's best they get back here." Walsh made a turn toward his office. "I just want them home."

Duncan and Quinn followed him into his office and Duncan began. "Is there anything we can do to, I don't know, get someone to check in on this guy? Mason Wylder?"

"Without cause?" Walsh returned to his desk. "What are we going to say? He was in Rio when we were and he might be a killer?"

"Why the hell not? What if we don't get anything back from that napkin?" Duncan appeared flustered. "For God's sake, we're relying on the possibility he left skin cells behind, a miniscule amount of DNA. There has to be another angle to this."

Quinn leaned against a file cabinet near Walsh's desk. "We're all assuming Wylder is the killer, but we have no hard evidence of that. It could still be too soon to leave. Not until we can give them a definitive answer."

"Hang on," Walsh said. "First you thought it was a bad idea for them to stay. Now it's a bad idea for them to leave? Which is it,

Quinn?" Walsh folded his arms across his square chest. "I'm trying to figure out who's team you're on because it doesn't feel like it's ours."

"That's even a question in your mind? That's new. How long have we known each other, man?"

"A long time. Which is why your behavior is so troubling. Look, whatever problem you have with Scarborough needs to be hashed out because it's affecting your outlook and we can't afford to have you showing bias. You're the profiler here, man. Your job is to give us some damn idea as to who we're looking for and you've provided zilch so far."

Quinn aimed his sights on Duncan. "Is this how you feel too? Like I'm pushing back on this entire investigation?"

"A little. Yeah. I don't know if it's Scarborough or if it's Reid, but someone's gotten under your skin and yeah, it's starting to become a problem. We're lost right now. Don't you see that? Half our team has been running for their lives and you sit here and question every decision our team leader has made? I don't get it."

Quinn eyed his colleagues. "Well, I guess it's better to know how you feel now rather than later. Glad to see we're all one cohesive unit."

"That's not on us, man. That's on you," Walsh said. "You need to take a look in the mirror and figure out some things because this can't continue, and I think you know that. When our people get back, you're going to have to step in line."

"This isn't the military, Walsh, in case you forgot."

"Maybe not. But there is a hierarchy and I think you've forgotten that."

"It's really good to know how you both feel. Gives me something to chew on." Quinn started to leave.

"It doesn't have to be like this, man. You just need to have a hard look at what you want from this team," Walsh said.

Duncan watched as he left and turned back to Walsh. "This entire investigation has felt disjointed. We haven't been behaving like a team and something's got to give."

"I know. I feel it too. Let's get through this. Get our people back home and get some hard evidence on this guy."

"Assuming he's our guy." She stopped a moment. "You haven't answered my question. What if we go check him out anyway before the others return?"

"Who? Wylder?"

"Yeah. Why not? We can do some digging. We can pull up his passport details. See when and where he's traveled, including Rio and get a feel for the timeline. That could be critical. We can pull phone records."

"That's where I'll have to stop you. We can't do that. Not without a warrant."

"Levi, come on. We know people. We already have records of our mysterious person who made calls in Rio."

"Then those are the ones we'll need to analyze. Check to see if any of the numbers match the phone number of Wylder. His phone number, we can get."

"That's what I want to hear. We'll pull up anything and everything on Mason Wylder until the others return and go from there."

"Agreed. We'll suffer the consequences later."

THE AIRSTRIP WAS JUST AHEAD AND A PLANE AWAITED THEM. The hour was late and the drive long, but the remaining BAU team made it to the secluded airstrip operated by their own where they would fly to Brasilia and then on to D.C.

Cain pulled up as close as he could to the plane when his phone rang. "Yeah?" He waited for the caller to continue. "I see. Thank you." He ended the call. "That was Lambert. He says it wasn't Varela. It was the AdA. Well, it wasn't entirely Varela. Apparently, his officers grew suspicious and informed the AdA. After that, they must've figured we didn't go through with it after all." Cain looked to Scarborough. "I told you we should've killed him. Now you're forced to run. Who knows what the hell will happen to me when I get back to Brasilia? Doubt I'll be able to show my face here in Rio ever again."

Guilt crawled up Kate's spine because she had wanted Varela to live and might've planted the idea in Scarborough's head. Turns out, she had been wrong. And now Nick would feel the brunt of the ill-conceived plan that once again, nearly cost their lives.

"Doesn't matter now," Scarborough said. "It's done and we're leaving. Should never have come to this God forsaken, shady country." He opened his door and stepped outside.

In the blackness of a tropical night where the trees blocked out the glow of the moon, and the sound of cicadas overwhelmed the skies, the three agents who remained in Brazil made their way onto the small charter plane bound for safety.

EVA DUNCAN EXAMINED HER COMPUTER SCREEN AS SHE submitted to the NCIC or National Crime Information Center database. The database itself comprised of roughly 18 different systems and inside one of those systems was the passport information she would need. The State department and the FBI shared material in circumstances when needed during the course of a criminal investigation. This was one such instance. She could search for Mason Wylder's travel information and determine when and where he traveled since he held the passport. For someone of his status, that could mean files upon files of information to sift through. A wealthy celebrity traveled frequently, but she would narrow down her search to the last two years and see what those results yielded.

She eyed the time and noted her team's plane should be landing in Brasilia at any moment. It was her hope that one of them would call in to confirm their location. She worried about Cameron and despite her siding with Scarborough on the call to remain in Brazil, her heart was torn. Cameron could handle himself, no question, but sometimes he was arrogant. Most of the time he was arrogant, and that could cost him. Knowing that they were aboard their first flight put her mind at ease, though she didn't know what they would face upon landing in Brasilia or how easy it would be to get on another flight and leave that place for good.

"Here he is." Duncan verified the name and address against what she already had and confirmed it. "I got you now." She typed in a few more commands and printed his travel data for the past two years. It was an extensive amount of information, much of which would have been gleaned by further drilling down, but she wanted everything. First things first, though. When had he left for Brazil and what was his history?

The murders, according to the now-deceased Pedro Sosa, had been an ongoing problem for at least a year, maybe longer. But records and reports were scarce in Rocinha, if anyone reported anything at all. Most feared retribution by either the gangs or the civil police. Neither of which were sympathetic to their cause.

She retrieved the information and highlighted the dates as reflected on Wylder's passport statement and marched headstrong into Walsh's office. "I have something you should look at."

"Come on in and let's have a look-see."

"Should we get Quinn in here?" Duncan pulled up a chair and sat down.

"That would be the right thing to do, yes." He appeared to pause on taking action.

"And so, that's what we'll do, right?" She persisted.

Walsh picked up his phone and called Quinn. "Hey, Duncan found travel information on Wylder. Do you want in on it?" He nodded. "Okay. Come on over."

"He's coming. You need anything to drink?" Walsh stood. "I'm going to the breakroom for a water."

"I'll take one. Bring one for Quinn, too."

"Sure thing." Walsh left his office and on his way to the kitchen, he spotted Quinn. "Go on in, Duncan's there. Just grabbing some waters. Care for one?"

"Please. Thanks." Quinn continued until reaching Walsh's office and walked inside. "Hey. I just passed Walsh in the hall."

Duncan patted the seat next to her. "Have a seat. This is good news."

He accepted her offer. "Listen, um, about earlier. It's something I need to work on. And I'm sorry for dragging you into it."

"It wasn't just me. Walsh too. All of us, Quinn. It's affecting all of us."

"I am now acutely aware of that fact."

Walsh returned. "Here you go." He sat back down at his desk. "Show us the goods, Duncan."

She laid out the reports that had been highlighted to show the dates when Wylder visited Rio. "As you can see here, he arrived in Rio in early May. Probably right after his show wrapped up taping."

"That'd be my guess," Walsh said. "Go on."

"And of course, we saw him there at the club, so that tracks. And if you look here, you can see a history of summer travel, however, each time, he stayed the entire summer. Didn't return until September."

"How long has he maintained this habit?" Quinn asked.

"At least the past two years. I could go back further, though, if need be."

Quinn nodded as if considering the notion. "What do we know about him here? Any run ins with the law?"

"Not that I've been able to find," Walsh began. "I did run a background check already."

"Okay. So no record, which makes sense. He probably wouldn't have a job if he had a record. During his travels, I wonder if he chooses to stay in the same place? Does he own a house there?"

"He does in fact own a very nice property in Gávea," she continued.

"That's near Rocinha, as we discovered," Quinn replied. "I'd like to know more about his background here. Trouble in school, what his family was or is like. That would help me decide if he's a likely unsub."

"Seems to me he's put himself right at the top of our list, given the time factors alone. Highly coincidental," Walsh said. "I mean, come on. The guy decides to return days after we arrive? When he had no history of doing so in his prior visits?"

"That's a fair point," Quinn replied. "And then a woman goes missing from the very place he also frequented."

"If that don't sound calculated, I don't know what does." Walsh turned his attention to Duncan. "When you and Reid were at that club, though, and this is what still confounds me. You two saw a different man who you believed matched the tipster's description of the person seen up that hill just prior to the discovery of the shallow graves. What do we know about him?"

"Well, he was next to Wylder. Close, you know? Talked to him for a while. But then things went south and we left."

"Is it possible to think the incident you two faced was triggered at the direction of Wylder himself?" Walsh added.

"If that's the case, then the man with him could be an accomplice." Duncan turned to Quinn. "That would change your profile. We don't see that often. A willing accomplice like that? Especially one of an extremely high-profile individual."

"That would throw a wrench into the works. I mean, who would keep quiet about such a thing?" Quinn pursed his lips. "Unless he was getting paid to keep quiet. This guy, this Mason Wylder, if he is who we think he is, he has the means to pay off anyone for just about anything. And we know how the cops there have their hands out."

"But why risk doing something here, stateside, when it doesn't seem there's been any indication of that before?" Duncan continued.

"He could be losing control of his urges. He had to leave shy of his usual plans. That could have thrown him off. The reporter's death. He might've felt boxed in and in being forced to return home, he was unfulfilled," Quinn said.

"Okay, so where are we on the cross-referencing of the phone records we received from the calls made near that tower in Rocinha?" Walsh pressed on.

"I was just about to get started on that," Duncan said.

"Let me pull this up and do a quick cross-check." Walsh opened the file that contained the phone records and ran a check against US numbers making calls during that timeframe. "If we get a hit with a New York number, or hell, any US number as far as I'm concerned, that's where we'll start getting some better details."

"We can trace it then," Quinn said. "We might not have a warrant, but right now, we have enough to get one."

22

T he actions leading up to this moment seemed unimaginable and in working for Mason Wylder, Scott had had plenty of time to imagine the impossible. There was shock, at first, but then it seemed like, well, like it didn't matter. No one was going to find out. No one gave a shit about those poor women. And Wylder was happy.

It had taken time and a lot of booze, but Scott adapted to the behavior and the ritual hadn't altered in the years since he'd been working for Wylder. Tolerance resulted because as soon as they would return to New York in the fall, everything would return to normal.

Now, all that has changed. Wylder was fully unhinged. And here they were, back home in New York. It was going to be hard enough diverting attention away from Wylder after the murder of the director's niece. In fact, that was an ongoing investigation that was growing in intensity, and it was likely only a matter of time before the NYPD would knock on Wylder's door. Scott had already devised an alibi, but with this? Wylder was out of control and he no longer believed he could contain the problem.

Scott finished rinsing out the bloodied rags and the woman was wrapped inside an area rug. He still needed to find a way to get her out of the house. There were certain people he could call on yet again, but questions would be raised that he would have no choice but to answer. Nevertheless, there didn't seem to be much choice in the matter right now. Scott had become the fixer and there was no escaping it. Wylder's words still echoed in his head. *"Do this, or you die."*

If he was caught, he'd be dead anyway. Either by way of suicide or waiting for the thugs in the prison to do it for him. He wouldn't see his 30th birthday come November.

Scott returned to his feet and peered down at his shirt. "Damn it. I love this shirt." It was soaked in the woman's blood. He didn't know who she was, which was probably best. And while Mason studied his script in his office, Scott was forced to finish the job and make everything appear as though nothing had happened. "Easier said than done."

He retrieved his cell phone and made the call. "Yeah, it's me. Look, I need your guys to come over as quickly as possible."

"What do they got to do?" the man replied.

"Clean up. It's a big job, so they should come prepared."

"They'll be there in an hour. Have the money ready."

Scott ended the call and peered at the rolled-up rug covered in silver duct tape. "Maybe I can leave the country."

"I wouldn't suggest it." Mason entered the room and stood next to him. "Good work, though. Is it handled?"

"Yes. It's handled."

He patted Scott on the back. "Great! How about dinner? I'm starved."

THE THREE AGENTS WHO WERE EXPERTS IN VARIOUS AREAS OF violent criminal conduct, joined together for the menial, but necessary task of combing through the phone records handed over to them by Varela in search of a match to Mason Wylder's number, obtained via not so legal means.

"I hate to bug out on you guys, but I have to head to the airport." Walsh stood and grabbed his keys. "I know it's late, so if either of you want to go home and get some rest, no one will take issue with that."

"I'm staying," Duncan said.

"I'll stay, too," Quinn replied.

"Okay. I'll come back with the rest of our team." Walsh started out the door and made his way to his car.

He drove through Quantico's gates and started on his way to Ronald Reagan Airport. It was the middle of the night and that didn't matter because all he wanted to do was see his colleagues back on American soil. So many things had gone wrong. It was easy to question Scarborough's decision in hindsight, but Walsh wasn't about to do that to his boss. He'd worked enough cases to know that sometimes, shit happened. It didn't usually happen in foreign countries, but there was always a first for anything. Regardless, he still felt torn by the entire situation. What was happening with Quinn, all of it made him question what he thought he knew about the people he worked with. He had become close to Kate, probably closer than he had to any of the others and he'd known them longer. There was just a way about her that drew him in. And she was smart. Scary smart and intuitive in ways he'd never seen before. It was no wonder Quinn was threatened by her, especially given his personality. But he felt all of this was about to slip through his fingers. The team as it now stood was fractured and he didn't know if there was a way to get whole again.

He pulled into the short-term parking and walked inside the terminal. A quick text to Scarborough to let him know he'd arrived and he waited. A smile masked his face as he spotted the petite brunette with the pulled back hair. "Kate."

Behind her trailed Scarborough and finally, Fisher. It seemed she spotted him too as indicated by her returned smile.

"Man, am I glad to see you." Kate wrapped her arms around his burly shoulders and kissed his cheek. "Levi. Thanks for coming to get us."

"Are you kidding? No way could I have waited at the office. No. I needed to see you. All of you. Just to verify you were okay."

"We made it out alive," Fisher said.

"By the skin of our teeth, but we're here," Scarborough replied. "Thanks for coming. We could've taken a cab."

"Now don't you start. Come on. We have a lot to catch up on."

Duncan waited in the lobby of the BAU offices, knowing the others were pulling in. In the distance, the three of them approached and relief consumed her. She would never admit it to him, but her concern for Cameron Fisher had grown to the point of agony. "Thank God you're all back safely."

Fisher threw his arms around her and pulled her close. "Feels good to be home." He pushed her to arm's length. "I wasn't sure I'd see you again."

"Me neither." She turned to the others. "Did Walsh fill you in on the drive?"

"Mostly. I'd sure like to find a connection between our anonymous man and Wylder's phone number." Scarborough started toward the elevators. "I know it's late, but now more than ever, I want confirmation so we can put this man behind bars. The sooner the better."

They returned to the BAU offices where Quinn waited at the elevator doors. "It's good to see you all."

Kate eyed him with doubt thanks to their prickly relationship, which had worsened exponentially. She still hadn't confronted him about his meeting with Georgia Myers, the former girlfriend of his boss. And it was all due to her good friend, Dwight Jameson, who dug up that little nugget of intel. Still, now wasn't the time to bring it up.

"Thank you," Scarborough replied. "I won't lie, it's good to be back. At least things make sense here and not everyone is looking for a payoff. Have you made progress?"

"Actually, I think so." Quinn started back toward Walsh's office where the files had been spread out on his conference table. "Duncan and I have been cross-refencing phone records and I think we might have something."

"That's right." Duncan returned to the papers she had been working on. "Right here, here and here." She pointed to three numbers that matched Wylder's. "We have a match to our unknown accomplice and Wylder, who may or may not be the killer."

"Is that enough for a warrant?" Kate asked.

"It's a crapshoot," Fisher said. "A couple of calls to a guy we don't even know and have no evidence to suggest he's a killer. I don't know. Scarborough, what do you think?"

"I have to agree. I don't think any judge will give us a warrant based on the circumstantial evidence we have right now. That said, if our lab makes a match with the DNA on the napkin Wylder gave to you, Duncan, and the samples we provided, that's a whole other ball game. Then we got ourselves a case and we'll get a warrant all day long with that."

"So we wait—again," Kate said.

"We have a lot that points to Wylder and the man who we assume works for him," Walsh said. "And thanks to Duncan, we also have passport information on Wylder. We've made more progress here than we did there."

"Then again, you weren't escaping a hail of bullets," Kate said. "Is there a way to pull employer records on Wylder?"

"You mean, the show he's on?" Quinn asked.

"No. I mean, his own records. Who he pays. His assistants, housekeepers, valets, whatever. We might find the guy on his payroll and we have a description so if we can match that, then all the better for us."

"I think that's doable." Walsh turned to Scarborough. "Look, the lab guys have gone home. It's late and I can't imagine how tired you all must be. Maybe we should call it for tonight. In the morning, we might have some answers and we can move on pulling more intel on Wylder."

"I guess you're right. We've all been through the wringer. You guys too. I know you haven't stopped since you got back." Scarborough peered at the team. "Walsh is right. There's nothing more for us to do tonight. We'll reconvene first thing in the morning."

THE WALK THROUGHOUT THE SOFTLY LIT CORRIDOR TO THE condo Nick and Kate shared was shrouded in unnerving quiet. Nick held open the door as Kate entered and on securing the lock behind him, he asked the question that hung over them since their return to D.C. "Are you okay?"

She dropped her bag to the floor and faced him. "No. I'm not okay. I thought I could handle it, but I guess I'm not as strong as I believed I was." Her eyes welled.

"You're the strongest woman I know." He wrapped his arms around her and pulled her close. "I'm so sorry for betraying your trust. It was my job to keep you safe. You and the rest of the team. I know what I did and there is no justification."

Kate walked into the kitchen and pulled two bottles of water from the fridge, setting one down in front of him as he joined her. "There are so many things you don't know. Sacrifices I've made." Kate wanted to tell him Quinn was blackmailing them and doing so with the help of Georgia Myers, a woman she once respected. His foolish demand that she work with him to break through whatever professional barrier he struggled with. And if she didn't, well, then everyone would know about Nick's battle with alcohol. She had given in to Quinn's demand.

"Why don't you tell me then?" he replied. "How do we get past this, Kate?"

"I honestly don't know. The only thing I do know is that I need sleep. I'm jet-lagged, my nerves are frayed. I have to close my eyes and try to find sleep. And you should do the same." She padded into the bedroom and once inside, shed her clothes and pulled on a t-shirt. It felt good to be in fresh clothes. The only thing better would have been to have a shower, but she was drained. The condo was too warm. D.C. had been in the midst of a warming trend since they left and the air conditioning needed to be turned on. She walked back into the passageway where the thermostat was fixed to the wall and pressed the button. Nick stood at the hall's entrance, as if in shock or disbelief. "What's wrong? What are you doing?" she asked.

"Trying to come to terms with what I did. That I let you down, my team down and myself down."

His gaze fell upon her in a way it hadn't in some time. She felt him stare at her t-shirt and her thighs and her hair as it cascaded down her shoulders.

He walked toward her and rested his hand on her cheek. "Please don't give up on me."

"You didn't keep your promise," she whispered.

His lips touched hers. She felt his shame; his fear of losing her; his fear of losing everything. She sensed every bit of it so much so that her heart broke for him. This man who had done so much to give her everything she wanted. Pushed her to be something she never knew she wanted to be. That was his true strength. He pulled from her a person and a life she never would have dreamed possible.

Nick pulled her up in his arms and carried her to their bedroom. He lay her down on the bed and in his eyes, she witnessed the love he had for her. The regret he felt for the decisions he had made. His soul was laid bare and she could deny him, or she could accept him for all his faults. She had placed him on a pedestal, and he fell.

"I love you."

He pulled back and held her gaze. "Even still?"

"Yes," she replied. "For now, that's all I can offer."

CAMERON FISHER RETURNED TO HIS APARTMENT ON THE edge of D.C. proper and switched on the lights. "Are you coming in?" he asked Eva.

"Right behind you."

"You want something to drink?" He walked to the kitchen. "Water or anything?"

"I'm fine, thanks. I was worried about you."

"I know. I was worried about me too." He smiled.

It was just like him to lighten the tone of a conversation no matter how grave the subject. It was a defense mechanism because she knew he'd been afraid. They all had. None knowing for sure if they would survive. "I wish you hadn't stayed with them."

"I wasn't going to let them do it alone. You know me better than that. We didn't get what we wanted exactly, but we walked away with our lives."

"Jesus." She turned away. "We all thought this was going to be a slam dunk."

"We both know it never happens that way." He returned to her side. "But I'm glad to be home with you." He started toward the sofa. "You know, I was thinking, with my contacts at NYPD, I bet I could take a look at the missing persons' file. The one we suspect could link us to Wylder and/or his cohort. I still have some friends there."

"It can't hurt. But what we need is DNA."

"That we do. At least it's something I can work on while we

wait." He reached for her hand as she approached him. "I really was afraid I might not see you again."

"You and me both," she replied. "Levi's afraid that after this case, the team's going to fall apart."

"Quinn?"

"He does seem to be the catalyst."

"Don't worry about him. He doesn't have the ammo to take down any member of this team, let alone Scarborough. He's blowing smoke and trying to make waves."

"We know what he's like, but Kate and Nick don't, and Nick's the one in charge."

"You know what? It's entirely too late to be worrying about office politics right now. We potentially have a famous New York actor decapitating women. Can you imagine what the optics on this are going to be?" He pulled her from the couch. "We should go to bed. You know the rules."

"Get sleep while you can because you don't know when you'll get it again," She replied.

It was Scott's job to drive Mason Wylder to most of his destinations, and tonight's dinner was no exception. He'd watched as his boss ate, drank and laughed all the while knowing what a monster he was and that he'd allowed the man to get away with abhorrent behavior.

The money had served as a deterrent and allowed him to look the other way while he brought those women to slaughter. Scott had become someone he never believed he could become. He was the monster. He played it off that they just wanted to be with the famous actor and deserved what they got for their vanity and lack of self-respect. But things were different now. It was as if he'd seen the devil for himself and it frightened the hell out of him.

Scott peered at Mason as he scrolled on his cell phone, three sheets to the wind. The idea of turning him in crossed his mind, though Scott would also end up in prison and a man like him would not do well in a place like that. Wylder would get some cushy isolated cell because of his celebrity status until the day he died, but not ol' Scott Brooks, no sir. He'd be left inside with the wolves.

So he considered another solution. Something that could save him from the fate that surely awaited him at the expense of Wylder. What did he care about Wylder now? The narcissistic homicidal prick meant nothing to him anymore. Could he do it, though? Did he have the balls to go through with it?

Scott waited for Mason to pay the bill and he reached for his keys. "You ready to go, boss?"

Wylder slowly pulled up from his chair. "I am."

Scott helped him to the car and opened the passenger door. After ensuring Mason was completely inside, he walked to the driver's seat and slipped in. "Thanks for dinner." It was all he could say in light of everything and even that was hard to do.

He started down the main road back to Mason's exclusive high-rise apartment, but then reconsidered the idea he toyed with in the restaurant. Could he actually do it? He set his sights on Mason for just a moment. He was drifting in and out of consciousness, by the look of him. So if he was going to do this, it would have to be now in order to achieve the best results.

Scott pulled off onto another road that led to another house Wylder owned. The house on Grovers. The one with the gym.

This was where he usually spent his holidays and had his family come around. It was in a nice secluded suburb and Scott carried on until they reached the narrow lane lined with trees. He was still a mile or two away from Wylder's house, but he figured he could make it work here.

Scott pressed on the gas and the car accelerated.

Wylder appeared alert enough to catch on that they were speeding up. "What's up, dude? Why are you going so fast? You got to take a piss or something?"

Scott ignored him and pressed harder and drove faster. He was doing 80 now.

"Dude? Slow the fuck down!" Wylder was starting to panic and appeared to be quickly sobering up.

Scott ignored him and watched the speedometer as it climbed to 100 before turning to Wylder and smiling. "Say goodbye to your life, you sick fuck." He pulled sharply on the wheel and swerved to the side of the road. The car's headlights shone on a hardy tall oak before barreling head-on into it. The front passenger side collapsed like an accordion while the car raised off its back wheels and fell again from the brute force of the stop. Steam rose from the engine high into the night air, glass was shattered and in pieces on the ground. Blood splattered in all directions.

And inside the car, both men lay against the deflated airbags, lifeless.

23

The strident noise from the horn of the Mercedes coupe was what eventually rallied Scott from unconsciousness. He pulled back from the wheel, pushing away the deflated airbag, and the blaring stopped. His eyes fluttered as he tried to clear his vision, though his brain suffered a splitting headache. The car's engine sputtered and steam still hissed from the mangled front end. Time had lost all meaning as the car remained wrapped around a tree on the two-lane road. It was still night, but that was all he could comprehend at the moment.

Awareness returned and Scott abruptly recalled what he'd done. A slow turn of his head to the passenger he intended to harm and there was Mason, doubled over amid metal debris and a collapsed airbag. "Mason?" He placed his hand on Mason's shoulder and nudged him. "Mason? Are you awake?" He waited for movement, a breath or some indication Mason was still alive. "Mason? Man, wake up!" He shook him harder to confirm his suspicions.

Then Mason let out a moan.

"Jeez!" Scott pulled away his hand, shocked Mason survived. He had failed. "What the hell?"

Mason moaned again as he tried to move and managed to form garbled words. "What happened?"

If he couldn't remember, Scott wasn't about to tell him that he'd just tried to kill him and nearly killed himself in the process. "We have to get out of here." He turned his head slowly and winced in pain as he tried to peer through the driver's side window. No headlights or sirens approached. At least he had that going for him. Witnesses would have been a real problem because while he hadn't accomplished his goal, he needed Mason Wylder to disappear for however long it took. Maybe forever.

Scott searched for his phone that had been inside the center console but was no longer. He didn't know the extent of his own injuries but felt a stabbing pain in his right leg. Blood soaked through his ripped jeans and exposed a wide gash. A piece of the console split and sliced his leg. But could he muster the strength to drag Mason out of the car and hobble a mile or two back to Wylder's home? All without being seen?

The phone was on the floorboard by his feet. With great effort, Scott retrieved it, noticing the screen had been shattered. "Please work." He pressed the button and the screen flickered on but was nearly impossible to read. "Thank you." The goal wasn't to call for emergency services, that was certain. It was merely to get a location and point them in the right direction. With the shattered screen, he tried to read Google Maps but couldn't. "Damn it." Onto Plan B, which was to wing it, like he had from the moment he saw the director's niece murdered.

"No cops," Wylder mumbled.

"I'm not an idiot." Scott shot back at him. "We're going to walk back to your house. I think it's a mile and a half, maybe two at the most. Can you walk?"

Mason tested his legs. First the right, that one seemed okay, then the left. "Ah!" He wailed with pain.

"I guess I have my answer. Shit." Scott tried to open the driver's side door, but it was stuck. He thrust his shoulder against it and his eyes clouded over with tears from the pain. "Come on. Open!" He tried again. "Open!" Another slam against the door and this time, it pushed open just enough. Scott slipped out, dragging his injured leg behind him.

He examined the car and couldn't understand how Mason survived, or either of them for that matter. The beautiful silver Mercedes was nothing more than a heap of twisted metal. Scott was supposed to be the sole survivor. That was the plan. A blown tire, failed brakes, any reason he could find would have sufficed. The cops would've bought it, too.

Now that Wylder had survived, Scott would have to devise another plan. He could leave Wylder here and hope he just died, but knowing his luck, some good Samaritan would stop to help. Perhaps pulling him out of the car and leaving him down farther on the hill where he wouldn't be seen? No. That wouldn't work either because chances were, Mason could manage to call for help.

Only one solution seemed obvious. Kill Wylder here and hitch a ride to a hospital, claiming his companion died at the scene. A simple hand over his mouth would do it. Wylder was too injured and too weak to fend off the attack.

Scott dragged his leg behind him and limped toward the passenger side. The door was jammed, just like his had been. The entire front end of the car was crushed, and it had bent the frame so the doors were fixed. He pulled hard on the handle, releasing a painful grunt as he tugged. Another pull and it creaked open. Scott pulled harder on the door until it opened enough to pull out Mason. "Come on. Let's go." As he peered at the psychotic killer who looked at him with eyes full of pain, he decided he couldn't do it. He didn't have the balls to kill someone with his bare hands, not even this man. He was a coward and had been since the beginning of this vile arrangement.

"Wait! Wait!" Mason protected his body with his arms as Scott reached inside. "I'm really fucking hurt here, man."

"I have to get you out of here, Mason. It's only a matter of time before someone comes and sees the car. We have to go now." He tried again and this time, with one arm under Mason's shoulder and another wrapped around him, he pulled. "You gotta help me, man!" Scott groaned as he pulled Mason from the vehicle and dropped him to the ground.

Mason winced and held onto this stomach. "Stop! I'm really messed up."

"I know you are, that's why I'm trying to get you out."

"No. Really. Something's really wrong here." Mason pulled away his arm.

Scott looked down at Mason's torn shirt. "Oh shit." Mason's stomach was black and blue and swelling quickly. "Dude, you're bleeding internally." Maybe this was his out. Mason was going to die of internal injuries, and Scott would be freed. His plan wouldn't have failed. But he still couldn't leave him here on the side of the road. He might be enough of an evil bastard to survive. "You're going to have to help me get you up. Once we get to where we're going, I'll call our people for help."

Mason pushed up on one side and tried to sit up. Scott was finally able to pull him back to his feet and the two started south.

Agent Elijah Cain was awakened by the vibration of his phone on his bedside table. He peered at his wife who had not yet been disturbed before he reached for it and sat up in bed. He answered the line as he walked into the hall. "Yeah?"

"I have a message for you from your friend in Rocinha."

Cain furrowed his brow as he shook off his sleep. "Who?"

"De la Costa."

At this, Cain stopped at attention. "I'm listening."

"Your man did not show up as he promised yesterday. Are we to assume he no longer wants the answers he seeks?"

"Funny you should bring it up." Cain continued into the kitchen as he grew more alert. "Circumstances prevented him from keeping said promise as his life and the lives of his colleagues, including my own, were placed in imminent danger. We were forced to revise our plans."

"Yes. We assumed that was the case. Your people have made powerful enemies during their short time in our beautiful city."

Cain placed his mug under the dispenser and waited for the single-cup brewer to finish. "Are you telling me you have the answers we need?"

"I'm saying that if you want those answers, we would like to make a deal."

"We had a deal."

"That's correct. However, it is my understanding that Inspector Varela still lives. That was not the deal."

"So what do you want? Varela is being protected by those who attempted to harm my people. There is nothing I can do about that."

"Then if you wish to discover who killed the women of Rocinha, we will need the FBI's assurances that the military police will rescind their troops and leave us to govern the favela as we see fit."

Cain laughed. "You can't be serious. I have no clout with the military police and even if I did, they wouldn't do as you ask. That's an impossible request and I think you and your people know that. So, I think we're done with this conversation. Unless you have something more realistic in mind."

There was silence on the other end before the man finally continued. "This will be an enormous victory for Rio's civil police should you find the person responsible. That said, at the very least, we would wish to establish parameters in an effort to maintain the status quo when the world discovers what has happened in our little favela."

"That is something within my capacity. An agreement could be reached with all interested parties if you provide the necessary details." Cain sipped on his coffee. "Do you know who killed those women? Because if not, you're wasting my time and I don't take kindly to those who waste my time."

"The man you are looking for is Mason Wylder."

"The actor?" Cain asked.

"Yes. He visits Rio every summer. The past two, maybe three summers, he has taken and murdered the women of Rocinha, for what reason, I cannot speculate except to satisfy a tortured soul."

Cain was silent as he processed the information. "Do you have proof of this?" He was already well aware that the new samples had DNA but had no match in the FBI's database.

"We will ensure the release of every known victim to submit to your doctors for testing. I am sure you will find the evidence you seek."

"How soon can you make this happen?"

"Today. Provided we reach an agreement."

"Of course. I'll start making the calls now. When will I hear back from you?"

"Four hours."

"I'll need more time than that. What you've asked requires coordination on a very high level."

"Four hours. Or you have no deal." The line went dead.

"Great. I'll get right on that." Cain set his phone down and walked into the living room. He gazed out onto the rising sun from his small house in Brasilia. "I think I just made a deal with the devil."

THE MORNING HAZE HUNG LOW AND STEAMY AS FISHER approached the BAU building while he spoke on his phone. "If you can pull it off, I'd like to take a look at the file you have on the missing woman from the café. I have a feeling it could coincide with a case I'm working right now." He listened. "Great. Hey, thanks, man. It's good to know I still have some buddies in the NYPD." He ended the call and walked inside.

Fisher walked onto the elevators and as the doors parted on the offices of his cohorts, he marched directly to Scarborough to relay the news. He stopped in the doorway upon noticing Scarborough was on his phone.

With a raised index finger, Scarborough held off Fisher for a moment. "Can you pull that off?" He continued. "It seems risky." Scarborough nodded. "Okay. Keep me posted." He ended the call. "Morning. Come in. That was Cain. He says he was contacted by De La Costa with the AdA. They are offering a deal. Proof that Wylder is the one who killed the women in Rocinha."

"What do they want in return? They've burned us before." Fisher walked inside and sat down.

"They want to keep the status quo. Make sure that nothing changes inside the favela."

"Cain has the ability to pull that off?" Fisher continued.

"He's going to try. So, if he gets them what they want, they've agreed to have the coroner release the victims to us for autopsy."

"That would virtually guarantee we get a match to the samples we already provided," Fisher replied.

Scarborough nodded. "And if that's the case…"

"Game over," Fisher said.

WORKING WITH QUINN SOLO WAS AN ARDUOUS TASK FOR Kate. But it was her job and she had to push aside the underhanded deeds he'd done in an effort to exploit her for his own personal gains.

As they convened in Quinn's office, it appeared he had seen the toll his behavior had taken on her. He sat at his desk and held her gaze for a moment. "This isn't going to work anymore, is it? You and me?"

"I don't see how it can. I wish that wasn't the case."

"What do you want to do?" he asked.

"I'll request a transfer after this investigation. And if you continue to try to blackmail Nick, I'll let it be known you gathered your information against him through illicit means. I don't know who you paid off, but I'll find out." She knew the source but had no idea if it was illegal. "He's done nothing but try to work with you."

"He's made decisions based on his relationship with you. That's a problem in my eyes," Quinn replied. "And he's damaged your career as a result. You could have been so much more than what you are."

Heat began to rise under her collar. "How can you say that? I've been at the Bureau for what, five years? And I'm with the BAU now. That's almost unprecedented. I'm an apprentice for the best profiler the Bureau has and yet you tell me that I've squandered my career? That Nick has squandered it?" She'd complimented him inadvertently, but it was true, and she couldn't deny Quinn was the best she'd ever worked with.

"I just think he keeps you too close. His decisions are based on how it will impact you, not an investigation."

"I don't agree..." She pressed on.

"I don't expect you to."

"Then what do you expect, Noah? For me to just roll over and let you take advantage of a past I've worked hard to keep private? You have no idea the nightmares I've faced down."

"I was hoping to learn from them. To help you use them to your advantage."

"You mean to help you use them to your advantage." Kate was growing tired of this same conversation. "Look, what's done is done. There's nothing that can heal this divide between us. You've left me with no choice. I wanted to be here. I chose to be put up for this position and you put me through the wringer to get it. I thought that was enough. I can see I was wrong."

Quinn stood from his desk and paced the room. "This isn't how I wanted things to go. You have to know that." He stopped and turned to her. "Can I do anything, at this point, to fix it?"

"Is that what you want? To fix the fact that you went to a former colleague to dig up dirt on Nick? That you in effect insisted I work with you on a paper for you to publish that would expose everything I've gone through? How do you fix that, Noah? How the hell can you fix that?"

He appeared taken aback. "How did you know about that?"

"I know the same way you knew to go to her in the first place. We both took drastic measures, it seems. And it also seems I'm the only one willing to give up my position to save the team. What happens when Cole finds out about all this? And he will, believe me. Even if I'm gone. Even if Nick's gone. Cole will know what went down. How do you think you'll come out of it?"

Quinn huffed. "I see. You have put a lot of thought into this, haven't you? You'd blow up your own career to sabotage mine."

"You sabotaged your career. This was all your doing, not mine." She sat upright in the chair and held his gaze with firm contempt. "The ball's in your court, Quinn. How are you going to play it?"

24

The rap on Quinn's office door dissolved the strain between he and Kate as he responded with an invitation to enter. Fisher walked in and appeared to catch on to the idea he had just stepped in the middle of something. "Sorry to interrupt. Can you two come with me? I've got a friend at NYPD who's working the case on the missing woman from the cafe. He'd like to talk, and I'd like to have my two greatest assets with me."

"Yeah." Quinn peered at Kate. "That's a very good idea."

"Good. Meet me in the lobby in five minutes. I'll drive us to the airport. Our flight leaves in 2 hours." He traded glances between them. "Are we good here?"

"We're good. See you in five," Kate replied. She waited for Fisher to leave. "I think the best thing now is to put this on the backburner. The team needs us to be on our game. I won't be the one to let them down." She turned to leave. "See you downstairs."

Kate continued into the corridor where she walked back to her office to gather her things. As she was about to head back out, Nick entered.

"Hey. I hear you're going with Fisher to New York to see the detective?"

"Yes. I don't know how long we'll be, so keep in touch and let me know if anything comes back from the labs."

"Will do. I should hear something in the next few hours. We did get some good news. Cain's working a deal with the AdA for them to give us proof it was Mason Wylder who killed the women. I don't know if he can pull it off, but if he does, their coroner will release the victims to our doctors."

"We aren't transporting the victims here, are we? They aren't US citizens."

"No. Cain's got a trusted forensic doctor who will perform the autopsies in Rio—at another facility. His samples will be turned over to us for analysis."

"That could take another week. Nick, we don't have that kind of time."

"You're right, but we can't afford not to do this. Even if we get evidence on Wylder, additional evidence will only strengthen the case."

"I suppose you're right. Listen, I'd better head down to the lobby. Fisher's waiting."

He placed his hands on her shoulders. "Are you okay? You look upset."

"I'll get over it. I have a job to do. I just hope Quinn remembers that. Talk to you later." She continued on, not looking back. The two most significant men in her life were causing her the worst stress she'd faced in years. It was all coming to a head. Once this case was over, a decision would need to be made and Kate felt as though she'd already made hers. But what would Quinn do?

"Sorry to keep you." Kate walked into the lobby to see Fisher and Quinn waiting.

"No worries. Let's go." Fisher led the way to the parking lot and into his car. "So this detective is a veteran. I never worked with him directly, but I know of him. His reputation is stellar. He's doing us a favor, so we need to keep that in mind."

"I hope it leads somewhere. Pinning everything on a napkin and waiting for Cain to pull off a miracle doesn't put us in a good position," Kate replied.

"Let's roll." Fisher started the car and pulled out of the lot and through the gates of Quantico.

"Seems odd to me, given how high-profile Wylder is, that they don't have more tips from others at the cafe," Quinn said.

"I think the reality is, no one would ever believe Mason Wylder was a killer. It just doesn't connect. So they aren't seeing it as even a remote concern that he was seen with that missing woman on the day she went missing," Fisher replied.

"And we have the advantage already knowing that Wylder has someone who works for him who was seen near the burial ground in Rio. We've already established a link to Wylder," Kate replied.

"Not yet. Duncan will make the connection through the phone records. I'm sure of it." Fisher continued on the drive. "And what Cain has, we might start pulling ahead on this one."

"I hope your detective can lead us to something viable. We need it." Kate stopped and peered at Quinn in the back seat. "With what we know now, what Quinn has derived at, his impulses have led him astray. It's not looking like he's going to stop voluntarily."

Quinn nodded. "If it's Wylder, and it seems very likely at the moment, then he's lost control. And the man with him? He has to be the fixer."

"Does the detective know the connection to Rio?" Kate asked.

"I've kept that under wraps for now," Fisher replied. "If it turns out they have something worthwhile, I'll let them in on the situation."

A NEW DAY ARRIVED AND MASON WYLDER LAY ATOP A SHEET of plastic under a blanket on his sofa. He peered down at his stomach, which had swollen to at least twice its size and was almost completely purple. He turned his sights back to Scott. "I'm not going to get out of this one, man. It's over."

"Don't say that. Let me get you to a hospital. It's not too late." It was an empty offer Scott knew would never be accepted. Risking a hospital visit where blood and DNA could be pulled wasn't going to happen.

"You know I can't go to the hospital."

"Why? No one knows anything."

Those FBI agents know something, and it would probably be enough to open an investigation. Nah man, it's over."

Scott tried to hide his relief because Wylder was right, it was over, and he would soon be free of this monster. A monster he turned a blind eye to and even helped. What it meant was that Scott would be cleared. They would discover who the real killer was with Wylder's DNA and that would be that.

Mason held his gaze. "It was you, wasn't it? You did this on purpose. You wanted me dead."

"No. No, that's not true. It was an accident. The tire or something."

"You were trying to save your own ass and this was how you chose to do it. Hey man, I don't blame you. I probably would've done the same thing. No, that's not true. I would've just killed you straight up. We had something good going there for a while, though. You'll be set, bro. Don't you worry about that. Of course, you'll have to explain why you didn't get me to a hospital. Why you let me die right here on my own couch after dragging me through the streets in the middle of the night."

"At least I didn't kill anyone." Scott's expression hardened. "I'll let you sit here until you die. Then I'll sort the rest out." His attention turned toward the front door where keys jiggled in the lock.

Wylder chuckled and coughed. "Did you forget about the housekeeper? What are you going to do, bro?"

Scott stood in a panic. He hadn't planned on anyone arriving here. "Shit."

"She's coming in, man. You better think of something."

"Shut up!" Scott said.

The door opened and a middle-aged woman entered. "Hola, señor. Good morning." She continued inside until stopping dead in her tracks at the sight of Scott hovering over Wylder while he lay bleeding on the couch. She thrust her hand over her mouth to contain a scream. Her eyes darted between the men as she tried to comprehend what had happened. "Mr. Wylder? What happened? You need a doctor. Quick, you need to call a doctor," she said to Scott.

"He won't be calling for any help, Mrs. Gonzales. But you might want to run the hell away from here."

Scott rushed her and tackled her to the ground before she could leave. He held his hand over her mouth. "Shhh. Shhh. Mrs. Gonzales, everything will be okay. I just need for you to be quiet, okay?"

Her eyes imbued with fear as she nodded.

"Okay. I'm going to take my hand away." He pulled it slowly back. "Don't scream or I'll have to kill you." He pointed to Wylder. "That man? Your boss? He's the real killer here. I'm going to need you to trust that I know what I'm doing. Can you do that for me, Mrs. Gonzales?"

Again, she nodded.

"Good." He pulled her to her feet. "Everything will be clear soon enough. For now, though, I'm going to have to put you in the room."

"Por favor, no."

"I'm sorry. It has to be this way, but only for a little while." He led her away but stopped when Wylder spoke.

"Who's the monster now, brother?"

"THANKS FOR COMING. I TRUST YOUR FLIGHT WAS uneventful?" Detective Sievers was an NYPD veteran of 25 years and was the lead investigator on the missing woman who was the niece of a prominent Broadway director.

"Hey man, no problem. It was fine and you're doing us a favor." Fisher returned the greeting. "These guys here are the real deal. This is Agent Kate Reid and Agent Noah Quinn. They're our expert profilers. They can help us figure out who might've taken the young woman."

"Come on back, we'll get started." Sievers walked to his office which was near the entrance of the frenzied 10th Precinct. "I got a team working on the missing persons' case, as you know, and so far, we got jack squat. So, with you guys jumping in the mix, I'm thinking we stand a better shot at finding this girl." He held open the door while the agents entered.

"Don't get me wrong, I'm happy you reached out to us lowly city cops, but you didn't mention why the keen interest?" He gestured for them to sit. "Care to let me in on the joke?"

"No joke here, I promise you that, detective," Fisher said. "Look, I didn't want to speak out of turn because we don't have squat ourselves, but we got an interest thanks to some similar cases we're working on an international level."

"What do you mean, international? What are you, the CIA?"

Fisher explained what had happened in Rio and how they came to be involved there before going into more detail as to why they think there's a connection to this case here in New York.

"You gotta be shitting me, Fisher. Come on." The detective swatted away the suggestion.

"I wish I was shitting you. We're working on DNA evidence as we speak. This is a matter of life and death, my friend." And we're going to need each other's help to find her before it's too late."

Sievers looked at the agents who were not laughing. He seemed to realize this was no joke. "Um, okay, yeah. So, where do you want to start?"

"Priority will be to keep a lid on the suggestion this is the work of a famous actor. That gets out and all hell will break loose," Fisher said.

"This is the craziest damn thing I've heard, but if what you people are saying is true, we got ourselves a real barn burner of a case."

"Don't I know it. We should take a look at your files and get started," Fisher said.

"Right here." Sievers opened the file folder for the team to view a picture of the missing girl and all information they had to date. "As you can see, we got ourselves some pretty slim pickings, but now that you got a bonafide lead, we can open some doors."

Fisher pulled the file closer. "She's nothing like the other victims."

"No," Kate said. "Which leads me to believe this was nothing more than an opportunistic killing. I don't think he intended for it to happen."

"I agree," Quinn said. "He's changed so much about his M.O. that I think we have no choice but to throw it completely out the window and move on the assumption he's lost all control over his will power."

"What about the assistant? The one we suspect helped him lure in his victims?" Kate asked. "Was he there at the café?"

"What's his name? We talked to a lot of witnesses at that café already," Sievers said.

"We don't have a name, only a vague description," Quinn began. "What about talking to his co-stars? They'd know who his people are. We'd have ourselves a name to run."

"That would open a can of worms." Fisher shook his head. "Don't get me wrong, it could open this up for us, but if word got out he was being looked at, I don't know, man. That might screw us."

"What about making a house call?" Kate asked. "Has anyone seen Wylder since the day the girl went missing? If he was there, why can't we question him about the girl? It seems like a logical step in an investigation."

"She's got a point," Sievers said. "We could do that without risking him taking a flying leap out of here before hand."

"That could work," Fisher began. "But you can't be there, Reid. He's seen you. He might not remember or put two and two together right away, but if he does, he'll fly the coop for sure."

"Fair enough. I don't need to be there, but Quinn should."

"Agreed." Fisher turned his sights to Sievers. "You and Quinn should go. He'll know what to ask and be able to analyze his response."

"Anyone know where he is?" Quinn asked.

"That's something we can dig up." Sievers stood. "Let me get an answer right now."

"I'll contact Scarborough and give him a heads up. Maybe see if he's made any headway." Fisher stepped into the corridor to make the call, closing the door behind him.

"Thanks," Quinn said.

"What for?" Kate replied.

"For acknowledging the fact that I know what I'm doing."

"I've never said you weren't good at your job. I've been a champion of your work. You know that."

"Yeah, but I mean with all this going on between us..."

"I would never let it interfere with an investigation. I thought you would've figured that out about me by now."

"I did know that. I also know what you're truly capable of doing and that would far outshine anything I can do."

"That's not true. I stand to learn a lot from you if you'd just let me." She turned squarely to him, her eyes pleading. "Stop what you're doing to further yourself this way. It will only backfire. If we were to truly work together, we could be an unstoppable team."

"I don't doubt that," he replied.

"Then why? Why are you doing this to me and to Nick? This wasn't how things started between us."

"You're right. This wasn't how it started, and it wasn't the way it was supposed to turn out."

"Then answer me. Why?" She waited for his response, which was slow to arrive.

"Because you're better than me. Better than I could ever be, and I don't think I can accept that."

Kate nodded. "You never wanted to find a breakthrough with me. You wanted to become me. Well, I'll tell you something, Quinn, being me isn't something I'd wish on my worst enemy. You think it's easy living with what I've been through? Or that I use it to build up my own skills? I use the tragedy in my life, the loss of my friends and loved ones to understand the worst of humankind. What does that make me?"

"It makes you as close to being one of them as you can be."

"You're right. I see things others don't—things you don't. I thought it was just a sixth sense, but maybe it's more. Maybe it's something deeper and darker. That's how I'm able to make the connections, find the missing clues. If that's who you want to be, then be my guest because I'd really like you to understand how it feels."

"There can't be two of us, Kate. I just don't see how."

"Then who will be the one left standing?"

25

The high-rise apartment owned by Mason Wylder was the intended destination of NYPD Detective Sievers and his new-found companion, the FBI's BAU profiler, Noah Quinn.

Sievers stepped off the elevator and into corridor where he cast his sights along the white walls that blended in with the marble floor. The only color came from the sconces mounted on the wall. "Nice place. They said this was where he'd be." He peered at Quinn. "Ready?"

"Yes, sir."

Sievers knocked on the door with his badge in hand. Quinn was only a step or two behind him and had his hand on his sidearm.

"Better give it another try." He knocked again. "Mason Wylder? NYPD. We have some questions for you."

"That might scare him off," Quinn said.

"Only if he's guilty. Besides, it's looking like he's not here after all." Sievers retrieved his cell phone. "Fisher, he's not here. Can you text me the address of his other residence? Thanks." He peered at his phone. "Here it is. Okay, looks like we've got a little bit of a drive heading into the 'burbs. Better get a move on." He started toward the elevators once again and waited. "If he is our guy, I have a feeling we won't find him."

They returned to Siever's unmarked car and pulled out of the parking garage.

"I wonder if Reid is having any luck at the studio." He looked to Quinn. "You mind calling her to find out? Let her know we struck out here but are heading to his other residence."

"Can do." Quinn picked up his phone. "Reid, it's Quinn. Have you made it to the studio yet?"

"I'm here now. I've talked to a few people. He's not here and no one's seen him in two days."

"Have they even heard from him? Did he call in sick or has he just been a no-show?" Quinn pressed on.

"No show. In fact they were about to start making visits to his homes as well."

"Did you tell them we were heading there? We don't want any of them involved in the real story," Quinn replied.

"I told them we had some people interested in talking to him since he was at the café when the girl went missing. They asked us to keep them posted. No one seemed overly concerned we were the ones asking questions. They're more concerned about getting him back on set."

"Okay. I'll let you know what we find. Are you wrapping up there or what are your plans?" He asked.

"I've got a few questions lined up for the director. We'll see if that gets me anywhere. Otherwise, I'll head back to the precinct and wait for you guys to return. Unless there's anything else?"

"Not that I can think of. We'll speak soon." Quinn ended the call. "She doesn't have anything new."

"Okay. I hope we aren't wasting our time going all the way there. I'm getting a bad vibe this is gonna end up a big fat goose egg."

"I THANK YOU FOR YOUR TIME, MR. HAGUE," KATE SAID. "IF you do hear from him, please let him know it's essential we speak to him regarding the young woman. He might have seen something without realizing it."

"Of course. Goodbye, Agent Reid." The director shook her hand and returned to his stage.

On her way out, a young woman caught up to her. "Excuse me, Agent Reid?"

Kate stopped. "Yes?"

"I'm Carey Phillips. I work with Mason. Not directly. My scenes don't usually include him, but I know him."

Kate studied the young woman who wasn't more than 22 or 23 at best. "Okay. Have you heard from him recently?"

"Um, no, but." Her eyes darted back and forth. "Could we talk for a moment?"

"Of course." She was led to a part of the studio toward the back that appeared empty. "What is it?"

"Well, I've been to a few parties with Mason in the past." She seemed reluctant to continue. "And I was with him in Rio last summer. Just as a house guest. I was only there for a couple of weeks. I don't make the kind of money he does, and I can't afford to go away for an entire summer."

"Sure. I understand." Kate anticipated news but didn't want to come on too strong. "Please, go on."

The woman with a short red bob and too-thin frame fidgeted with her hands. "Well, when I was there last year, Mason, well, he hosts a lot of parties and I thought maybe I might have seen something weird." She kept her eyes fixed on the ground.

"Carey, whatever you need to say, it's okay to say it. I'm here to help. You won't get in any trouble. I promise you," Kate replied.

"I was drinking kind of a lot, but I thought maybe I saw a woman who looked like she was hurt. Some of Mason's people, like, threw her into this room and I didn't see her after that. I don't know what happened to her. I just kept on drinking and then went home." Her eyes welled with tears. "I should've said something. I didn't know. I mean, what if he took that girl? What if it's my fault cause I didn't say anything?"

Kate reached out for her. "It's not your fault. Now, we don't know if Mason is responsible for the missing girl. We only want to talk to him because he was at that café. But if what you're saying is true, then I imagine we'll want to have a sit-down with him and figure all this out. Is there anything else you can think of that you want to tell me? Anything at all?"

Carey shook her head. "That's all I know."

"Okay. Thank you. I can't tell you how important your cooperation is. If we need anything, I'll give you a call, and vice-versa." Kate handed her a business card. "You should go take a breather and relax a minute. You'll be fine. You've done the right thing."

She nodded and walked away.

Kate marched across the studio, phone in hand, and pushed

through the exit doors. With her phone to her ear, she began. "Are you two there yet?"

"No. It's still a few miles away."

"Listen, can you hang tight? I'm not far and I want to be there. Actually, we should track down Fisher too. He's still at the precinct working on the files. We've got ourselves some new information."

"And that is?" Quinn asked.

"I just got some very interesting news from one of Wylder's co-stars. She saw something in Rio. Can you just wait? I won't be but a few minutes behind you. I want to see his reaction when I bring her up."

"I'm with Detective Sievers, this is his show," Quinn said.

"Please, Quinn. I'm asking you. Can you wait? I need to be there. I need to see his face to know the truth."

"I'll ask him."

The line went dead and she peered at her phone. "You just hung up on me. Are you serious?" Kate made her way to the car and pulled out onto the road, heading north. "You screwed up, Wylder."

Sievers checked the time. "Christ. How much longer are we going to have to wait?" He peered through the rear view in search of the other agents.

"We don't have to wait. We can go in and do this ourselves. I don't know why she's being so adamant about it," Quinn replied. "She had to go back and get Fisher too. She could be a while still."

"Hang on. That looks like them now."

Fisher rolled to a stop behind Siever's car. They stepped out and approached him while he rolled down the window.

"Welcome. Glad you could join us."

"Thanks for waiting," Kate began. "I know we agreed I shouldn't be here because he'll recognize me, but with this new information, I need to see his reaction. I have to understand how calculating he is or can be. He'll reveal something about the woman in the café. He won't be able to stop himself."

"What she said," Fisher pointed to her and smiled.

Sievers and Quinn stepped out and the four started toward the driveway of the suburban home. Fisher walked beside the detective. "I appreciate you doing this."

"He's an interesting guy." Sievers thumbed back at Quinn.

"Ah yes, but he's damn good at his job. And so is she." Fisher eyed Kate who trailed slightly. "There's still the question of whether Wylder's even here."

"We should get an answer on that in a jiffy," Sievers replied.

Quinn moved in next to Kate. "I'm glad you're here. I think it's a good idea."

She regarded him with mild suspicion. "I wouldn't have expected to hear that from you, all things considered."

"Yeah, well, I know how to concede when I'm wrong."

Fisher turned back to his junior agents. "I don't know what we'll find in there, if anything. So I suggest you both have your weapons ready."

Sievers knocked on the front door. "Mr. Wylder, NYPD. We have some questions for you."

A curtain blowing through an open window on the second floor caught Kate's eye. "He's here."

"If he won't answer, we can't just bust in there without cause,"

Quinn said. "We need to find a cause." He started toward the garage that was below grade, and peered through the windows as best he could, but they were obscured glass.

"I'll give it one more time." Sievers knocked again as he turned his sights from Quinn back to the front door. "Mr. Wylder? NYPD. Open up." He looked back to Fisher. "Well? Any ideas?"

Kate set her sights on Quinn who still skulked around the home in search of something to possibly use to give them reason to enter. "Unless he finds something, I don't know what we can do without a warrant. I thought he'd be here. We've checked his residences, his workplace. Where else could he be?"

Sievers' phone buzzed and he peered at the caller ID. "Hang on, it's one of mine. "Franklin, we're here at the Wylder home, but..." He stopped cold. "What's that? Okay. We're going to see what else we can find here and then head your way. Thank you for the heads up." He ended the call and looked to Fisher. "Wylder's car was found wrapped around a tree a few miles from here."

"Is he there? Is he alive?" Kate asked.

"No one was there. Both doors of the Mercedes were open, but no one was inside. My guys are there combing the scene to locate any survivors. It's surrounded by woods, so maybe they, whoever 'they' are, got out and tried to go for help."

"Something's not right," Kate said.

"You're telling me." Fisher again turned his sights on Quinn. "I don't know what the hell he thinks he's going to find. Maybe you should go over there and show him how it's done?"

"Therein lies the problem," she replied.

"What do you mean?"

"Nothing. It's not important right now. Let me go see if he's found anything. Otherwise, I think we're screwed." Kate walked over to the side of the house where Quinn stood. "Any luck? We got no answer at the door and turns out, the cops just spotted Wylder's car on the side of road, wrapped around a tree."

"And?" Quinn's interest piqued.

"No one's there. The consensus is there were two people inside, likely with injuries. That's all we know right now."

"Where does that leave us?" Quinn asked.

"You tell me. Anything stand out to you that we can use to bust down that door?" She surveyed the area where he stood.

"I don't see anything unusual and now with this, I don't know where we stand. It doesn't look good, though."

"It does not." She turned and looked at the garage door. "You couldn't see inside?"

"Windows are frosted glass."

"Right." She walked to the driveway and looked for signs of forced entry around the door. "Doesn't look like anyone tried to get in." And then she stopped and cocked her head. "What's this?" Kate crouched down near the corner of the door where it rested on the driveway.

"What is it? What do you see?" He quickly approached her.

"Tell me that doesn't look like blood to you?" She pointed to several microscopic drops of blood that looked like they lay just underneath the door itself and then within inches of the driveway.

"That looks like blood. How the hell did you see that? I've been standing here for the past ten minutes looking for something."

"You just needed a fresh pair of eyes. That's all," Kate replied.

"Sure."

"What matters is what Fisher has to say about this." She stood back up and called out to him. "Fisher, come take a look at this."

He started toward them. "Did you work your magic again, Reid? I knew we could count on you."

It was as if Fisher was commenting on purpose, knowing it would annoy Quinn. She cringed at the accolades because it was exactly the reason Quinn had gone off the rails. He couldn't handle someone being better than he was, even if she didn't really believe that herself. Whatever gift was given to her that allowed her to see the minutia was a gift he didn't possess and it was what had really caused the riff between them. "This looks like blood spatters. Don't you agree, Quinn?"

"Yeah. What she said."

He was angry and while that shouldn't concern her any longer, given what she knew about him, it still did. Deep inside, she wanted his approval. He was the better profiler, for now, and she did still stand to learn from him, but at this point, it didn't seem like that was going to be possible.

Fisher leaned over and placed his hands on his thighs. "Yep. Looks like blood to me. That's all I need." He pulled up again and started back toward the door. "We're getting inside this house, Detective. Found some blood over there by the garage. Between that and the accident down the road, well, we have cause." Fisher brandished his weapon and knocked a final time. "Wylder? FBI. We're coming in."

As the others joined him, Kate looked on figuring he was about to smash a window. "You sure this is how we play this? You remember what happened in Boston."

"What? So we get into a little bit of trouble. We have blood on the ground and a missing actor whose car is hugging a tree. We have enough. I'm going in. So, are you all with me or not?"

"Don't need to ask me twice," Sievers replied.

I'm with you," Quinn said.

Kate eyed the others. "I guess that means I'm in, too."

"That's what I thought." Fisher raised the butt of his gun to the glass insert in the door. "Here we come, ready or not." He smashed the glass and it shattered in front of him. An alarm sounded as he reached inside to unlock the door. "That'll bring the cops for sure. We won't have much time to look around before they come in and contaminate everything. No offense, Detective. But those guys won't be from your precinct. We should split up and see what we can find."

Fisher walked inside and stepped on the broken shards until making his way to the alarm keypad. "Shut up!" He ripped it off the wall and when that didn't work, he shot at it. "That should do it."

The three made their way inside and it didn't take long for Quinn, who was headed left, to spot the body.

"Oh shit!" He rushed toward Wylder who lay on the sofa appearing lifeless. "Hey! Wylder's here. He's in here!"

Kate, Fisher and the detective dashed to the living room. Kate approached Quinn. "Please tell me he's still alive."

Quinn checked for a pulse. "He's dead. Looks like he sustained internal injuries. Look at his chest and stomach. They're purple."

"Damn it! What the hell do we do now?" Fisher paced the room. "Where's his accomplice? Was he the driver?"

"We don't know." Kate returned upright and started back into the hall. "We need to clear the house and find any detail we can about where the other man went. I guarantee you, Wylder didn't make it back here alone." She stopped. "I hear the sirens." Kate steered through the extravagant home. "FBI. Anyone here? Identify yourself." Her raised voice echoed as she walked atop the dark wood floors, peering around the grey walls into every room. She walked purposefully, intent on finding something that would tell them where the other one went.

A voice or something like a voice drifted toward her. Kate stopped on a dime. "FBI. Is someone here?" She shouted again and moved toward the sound. "Hello? Keep talking. I can hear you. I'm coming." It was clear the voice was from someone in trouble. She prayed it was the fixer. That would put a tidy bow on this case and it would be all over.

She stopped at a tall white door that appeared different than the rest. Slighlty thicker, heavier looking. She tried the handle, but it was locked. "Shit. Hello? FBI. Is someone in here?"

Through the door, a muffled voice was barely audible.

"It's okay. I'll get you out of there." She scanned the area for a key or something that could help her open the door. "Hey!" she turned and shouted. "I need some help back here!"

Fisher and Quinn appeared only moments later, weapons drawn.

"There's someone in there."

Fisher studied the door. "It's a panic room. We aren't going to get inside without the key."

"We have to. I think there's a woman in there. Could be the missing girl," Kate replied. "Hang on. She's trying to talk. I think her mouth is covered. "Can you try to speak up? Please. We can't get in the room."

Quinn placed his ear near the door. "She's trying to say something. Damn it. I can't hear her clearly."

"She knows where the key is," Fisher said. "I can shoot the lock, but this thing looks military grade or some shit."

"She must be gagged." Kate faced the door. "Where's the key?" She listened and tried to understand the woman. "Where? I'm sorry, you have to try to speak slowly and as loud as you can." She pressed her ear against the door. "The key. It's in a fireproof box." She turned to the others.

"You mean this box right here?" Sievers approached with a metal box in his hand. "Found this is the master bedroom."

"Set it down." Fisher aimed his gun and fired. The box kicked up off the ground and popped open. "That should do it."

Kate reached for the key." I'll get her out. You three need to keep looking. If we let the accomplice go, we're screwed. Wylder couldn't have put her in here with his injuries. It had to be the other guy."

Fisher held Kate's gaze. "You'll be okay?"

"I'll be fine. I just need to see what condition she's in and if she knows where the fixer went."

26

The numbers didn't lie. Back at Quantico, Walsh had found a match. The phone call made to Mason Wylder's cell matched the number that had been found on the records from the Rio calls made to both Gustavo Varela and the member of the AdA. And now, maybe Agent Cain didn't need to make the deal with the devil because none of that mattered any longer.

Walsh snatched the papers and hurried to Scarborough's office. "I got it." He waved them around. "I found the match. We now have proof that the man in Rio who was seen at the burial ground is the same man who was in contact with Mason Wylder and Gustavo Varela."

Scarborough appeared reticent. "Wylder's dead."

Walsh advanced with guarded steps. "What's that now?"

"Fisher just called. They found Wylder on his sofa, apparently having died from injuries sustained in a car accident. One in which another was involved. And a woman was found inside his panic room, bound and gagged. Reid was searching the corridor to clear the house when she heard a noise. They got her out, but it took some work. The woman explained that Wylder's assistant, Scott Brooks, put her in there and left."

"He's the one who did Wylder's dirty work," Walsh said.

"That's right. And now that you have proof, looks like we've got ourselves an accomplice on the run."

"And a dead serial killer." Walsh's gaze shifted as he appeared to consider their next play. "Do we take this to the public? Get eyes on the ground for us?"

"That's one way to go."

"But you're not so sure?" Walsh added.

"We're dealing someone with ties to powerful government officials in Rio and maybe beyond. He could be using those connections as we speak to find a way out of the US. Initiating a media blitz might expedite his plans."

"The killer is dead," Walsh replied.

"Yes, it certainly looks that way."

"Maybe that's what will work in our favor." Walsh raised his index finger. "Hear me out. What if we use what we know right now to pin the murders on this Scott Brooks? Suggest that we have a team in Rio that is receiving cooperation from officials to ensure he doesn't enter the country."

"I like the sound of that. Go on," Scarborough said.

"If this guy thinks he's going to take the fall for what his boss did, he might have second thoughts about fleeing."

"He must understand that he'll still face a lifetime in prison for his part. He has no opportunity for a plea bargain when the killer is already dead."

"Good point. Regardless, say we find him. We convince him

that by giving us the names of the Rio officials he received help from and the names of the AdA members, he'll get a more lenient sentence. Maybe even just a few years for cooperating in a sting to oust corrupt Brazilian officials."

"Can we do that?" Scarborough asked. "We would need assurances from the CIA, the State Department and a host of other officials. CIA Officer Lambert insisted we wouldn't be able to touch the Rio government."

"We just need to convince this man that it's either he gives us names, or he will face a lifetime on the run. He'll run out of money and friends. He'll have no place to turn and his plans for a plea bargain will be out the window."

"Okay. I get where you're going with this. The question is, how do we communicate this to him? We have to find him first."

"We have phone records. We know how to reach him, either through the people who helped him or the AdA." Duncan walked into the room.

"And here's our woman of the hour," Walsh said. "Without her help, we wouldn't have gotten this far."

"That's what I'm here for." She patted him on the back before adding, "So we attempt to make contact. The question is, who are the people who helped? Given what we have right now, there's no question we'll get cooperation from the DOJ regarding warrants on Brooks' property and Wylder's property here in the US. But that will only tell us so much. We need Cain to search Wylder's property in Gávea. If there are people who helped him, and we know he had to have a few, then Scott Brooks will likely reach out to them for help. We get a message to them. Cain's going to have to be our point man on this one."

Scarborough considered her plan. "I'd sure as hell like to find him before he leaves the country. There's still a slim possibility of that. But I'll give Cain a heads up and test the waters."

Fisher walked into the living room where Kate waited with the woman who had been Wylder's housekeeper. "How's she holding up?" He pushed around the toothpick in his mouth awkwardly.

This nervous habit of Fisher's was something Kate often used to understand his moods, and, in this instance, it revealed how sorry he felt. "She's okay." Kate turned her attention to the middle-aged woman who had a slight paunch and thinning gray hair. "And you're sure there's nothing else you remember Mr. Wylder saying, or Mr. Brooks?"

"I came to the door and Mr. Brooks let me in. I knew something was wrong as soon as I got inside. He had wild eyes. I thought he was on drugs."

"Mr. Brooks—Scott?" Kate asked.

"Yes. Then I saw Mr. Wylder and I knew then," she shook her head. "I wasn't going to be allowed to leave."

Fisher moved in and squatted in front of the woman to meet her at eye level. "Mr. Brooks put you inside the room. Did he say anything at all that might suggest where he was going?"

"No. Nothing. He just left and no one can hear you inside there. It's a terrible place. I only know that Mr. Wylder wasn't the same when he came back from Rio this time."

"She doesn't know anything else." Kate stood up. "We're going to have to make a move or risk letting Scott Brooks disappear for good. What did Scarborough say?"

"He was going to get with the others and put together some ideas. We should hear back from him soon."

Quinn entered the room. "Brooks can't have gone far, but the longer we wait, the more chance we have of losing his trail. I didn't find anything that might suggest where he would go. I can only think, based on what we know of how things went down with Wylder, I have to think Brooks played a big part in causing the accident. He wasn't injured, at least not badly enough that he couldn't escape on his own. According to Sievers, the car showed no signs of mechanical failure, tire failure. Nothing. It appears to have been human error." He turned to Sievers who had returned from the scene. "Isn't that right?"

"It's shaping up to be that way."

"It's possible he intentionally crashed," Kate said. "Brooks might have been fearful Wylder would get caught."

"He must've gotten tired of cleaning up the messes. And then when Wylder started acting up here, that was probably the final straw," Fisher said. "That must've been the moment he realized Wylder had gone off the deep end and couldn't be contained."

"Let's get her to a hospital to get checked out," Quinn began. "Then we should head back to the precinct and formulate a plan. We don't have much time before we lose our window."

"I agree," Fisher said. "Sievers' team will be here shortly to collect evidence and seal off the house. I'll hang back until they arrive."

Sievers nodded. "Sounds good."

Fisher continued, "you two should go and take her. By the time you get back to the stationhouse, I'll be there waiting."

Quinn and Kate made their way out with the housekeeper and

started toward the hospital. Kate was in the back seat with her. "You're sure you're still doing okay?"

"Yes. I'm fine. He didn't hurt me," she said.

"Thank God for that. You were one of the lucky ones." Kate pondered an idea. "You didn't travel with Mr. Wylder to Rio for the summer months?"

"No. I stayed here and took care of the property on a monthly basis. I have a family, I could not leave."

"Do you know who was on his staff at his home in Rio?"

"I don't. Mr. Brooks would know. He took care of everything for Mr. Wylder when he was on vacation." Her head sank. "Not so much a vacation, was it?"

"No. I'm afraid it wasn't. Not for the women he killed."

The housekeeper sobbed. "I'm so sorry. I didn't know. I swear I didn't know."

Kate placed her arm around her. "Of course you didn't. You're not to blame. Wylder was a sick man and now he's dead. That's the good news. And it'll be our jobs to find Brooks and ensure he sees justice."

"We're here." Quinn shifted the car into park at the hospital's entrance before opening his door.

Kate watched as he walked inside and soon returned with a nurse and a wheelchair. "It's time to go now." She stepped out and helped the woman into the chair, eyeing the nurse. "This is Mrs. Gonzales. She still needs to contact her family, but we'd like her to stay here overnight for her own protection."

"Protection?" the nurse asked.

Kate traded glances with Quinn. "Yes. This will all be explained later. I'll make sure the NYPD gets here soon. They'll want to speak with her too."

"What's going on here?" The nurse pressed on.

"That's all I can say for now," Kate replied. "Please use discretion. This woman has been through a lot today."

"Of course."

Quinn started back to the car but stopped at the entrance and turned back. "Reid?" He tossed his head toward the door.

She caught up to him at the car. "We have to find Scott Brooks tonight. He knows where the bodies are—in Rio and here. We can't let him get away."

"We won't." He placed his arm on her back and opened the passenger door for her.

She slipped into the seat and eyed Quinn with concern. What game was he playing now? The part of the concerned law man who only wanted justice, or was this some other ploy to get into her head like it was his own personal playground?

A CONSENSUS HAD BEEN REACHED. THE REST OF THE TEAM would join the effort in New York to track down Scott Brooks, the man they knew had served as an accomplice to the now-deceased killer, Mason Wylder. He could not be allowed to escape justice.

Within a few hours Scarborough and the rest of the team arrived at LaGuardia airport and made their way to the 10th precinct. A man hunt was about to be initiated for the missing accomplice.

"Before we arrived here, I was on a call with Agent Cain in Brasilia." Scarborough handed out a detailed report provided by Cain. "Mason Wylder's home in Gàvea was raided this morning by Cain and his team in International Ops. They received no cooperation from the civil or military police in Rio. Unfortunately, no evidence was discovered of any additional victims inside the home, nor was there any documentation of payment to government officials. That's the bad news. The good news is that they did discover a very sophisticated room, which can only be described as a kill room where Cain believes he'll be able to retrieve enough physical evidence to put Scott Brooks away for the rest of his life. It appears he was tasked with disposal of the victims."

"Can we get Brooks on a watch list to prevent him from leaving the US?" Fisher asked.

"Absolutely. Given what Cain's team uncovered, no question there."

"Why are we not discussing the missing girl from the café? Can we assume Brooks is holding her hostage?" Kate asked.

Detective Sievers raised his index finger. "I'll field this one. Agent Reid, I have five of my officers working that investigation. We haven't given up on her. Nevertheless, it appears doubtful Brooks had taken her. I think the housekeeper would've mentioned if he was holding anyone else. Don't misunderstand my meaning, we haven't given up on finding her, but our window is closing fast."

The words he chose must've come straight out of a police manual that scripted precisely the right words to assure families of victims the police were doing all they could. The problem was, Kate knew the script, too. It didn't work on the families and it wouldn't work on her either. They'd given up on finding the girl. Maybe it was time for her to accept it because if Brooks didn't have her, she was probably at the bottom of a river somewhere.

"A watchlist is great," Duncan began. "But we need eyes at the airports, train stations and subways. We believe Brooks is injured.

He shouldn't be that hard to spot. We're giving him too much credit to assume he can manage to flee the country."

"Do you have any idea how much area that is to cover?" Sievers asked.

"I understand you're putting your efforts into finding the missing girl, but how else do we find Brooks? He's here in New York." Duncan added.

Scarborough flipped through the report. "Hang on. We have Brooks' cell phone number. Why the hell aren't we tracing it right now? He's going to be looking for help."

Fisher leaped from his chair. "You're right. We need to jump on that now. We can contact the field office for assistance. That needs to happen like yesterday."

"Have the field office agent come here and get it set up ASAP," Scarborough said. "In the meantime, we'll get the travel restrictions in place."

Fisher eyed the detective and both agreed.

"We're on it." He hurried away with Sievers trailing behind him.

Scarborough set his sights on Kate. "When was the last time you talked to Marc Aguilar? He's still a reporter here in New York, right?"

"He is. It's been a while. Why?"

"See if he can get the word out, via social media, or an anonymous tip, whatever. But have him plant information that Scott Brooks is the killer and that he killed Mason Wylder. If he's paying attention, which is an almost certainty, and he's looking for a way out, he'll hear the news."

"And your goal?" Quinn asked.

"Put him in panic mode. He'll get desperate and start making calls to his people for help. That's where we'll catch him as soon as the trace is set up," Scarborough replied.

"I'll get on it." Kate stared out the door. "Duncan, you're the social media guru, you want to help me out with this?"

"I'm with you." She followed Kate into the corridor.

"Where does that leave us, Boss?" Quinn said to Scarborough as they were the only ones left in the room.

"You and I are taking a drive."

"Where to?"

"Cain mentioned that he'd found a calendar that appeared to belong to Wylder in his home in Gávea."

"Why didn't you say anything about this to the others?"

"This is something we need to handle ourselves. The calendar had an entry written by Wylder to the effect that Scott Brooks was at his parents' home in Hempstead. Looks to be about an hour or so drive from here."

"You think he could be there?"

"Someone's shielding him right now. What better place? We'll go there while Fisher and Sievers get the all-clear to set up tracking on his cell phone. Between taking a drive there and monitoring his calls, one of is bound to strike gold. Are you with me?"

"Let's move."

"I'll drive." Scarborough continued into the halls of the precinct and stopped when Fisher appeared.

"Where are you two off to?"

"Got a lead on a possible sighting in Hempstead. Don't know if it'll pan out. We're going to give it a shot while you arrange for the phone to be monitored."

Fisher appeared skeptic. "Since when did you..."

"I don't have time to explain. You have your job to do. This is something we can do. It's better than sitting on our thumbs. You good with that, Fisher?"

"Yes, sir."

Scarborough brushed past him with Quinn in tow.

Fisher watched with concern as they darted away but said nothing further. "Whatever you gotta do, man. You're the boss."

DAYLIGHT SURRENDERED TO A FIERY RED SKY AND threadlike cloud trails drifted in the mild breeze. The road glistened from an earlier summer rain, spraying water on the windshield as Scarborough drove to a destination of which he alone had knowledge.

He was quiet, unusually so, and Quinn appeared to take notice as he sat in the passenger seat. The awkward silence forced him to fidget with his seat belt and scroll through his phone. "No news yet." This stalemate had to end.

Scarborough kept his eyes fixed on the road. "It's early. It takes time to set up the call tracking."

Quinn seemed to have had his fill. "Is everything okay? You seem angry."

"I just want this to end, same as you, I imagine."

"Right. Yeah." He turned his sights ahead. "How much longer do you think?"

"GPS says about half an hour. We might be able to shave off some time. The sooner the better, in my opinion." Whatever Scarborough's intentions were appeared to be working. The pressure built between them. "Are you up for this?"

"I can handle it. I don't know if we'll find him there, but like you said, it's worth a shot."

"Yep." He let the silence linger until it choked all resistance from Quinn. "I hear you met my ex-girlfriend."

Quinn appeared alarmed. "I'm sorry?"

"My ex, Georgia Myers. I hear you two shared a few drinks not too long ago. I didn't realize you were acquainted with her."

"Um, yeah, well she's a profiler too, so I like to keep up with others in my field."

"Sure. Sure. Of course, you know how exes can talk sometimes. She must've given you an earful after hearing you work for me. We didn't exactly end our relationship on a high note."

"No, not really. I'm not even sure you came up at all, actually."

He could hear Quinn's voice tremor with uncertainty. "Uh huh." Scarborough yanked the steering wheel toward the shoulder of the road and slammed on the brakes.

Quinn's hands shot out in front of him to brace against the dash. "What the hell?"

Smoke from the tires suspended in the headlights. Cars whipped past them, some honked their horns and others displayed their middle finger. Scarborough shoved the gearshift into park and turned squarely in front of Quinn. "You think I don't have friends at the Bureau? That I haven't worked here since before you finished high school?"

Quinn raised his head and pulled back his shoulders. "I'm sorry, but what exactly are you talking about? Are you crazy? You could've caused an accident."

Scarborough chortled. "So this is how you want to play it? Denial? I figured you for a more creative type."

"Look, I don't know what you're getting at..."

"Stop!" He shouted. "You met with Myers to get dirt on me and she willingly handed it over to you on a silver fucking platter, didn't she?"

Quinn's expression turned cold. "You screwed this team, Scarborough, on multiple occasions, including in Rio where I was almost killed. Where your girlfriend was almost killed. Did you really think there wouldn't be repercussions?"

"Oh, I imagine you hoped there would be. Seems Cole has a different take on things than you do. I don't know man, blackmail? You screwed yourself on that one. And the real problem I see isn't that you wanted to take me down. It's that you wanted to bring down Kate too. See, now, that's where I have a problem. And now it's your problem." Scarborough threw the gearshift into Drive and spun the tires, returning to the road ahead.

"What are you going to do?" Quinn's blasé tone tried to rise above Scarborough's threat.

Scarborough turned to him and smiled. "Me? I'm not going to do anything. It's not me you should worry about."

27

The old television in the basement received poor reception from its rabbit-ear antenna, not that it mattered to Scott. It flickered staticky images that he ignored while he lay slouched low on the sofa and scrolling through his phone. What he wanted was to see if any of his social media had news on Mason Wylder that might implicate him. It was only a matter of time before they found Mason's body in his suburban New York home. And the Mercedes crumpled against the tree. Putting two and two together after that would be fairly simple. Still, he had hoped the body would be discovered because that would mean the housekeeper would be freed. Guilt consumed him over what he'd done to her.

Everyone was safe now that Wylder was dead. They just didn't know it. Only Scott knew what he had done and didn't regret for one second letting him bleed out right in front of him on his pristine couch. But he played his part in this gruesome drama and they would figure that out, too. According to a well-placed source, the agents who followed them to Rio had returned and those people were experts.

All he could do was monitor the news and wait for help that may or may not come from those whom he had called upon to cover up Wylder's misdeeds. It seemed all were willing to help if the price was right. However, Scott had no money and he was relying on their good nature. That was a laugh.

"Scott, do you want anything to eat?" A voice from above traveled down the staircase.

"No. I'm fine. Thanks." He continued to scroll through his news feed until a text message arrived. It was from a number he didn't recognize, but one who clearly knew who he was.

"Do you have any comment about the death of your employer, Mason Wylder?" The message read.

"What the?" Scott re-read it, trying to figure out who this was, and feared replying. "They know. And they're looking for me." He turned his sights to the television flipped through the channels until landing on a local evening news broadcast. Through the snow on the screen, he watched and listened. But there was nothing. No mention of the dead Mason Wylder. Why? Clearly the authorities knew. They had to. Something this big would have been leaked by someone. Why else would he have received the text message? He wanted to reply by asking who the hell this person was, but that would be a mistake. "I have to wait this out."

Whoever sent the message got his cell number from somewhere. And if the sender got it, the cops could get it. That would mean they could track him down through GPS. "Ah, shit." He pressed the "settings" button on his phone and disabled the location tracking. That was something he probably should have done before leaving Wylder's, but he was too busy trying to figure out where to go with a bum leg that still throbbed but had now been bandaged.

Footfalls sounded on the staircase. "I brought you a pillow and some blankets. It gets cold down here."

"I remember." He took the linens. "Thank you. I won't be here for long. Probably take off tomorrow."

"Okay. It's not a problem. Stay as long as you like, Scott. I'm heading up to bed. I'll be setting the alarm, so be careful not to open the doors or windows."

"I won't. Good night, and thanks."

"Sleep well."

SCARBOROUGH RAPPED ON THE DOOR AGAIN. "THIS IS THE FBI. We need to talk to you." He stood under a dim porch light encased in its yellowy hue and turned his attention to Quinn. "No answer."

It wasn't until the door opened just a crack that his attention returned. He held out his badge. "I'm sorry to disturb you so late, I'm FBI Agent Scarborough and this is Agent Quinn. Are you the mother of Scott Brooks?"

A heavy-eyed woman with unkempt, wispy grey hair cleared her throat. "Yes. He's my son. Is he okay?"

"As far as we know, ma'am, he is. We're looking for him actually and thought he might have come here."

"No. No, we haven't seen him in months, I'm afraid. He doesn't stay in touch with us often. What's going on? Why are you looking for him?"

"Ma'am, this is very important. Please. If he's here, we need to talk to him," Scarborough said.

"He's not here. I assure you, I'm no liar."

"Ma'am, my supervising agent isn't implying you are. We're in need of locating your son. It's absolutely critical we find him," Quinn said.

Scarborough shot him a glance. "I know it's very late, but can we come in, please?"

The woman studied him for a moment before relenting. "Fine. See for yourself."

She was being awfully cooperative for a mother Scarborough suspected was hiding her son. "Thank you." He stepped inside.

Quinn followed and both stood in the small foyer. He added, "You say you haven't heard from your son in some time?"

"That's right." The woman pushed back her hair and tugged on her nightgown. "Last we spoke, he was leaving for Brazil with his employer as they do every summer. He's probably still there."

"What do you know about his employer?" Scarborough asked.

"Not much. Except that he's an actor on a TV show. Look, I'm not sure what he's done or why you're looking for him, but he's not here."

Admitting defeat was never Scarborough's strong suit, but the chances Brooks was here appeared to be slim and none. "I'm very sorry we wasted your time." He retrieved one of his cards. "If you do hear from him, please give me a call. That's my personal cell number. It's urgent we speak to him as soon as possible."

She viewed the card and turned her sights to the door. "Good night then."

Both agents retreated to the porch where Quinn awaited orders. He seemed pleased Scarborough had failed in his efforts. "Do you want to have a look around?"

"Damn it. I thought he'd be here. Where the hell else would he go?"

"I don't know. The team might already have set up the tracking. We can head back there and put our heads together."

"We'll have a quick walk around the perimeter to see if she's lying to protect her son, like any mother would do. If we get nothing, we'll head back to base." Scarborough started around the left side of the home. "You take the right and I'll meet you back here." He made his way to the side yard fence and turned on the flashlight on his phone, aiming it at the ground in search of fresh footprints, but he saw none. "Damn it. Where the hell are you?"

He soon returned to the front of the house where Quinn waited by the car. "Nothing?"

"No. You?"

"No." Scarborough approached the driver's side door and stepped inside. His phone buzzed. "It's Reid." He pressed the answer button "Tell me you have a location on Brooks. He's not at his parents' house."

"His parents' house? What are you doing there?" she asked.

"I'll explain later."

"I asked Marc Aguilar to send him a text to throw him off. He didn't take the bait. However, we were able to home in on an area but we lost the signal too quickly to pinpoint an exact location. I think he must've figured out when he got the text that we were tracking him," she replied.

"He must've turned off his GPS. Any calls we can trace to a tower?"

"We're working on that now, but we have nothing for you. How did you figure out where his parents lived?"

"Cain. Doesn't matter because it was a bust anyway. Quinn

and I took a brief look around for footprints but saw nothing. We're going to head back to the precinct now."

Kate was quiet on the other end for a moment.

"Kate? You still there? Kate?"

"Sorry. Hang on. I think..." She trailed off and muffled voices sounded in the phone's speaker.

"Kate? What the hell's going on?"

"Nick, we just got a hit on a location. He's at his sister's home."

"How do we know that? You said he turned off his GPS."

"You're never going to believe this. He bit. It just took him longer than expected. Nick, you two need to get back here."

"We'll go to the house. Where is it? We can't afford to let him slip through our fingers now."

"Queens. It's going to take you too long. We'll assemble our team and head there now."

"Text me the address. We'll start that way. I won't sit here while you all take him on."

"Fine. I'll text it now. Be careful."

He ended the call. "They found him. In Queens."

"We won't get there in time. It'll all be over," Quinn said.

"We're going anyway."

This was Detective Sievers' jurisdiction. The BAU team had been trailing after a killer for the better part of three weeks, globetrotting and evading gangs and corrupt government officials, and no one could dispute the facts. This was New York and this was going to be the detective's collar.

"We can only offer backup, if he asks," Fisher began. "That's the deal."

"We've been after this guy for weeks. Wylder, anyway. They tried to have us killed. You can't think we're just going to sit here and wait it out," said Kate.

Walsh stood up from the table. "We're the ones who know what Brooks is capable of. They don't. He won't go down without a fight. He has nothing to lose."

"Look, all I can do is ask. Technically, this should be an FBI matter given the crimes and the international situation." He turned to the local field agent. "Would you agree?"

"I'll be honest, this isn't something I want to put my two cents in. It's clear there's a serious situation going on that involves a whole host of jurisdictions. I'll sign off if you want to pull this from the detective. But I don't think you'll win over too many friends and we might need their help. They can dispatch air support and backup quicker than we can, if it becomes necessary."

Detective Sievers returned to the communications' room. "Well? What's the good word? You folks coming with or not?"

"If you need us to provide support, we'll be happy to offer it," Fisher said.

"Good. Hey, I'm not looking to cut you folks out of the deal. I get what you've been through to find this guy. I'm just staking my claim, you understand?"

"We understand." Kate strapped on her tactical gear. "It's time to come together on a plan to bring him in."

The sister's address had been pulled up on Sievers' computer and the home was displayed on Google maps. Sievers viewed it in 360-degree mode. "We can see there are two entrances. Front and rear. Simple enough."

"And neighbors in close proximity." Fisher studied the map. "We'll have safety concerns."

"I'll have my guys ensure the protection of the immediate neighbors while we approach the suspect in the home."

"We'll want to flank the sides and have a man posted at each exit." Walsh peered at the team. "It's going to require all of us to make this happen swiftly and without incident."

"I couldn't agree more." Kate turned to Sievers. "I think we understand what we all need to do. So, with your permission, detective, we should move out."

"Listen to the lady, folks. Let's roll out," Sievers replied.

Scott replied to the text as a last-ditch effort to offer a diversion. Anything he could do to delay what appeared to be the inevitable. But maybe there was a way out of this. He'd always wanted to live in Sweden. They were neutral, right? Did that mean they didn't extradite? Perhaps he should look into the countries where he could get safe harbor instead of taking a shot in the dark. He wasn't the strategic one of the bunch. Wylder—he was a calculating son of a bitch with a dark side that couldn't be rivaled, except maybe by Ted Bundy, and he was dead too.

The sound of exploding glass pierced his ears and forced Scott to jolt upright. A heavy thud hammered above his head. He set his gaze to the ceiling and his heart beat through his chest from an adrenaline overload. "Oh God. They found me. They fucking found me." He sought frantically for a place to hide in the small basement or maybe a way out through the window well. Yes, maybe he could make it out through the window well. He hurried toward it, but an iron grate was fixed to the outside. "What the..?" Weren't they supposed to be accessible as a means to escape? Christ! Can't anything go his way?

Jarring footsteps broadcast above. Loud, deep voices shouted. "They're in. No. No, this can't be happening. Denise!" He cried out to his sister as if she could do anything to stop them.

"Down there!" Another voice cried out.

Scott froze in place and raised his arms. "Don't shoot! Don't shoot! I didn't do anything."

Officers in riot gear, tens of them, rushed the stairs.

"NYPD! Stay where you are. Keep your hands up!" One of them screamed.

Denise cried aloud upstairs and Scott listened, impotent to offer help. So many cops were there, he couldn't count them all. So much noise, it was like a movie and he knew what that would look like. "I'm not moving. Please don't hurt my sister."

Detective Sievers descended the steps and confronted him. "Scott Brooks? You're under arrest for the murder of Mason Wylder, Adriana Santos, Rosella Ortiz and countless other crimes."

"Wait. I didn't kill anyone. I swear it. It was Wylder. He's the murderer."

An officer pulled his arms behind him and locked cuffs on his wrists. He pushed Scott ahead and guided him up the staircase. The officer pressed on his radio button. "Coming up now. Suspect is in custody."

Kate waited in the living room upstairs, her gun face-down in her hands. Walsh stood near while Fisher assisted the other officers. Duncan held back the sister, and they all looked on as Scott Brooks appeared at the top of the stairs.

"I didn't kill anyone. It was Mason. He was a psycho. It wasn't me," he pleaded.

"It was you who tried to have us killed," Duncan began. "So, you're looking pretty guilty from where I stand." She continued her grip on Scott's sister. "I don't think she'll forgive you either."

Scott's head shook fervently in denial as the officers escorted him outside to a waiting patrol car.

"Now we need to get him to tell us where the rest of the bodies are buried. Here and in Rio." Fisher started outside. "Sievers wants this collar, that's fine. But we're getting those sons of bitches in Rio who tried to take us out."

Kate emerged from the home and waited for Duncan to place the sister in another patrol car. On her approach, she began, "somehow I thought this would end differently. I thought Wylder would see justice."

"So did I, but we both know things don't go as we plan." Duncan turned to her. "The good news is, it's over."

"What about the missing girl from the café? Is it over for her?"

"I don't know. I think it probably is." Duncan craned her neck to see outside. "Hey, is that Scarborough and Quinn? Jesus, they got here fast. Too bad they missed the whole thing."

"Better late than never." Kate started ahead, but Duncan reached for her arm to stop her.

"Hey, whatever happens after this. After we close this investigation. I want you to know that I'm with you. You understand? Whatever you decide, I'll back you up."

28

Scott's brow dripped with sweat in the sweltering interrogation room of the 10th precinct. It was clear his discomfort was intentional and used as some sort of tactic to get him to talk. Little did they know, Scott was more than willing to sing if it meant saving his own ass. He'd already proven himself a man who lacked integrity or any sort of moral authority.

"I'm telling you, I don't know who Mason paid off in Rio. You'd have to talk to his accountant or something. I wasn't party to that type of information. I was a grunt. Nothing more."

"And yet you brought women to him, like lambs to the slaughter," Fisher said. "He must have trusted you enough to believe you wouldn't squeal to the cops about it. You had to have known who was getting the kickbacks to look the other way."

Kate observed the questioning from the other side of the wall via a live monitor. "Did you tell Cain we got him?"

"I did," Scarborough replied. "He thinks if we can get some

solid intel on the corruption, he might be able to take it to his bosses."

"He actually thinks it could go somewhere?" Walsh asked.

"He believes something good can come from all this. What that is, time will tell. I just want to see this asshole fry for helping Wylder the way he did," Scarborough added. "We should probably head back out there. It's time to clean up now that the party's over. We've done our part, now the local office is going to have to jockey for position with NYPD and the press that's going to converge on this place in droves." Scarborough opened the door and stepped out into the stark corridor while Walsh and Reid followed. "There's something Reid and I need to take care of back at Quantico."

This was news to her, but by the look on his face, it appeared to be a priority. "You'll keep us posted about whatever happens in there?" Kate thumbed to the room they had just monitored.

"We will," Walsh replied. "Go. We can tidy up things here." He patted Scarborough on the back.

Quinn, who had waited in Sievers' office, stepped out into the hall upon noticing the two emerge. "How's it going in there? Are they getting anywhere with him?"

"They appear to have things under control. Reid and I are heading back to the shop. We'll take a commercial flight. You guys can take the plane back when you're no longer needed here."

Quinn studied them for a moment. "Um, before you go, can I talk to you both for a moment, in private?"

He and Kate exchanged worrisome glances before Scarborough answered, "sure." He walked inside Sievers' office and Kate followed.

Quinn closed the door. "I've had some time to think about

things. Things I've done. Things I've said. And I've had a chance to think about the future that I want for myself. This isn't it. I have struggled, admittedly, with the idea that my place on this team isn't what I thought it was, or what I wanted it to be."

Kate bared a cynical gaze. Quinn had already proven himself a liar and a blackmailer. Nothing he could say would sway her. His words, whatever they were, would fall on deaf ears.

"I was wrong to do what I did," Quinn continued. "Searching for something I could use against you, Scarborough, in particular, because I believed Cole wasn't doing enough to rein in your actions."

Scarborough folded his arms across his chest. "I didn't realize they needed to be reigned in."

"I suppose that's how I perceived it. I think it was more of a case of envy than anything else."

"Do you seriously expect me to forget what you did, Quinn?" Kate asked. "You went behind my back. You dug into a painful past for your own gains. And you tried to blackmail me."

Scarborough looked at her. "Jameson told me what happened."

She eyed him for a moment. "Regardless, you have a lot of nerve asking for forgiveness now. Why? Do you think you'll be fired? Is that it?"

"Kate, I'm just saying..."

"Don't call me that. You don't know me. I'm not your friend."

"Calm down," Scarborough placed his hand on her shoulder.

"I won't calm down." She pulled away and confronted Quinn. "You believe this is how you get away with what you've done? To issue a half-assed apology?"

"No, but I think it could be the start of my admitting I was wrong and selfish and a prick."

Kate shot a glance to Nick. "You don't believe him, do you?"

"I'm hearing him out, which is what you should be doing."

She smiled caustically. "Go on then. Shovel some more bull-shit our way. Try to dig yourself out of that hole."

"Maybe this is the wrong time to be discussing this. We're all tired. It's been a long few weeks," Quinn added.

"That's right. Weeks that saw us nearly killed. So yeah, maybe I'm not in the mood to hear you out right now." Kate's tone dripped with contempt.

"Fair enough." He opened the door and held it for her. "Maybe another time."

Scarborough followed but stopped short and turned to him. "I told you it wasn't me you had to worry about."

Kate fumed as she waited in the car for Nick. She spotted him exit the precinct and watched as he walked toward the car and step into the driver's side. "Can you believe him?"

"I figured we weren't finished with this." He keyed the ignition.

"You're damn right we're not. Quinn tried to blackmail us. I know I should've told you, but I thought I could handle this on my own. Dwight helped me out and well, I guess he must've contacted you about it."

"It was me who called him. He didn't want to tell me, but I knew something was up and I dragged it out of him. Look, Quinn is in the wrong here, but the fact of the matter is, he does have damning evidence. Proof that I've hidden my battle with alcohol. I don't know how Cole will react to that."

"Probably better than he would knowing his own agent tried to blackmail a Senior Unit Agent." Kate huffed as she peered through the passenger side window.

"What do you want me to do, Kate? I have to work with him. You have to work with him."

"Why? I don't understand. What would have to happen for him to actually pay for what he's done?"

"He hasn't *done* anything. That's the problem. So he talked to Georgia. She's a colleague. What am I supposed to do with that? Tell Cole that hey, Quinn talked to my ex?"

She felt she was losing this argument and it annoyed her even more. "Well, maybe if you hadn't jeopardized our safety in Rio by stopping in the local bar while we were running from gangsters..." she trailed off.

Nick kept his eyes fixed on the road.

"I'm sorry. I didn't mean that. I'm just angry," Kate replied.

"I can tell. Good to know how you really feel."

She regretted it, more than anything, but as they say, you can't put the toothpaste back in the tube. It was out there. Maybe that was how she really felt. She was angry with him too for disregarding everything because of booze. He'd done it before. Why should she be surprised?

Kate pushed her hand through her brunette hair that had now grown past her shoulders. She felt as though she'd lost control of everything. Quinn was after her, Nick betrayed her trust. She was losing it and wanted to break down in tears, but there wasn't a chance in hell she'd start crying in front of him. He would only try to console her and feel as though he was the big strong man offering comfort in her time of weakness. Well that wasn't going to happen. Kate was tired of feeling weak and used and lied to. "Let me out."

"What?" Nick said.

"Pull over the car and let me out. Now."

"Here? We're almost at the airport. Come on, Kate. It's a short flight back to D.C. and we'll be in the office in a few hours. We can sort all this out there."

"I swear to God if you don't stop this car, I'm going to scream."

Nick pulled over to the side of the road and didn't say a word.

Kate opened her door and ripped her laptop bag from the backseat before slamming both doors shut. And in the early morning light, she walked with no idea where she would go or what she would do. But she wasn't going to look back.

"KATE?" HER FRIEND AND FORMER COLLEAGUE, DWIGHT Jameson called out to her while she rested on his sofa. "Kate? Your phone's been ringing off the hook. It could be important."

She roused and sat up, peering at the time. "Shit. How long have I been asleep?"

"Several hours."

"It's dark out. I missed the entire day." She reached for her phone. "I'm so sorry about this. I shouldn't have just shown up at your doorstep. I hopped on a train and ended up here."

"Don't be. You needed sleep and it was no big deal to run home and let you in. How are you doing, anyway?"

"I've calmed down. I guess that's what's important." She began to scroll through her messages. "I see Nick's on top of things. He's called ten times."

"Maybe you should go see him? I'm sure with all that's gone on, he's still at the office. I can give you a lift."

"Yeah. Thanks. I should probably go in." She stood. "I'm just going to go freshen up."

He nodded.

"Thanks, Dwight." She kissed his cheek. "You're a good friend."

"He loves you, you know."

"I know."

"THANKS FOR THE RIDE." KATE STEPPED OUT OF THE CAR. "I'll call you later. Thanks for everything."

"No problem, friend. Good luck in there."

She closed the door and watched Dwight pull away. Behind her was the BAU building and inside awaited God knew what. But she had to face it. "Let the chips fall where they may." She pressed on and made her way to the floor of her unit's offices.

The elevator doors parted and she stepped out. No one noticed. Her colleagues were busy working cases and finding criminals and killers. Her little outburst didn't matter to them. Kate continued through the maze of corridors until reaching her office. She hadn't told Nick she was coming in. Hadn't called him back or anything, actually.

"Hey."

She spun around. "Figured you'd still be here."

Nick walked inside. "I called you."

"I didn't answer." She set her things down on her desk. "Where's Quinn?"

"In with Cole."

"Really? That was fast."

"He's requesting a leave of absence. In light of the situation, we felt it was the best solution, short term."

"Wait, what? A leave of absence?"

"Yes. He's going to take some time off, and if he comes back, he comes back."

"He gets a choice? That's what you're telling me? A sociopathic blackmailer gets to choose to keep his job."

"Mistakes have been made all around. By him. By me. And by you." Nick drew in a deep breath. "You tailed an agent without cause or permission."

"He threatened..."

"I know what he threatened. And the thing was, Kate, it wasn't your responsibility to fix it. It was mine. I should have been made aware of the situation. I would've made the call to bring him in to Cole and if it meant my own disciplining or God-forbid, firing, then so be it. But it shouldn't have been you."

"What about Dwight? Is he going to..."

"No. His name wasn't mentioned."

"So what's my punishment?" Kate stood firm.

"Cole doesn't want this to go beyond our team. He won't open an investigation if you admit wrong-doing. He wants this entire fiasco to be put behind us. What happened in Rio. Here. He wants it all to go away. And because of the work you did in Rio, the risks you took with your life to get to the truth, and the fact that your work will lead to corruption charges for the Brazilian authorities, the worst you'll receive is a letter of censure."

"I see. Quinn gets a vacation. I get disciplined. Seems fair."

"I said Quinn was taking a leave of absence from the Bureau. I didn't say he was coming back here."

She lowered her arms and appeared deadpan. "He's being fired?"

"If he chooses to return, he'll be transferred from our unit. It's clear the personnel issue is irreparable, according to Cole."

Scarborough started to leave. "And as for me, I'm begin demoted."

"What?" she walked toward him. "What for?"

"For withholding information about myself that could have placed the team in danger. Information that *did* place the team in danger."

"Demoted to what?"

"I'm no longer the senior unit agent. You'll be answering to Cameron Fisher from now on."

THE END

ABOUT THE AUTHOR

Robin Mahle has published more than 30 novels in the mystery/thriller genre. She also writes historical fiction as <u>Christine Chase.</u>

It is Robin's fast-paced style of storytelling combined with tense action and thrilling twists that bring her readers back for more. So be sure sure to subscribe to her newsletter to keep up on all the latest releases, sales, and giveaways. Go to robinmahle.com and sign up today!

Robin lives in Coastal Virginia with her husband and two children.

If you enjoyed Ms. Mahle's work, please share your experience by leaving a review on <u>Amazon.</u>

ALSO BY ROBIN MAHLE

The Kate Reid FBI Thriller Series (17 books)

The Chef (stand-alone psych thriller)

The Man in My Attic (stand-alone psych thriller)

The Compound (standalone psych thriller)

The Remy Fontaine Fugitive Hunter Thrillers (4 books)

The Det. Rebecca Ellis Thrillers (5 books)

The Allison Hart PI Thrillers (5 Books)

The Lacy Merrick Thrillers (4 books)

**Sign up to receive Robin's Newsletter on her website robinmahle.com so you can stay up to date on her new releases, events, contests and even exclusive new material!